Profound River

JOHN GUBBINS

Profound River

SWEETWATER BOOKS
SPRINGVILLE, UTAH

AN IMPRINT OF CEDAR FORT, INC.

ISBN 13: 978-1-59955-933-9

Published by Sweetwater Books, an imprint of Cedar Fort, Inc., 2373 W. 700 S., Springville, UT 84663
Distributed by Cedar Fort, Inc., www.cedarfort.com

LIBRARY OF CONGRESS CATALOGING-IN-PUBLICATION DATA

Gubbins, John (John L.), 1943- , author.
  Profound river / John Gubbins.
    p. cm.
  Summary: The story of Dame Juliana Berners, an accomplished sportswoman and devout Catholic nun. Dame Juliana was the first to document the habits of fish and other wildlife, and is also credited as the inventor of fly fishing.
  ISBN 978-1-59955-933-9
  1. Berners, Juliana, b. 1388?--Fiction. 2. Naturalists--Fiction. 3. Fishing stories. I. Title.

  PS3607.U235P76 2012
  813'.6--dc23

                                2011036506

Cover design by Danie Romrell
Cover design © 2012 by Lyle Mortimer
Edited and typeset by Kelley Konzak

Printed in the United States of America

10 9 8 7 6 5 4 3 2 1

Printed on acid-free paper

this book is dedicated to

My mother, Clara, who gave me life,
My wife, Carol, who saved my life,
Dr. Gabe Logan, who gave my life direction,
And Eleanor Jackson, my unerring guide in writing about it.

praise for
Profound River

How ironic that a sport long considered the domain of men was officially started by a woman! Not only is Dame Juliana Berners' treatise on fishing, published in 1496, the oldest known document on the subject, it's also one of the best how-to guides ever written. Allegedly penned before Columbus was born, the work was filled with precise advice on everything from how to build a rod to constructing a hook, dying horsehairs and braiding lines. There was also expert advice on where and how to catch fish, stern cautions against trespassing and poaching, and words of wisdom on the need for conservation. Yet Dame Juliana has remained a mystery, until now. Painstakingly researched and exquisitely written, John Gubbins' *The Profound River* reels in the legend to give us the real woman behind the greatest milestone in angling history.

—Lyla Foggia
author of *Reel Women: The World of Women Who Fish*

John Gubbins has done a remarkable job of creating for us the person of Dame Juliana Berners, Prioress of the St. Mary of Sopwell Priory—the first woman to be published in English and the first person to have an illustration in a published book. We know her as the Mother of Fly Fishing, but there is so much more. . . . John's descriptions of her times, the circumstances of her life, her thoughts, and her shrewd maneuverings have given us a real page-turner that makes one feel [he has] known this remarkable woman in a most personal way.

—Gary Borger
Fly-Fishing Expert and Author

Academics will always ask: Was there really a Dame Juliana Berners, and if so, did she really write *A Treatyse on Fyhshynge wyth an Angle*? After you read *Profound River*, you'll never again be among those who ask those questions. John Gubbins has removed her from the mists of time and too little historical information; he has given her life, told her story. She will forever remain real to you.

In Dame Juliana's famous little book, fly-fishing is an ironically small but very important part, tacked on almost as an addendum in three pages at the end. In this historical novel about her imagined life, she as a fly-fisher and a writer about that sport, is as major a thread as we would expect. It's a good story, but just as it's only part of her own book, it's only part of this book about her.

The two more major, and perhaps more interesting, threads that run parallel through the book are first, how Dame Juliana, a young noble lady who loved hunting, hawking and fishing, became a nun in a priory north of London, where she wrote the book that made her famous, and second, how this nun, as eventual Prioress, tried to save the satellite sanctuary from the venality of her superiors at the controlling abby. They're both mysteries that you'll solve when you read *Profound River*.

—Dave Hughes
author of *Trout Flies*

contents

Acknowledgments xi

Chronology xix

Chapter One: Matins 1

Chapter Two: Lauds 31

Chapter Three: Prime 69

Chapter Four: Terce 97

Chapter Five: Sext 119

Chapter Six: None 148

Chapter Seven: Vespers 176

Chapter Eight: Compline 192

Epilogue: The Great Silence 203

Glossary 206

The Benedictine Hours 219

Who Was Dame Juliana Berners? 221

Suggested Readings 234

About the Author 235

acknowledgments

To my wife, Carol, my own Juliana, gifted fly fisher, wise counselor in all things medical and altruistic, for supporting me always and without question. She is a much better fly fisher than I am.

To Eleanor Jackson, fly fisher, the indispensable person. She knew my best writing before I did. But for her intelligence, perception, and patience, you would not be holding this book in your hands right now. And if you find you like this book after reading it, you know that there are no words that could discharge the debt we owe her.

To Jane Milkie, friend and artist, who made this a magical book by her maps and sketches.

To my son Alex, published poet and Arabic translator, an excellent fly caster and fisher, and an even better companion, for his many contributions to this text. He is now writing a better novel than I could ever hope to write.

To our friend, the poetess Beverly Matherne. Evenings at Beverly's house are always an occasion, as Dame Juliana would say, "a merry respite," where Sophocles, Plato, Augustine, Elizabeth Bishop, Dylan Thomas, Robert Frost, and so many others pull up a chair to chat.

To my sister Mary Gubbins Davis, who, although younger than me, has always been my older sister, sending me the classics to balance a literary diet dominated by crime and spy novels. Of course I read them; otherwise I would have lost her respect and I could not bear that.

To my sister-in-law Mary Patricia McCreary, a pure soul and

talented nature photographer, for reminding us to be kind to fish. And to her husband, Joseph Bourgoigne, experienced outdoorsman, who shares my love of the rushing Escanaba. A day in the company of Pat and Joseph is always a good day.

To my sister Nora and her husband, Jim, skilled artisans and determined fly fishers—our fishing buddies. Nora served an early apprenticeship in never-never land and considers Tinkerbell a sister. Also to my sister Margaret, my family's most committed exponent of Dame Juliana's "merry spirit."

To my sisters-in-law Julia McCreary Laws and Nancy McCreary Zurawka, who have maintained their enthusiasm for this project beyond all reason.

To Lori Burns and Louise Dotter, Louise for reading and editing the very earliest drafts, and Lori, a skilled fly fisher, for camping and fishing the Brule River with us. We are looking forward to the day we shall see Lori and her daughter, Anaveja, wading the Brule together. At age three, Anaveja owned her own fly rod.

To Rebecca Maker, a new friend, my Guidepost Books editor, who found new depth in what I thought was worn ground. This is a much stronger book because of her suggestions.

Mom, Carol, Eleanor, Beverly, Rebecca, my sisters, my sisters in law, my nieces, and our friends, Lori and Louise, I say you will each hear your voice in the intelligent and wise voice of Dame Juliana.

To my father, Joseph, and my grandfather John Charles who brought me fishing once I proved to them I could sit still in a boat for eight hours. They will not turn the pages of this book, but they understand every word of it.

To Mr. Arlen Sunn and Reverend Dr. Robert Harris for many enjoyable hours fishing together. So much of what I know about fishing and fly tying comes from their observations, generously shared.

To Mrs. Elaine Sunn, her daughter, Jennie, and her grandchild, "Peanut," who practice hospitality to strangers as Dame Juliana did.

To my son James, his wife, Emmy, and their two great sons, Gianni and Domenick, anglers all in the making.

To Dr. Gabe Logan, who changed my life by accepting me, a late applicant, into his oversubscribed classes on sports history and then by taking a personal interest in my essays on field sports history, even suggesting I submit them for publication. But for Dr. Logan, I would not have thought sports history worthy of serious thought.

To Dr. Keith Kendall, who was the first person to whom I suggested this book project, whereupon he enthusiastically turned it into a semester of directed study. Dr. Kendall introduced the rigor of scholarship into my thinking about Dame Juliana. There is no better person than Keith for thinking with a student. To Cindy Sue Kendall, Keith's wife, for reading an early manuscript, offering many helpful suggestions, and patiently answering my questions.

To the history department of Northern Michigan University, home to not only Dr. Logan and Dr. Kendall but also my teachers and mentors, the Drs. Chet DeFonso, Rebecca Mead, Howard Nicholson, and Bill Bergmann, for the time they made available to me, even when I arrived at their office door, as the spirit moved me, to ask questions out of the blue about fishing, sports clubs, Native American guides, tuberculosis, and business corporations.

To Robert Wulkowicz, arborist, the smartest man I know.

To Emeritus Professor Dr. Stephen Born of the University of Wisconsin and Dr. Harry Peterson, former president of Western Colorado State University, whose reading of early drafts of this book buoyed my efforts to complete it.

To all librarians, the true leaders of any civilized society, but especially Mrs. Debra Ely and Mrs. Cindy Mack of the Ishpeming Carnegie Public Library and Ms. Beverly Evans and Ms. Michelle Kimball of the Northern Michigan University library.

To all those Trout Unlimited members who have struggled for years to keep our trout waters pure, cold, and public.

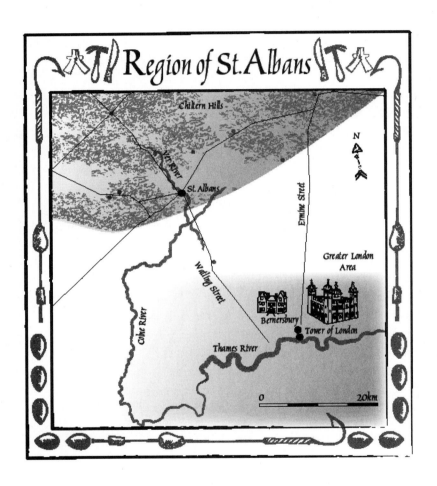

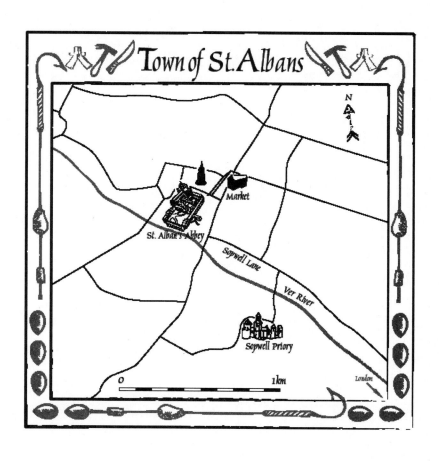

Town of St. Albans

Market

St. Alban's Abbey

Sopwell Lane

Ver River

Sopwell Priory

N

O 1km

London

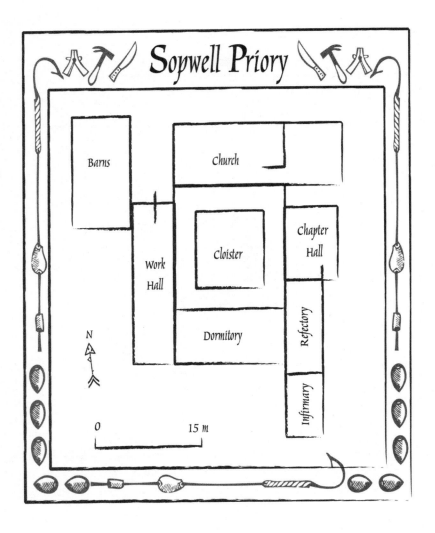

Sopwell Priory

Barns

Church

Cloister

Chapter Hall

Work Hall

Refectory

Dormitory

Infirmary

N

0   15 m

Anonymous portrait of Dame Juliana Berners

Wynken de Worde's illustration from his 1496 edition *Treatyse of Fysshinge wyth an Angle*. It is the first illustration in the history of English printing.

chronology

1373   Edward of Norwich, Second Duke of York is born.

1381   Dame Juliana Berners is born on June 19th to Lord James Berners and Anne Berew.

1388   Parliament votes to remove the counselors to Richard II. Dame Juliana's father, a knight of the chamber, is executed for treason; Parliament enacts legislation forfeiting all Lord Berners's estates except those protected by entailment, leaving the family with Bernersbury Manor.

1394–99   Dame Juliana and her brother, Richard, hunt from time to time with Edward, Second Duke of York.

1397   Edward, Second Duke of York, marries Philippa de Mohun, who was twice widowed before marrying Edward. Their union produces no offspring.

1399   Richard II is deposed by Henry Bolingbroke, who is crowned Henry IV.

1400   Richard II dies in the Tower of London.

1402   Dame Juliana's stepfather, Sir Roger Clarendon, is executed by Henry IV for treason.

1404   Dame Juliana begins her studies at Sopwell Priory.

1405–6   Edward, Second Duke of York, is imprisoned. While in prison, he translates *Livre de Chasse* by Gaston de Foix and adds five chapters of his own on hunting. Edward names his book *Master of Chase*.

1407–12   Dame Juliana begins her works on fishing, hawking, hunting, and heraldry and several years later takes her vows as a Benedictine nun.

1440   Dame Juliana is elected prioress of St. Mary Sopwell Priory.

1450   Earliest extant manuscript of the *Treatyse of Fysshinge wyth an Angle*, Dame Juliana's work on angling, is published.

1455   On May 22, the Wars of the Roses begin with the First Battle of St. Albans. The Town of St. Albans is sacked.

1461   On February 17, the Second Battle of St. Albans takes place. The Town of St. Albans and Sopwell Priory are sacked.

1480?   Dame Juliana dies in Cornwall.

1486   *Boke of St. Albans* is printed and published by the Abbey of St. Albans in partnership with the schoolmaster of St. Albans. The Boke is the first printed sports book in the English language.

1496   Wynken de Worde prints and publishes *The Boke of St. Albans* in Westminster at the sign of the Red Pale. He interposes Dame Juliana's *Treatyse of Fysshinge wyth an Angle* in the treatise on heraldry. The *Treatyse* becomes the first printed fishing book in the English language. More than sixteen editions of the *Treatyse* are published over the next century.

matins

The Annunciation
Midnight
March 25, 1477

he doves wintering in Sopwell's gables woke me just before midnight. Gusting drafts swept them from their perches. Again and again, they beat their wings to regain our sills— the sound of clapping . . . polite clapping. Almost ninety years ago, I heard such polite clapping the day my father was executed for treason. And thirty years ago, I heard it the day Sopwell elected me prioress.

I am Dame Juliana Berners, prioress of St. Mary of Sopwell Priory, the ninety-five-year-old shepherdess of twelve women and their souls. I look to holy Benedict of Nursia and his Rule for guidance. But it is the trust of my community, my sisters, which steels my purpose. It is my duty to ensure that tomorrow will be as today. I know when it has been a good day. All has been timely. Our chant is vigorous. The refectory bread is warm and fragrant. My sisters step a silent joy when they hurry to their chores. They do not murmur. They do not hesitate. I think of the good days, and for the sake of my sisters, I do not want them to end.

The sacristan's bell calling us to Matins will ring soon. From my window, I look across the Ver River to the silent town of St. Albans and its great abbey, a wandering mass of stone interrupting Watling Street, the centuries-old road to London. Rome engineered Watling Street to move its armies quickly north. Five hundred years later, the abbey diverted the street's linear path to make a fit resting place for the bones of St. Alban, Britain's first Christian martyr. The town now thrives on St. Alban's bones and the abundance of grass for grazing sheep. Pilgrims and wool. The town would not survive without them.

All is quiet. All is dark.

I went to bed worrying about the Abbey's plans for Sopwell and woke thinking about my father, Lord James Berners. Spring nights recall my father's arrest in Berners's hall when I was seven. It was near midnight, and the great hall door, our own oak trees, boomed and crashed open. His dogs rose about him and stood snarling at the intruders. Disarming our men at arms, Parliament's soldiers surrounded my father. The skirts of our tablecloths dripped red with hounds' blood as the dogs and my father struggled briefly but were overwhelmed. He slipped in the running blood and was dragged away. His arrest put us all on edge.

Ever since that spring, cold nights worry my sleep. I had missed the signs. It was true I was young and my father reassured my mother and me until the end. It did not matter. I had no excuse. I had missed the signs warning me that tomorrow my father's chair at our head table would sit empty and would sit empty forever.

King Richard II loved my father. He named my father a chamber knight, making him a trusted member of the young king's inner circle of young men, and he showed his affection by giving my father and his confidants manors and wardships with substantial income. My father supported the king unquestioningly and named his first son after him.

But the king's favors brought jealousy. And there were other irritants for those beyond the inner circle. Richard temporized in all matters, proving that he had not the expansive vision of his grandfather, Edward III, Britain's last great king. Edward was a born warrior invading France and pushing the Scots back farther north. Now ten years later, with Edward gone, France raided Britain's southeast coast, jeopardizing wool shipments to the continent, and Scotland took up residence in the northern towns it lost to Edward. Dominated by wool merchants, Parliament twice appropriated money for the invasion of France. It was an empty exercise, for Richard never raised an army. London was fuming.

Edward's old friends and counselors saw Britain slipping into lethargy and chaos. And they took action. Richard and his inner circle, for the most part inexperienced in war and diplomacy, were no match for seasoned professionals. John of Gaunt and his son Henry Bolingbroke, typical of the nobles arrayed against Richard, traveled with their armies to London to meet with the king. Faced with their superior strength, Richard temporized once more. Once too often. He suggested their dispute be laid before Parliament. Richard's ploy lost my father his life. Richard could not predict the outcome of delay. Nor could my father predict it. Not even Gaunt and Bolingbroke could predict it. No one but the London merchants could predict it, for they held Parliament, and they kept what they planned for the future to themselves.

The signs were plain. Night after night my brother and I heard my father's and mother's anxious discussions in Bernersbury's great hall. First Richard fled to the Tower of London for safety. Then his favorite, Robert de Vere, the Duke of Ireland and the most publicly hated of Richard's inner circle, raised an army, and on December 19, 1387, promptly lost it to Bolingbroke at Radcot Bridge. With Richard's army surrounded, de Vere swam the Thames at night. Jettisoning his armor, he slipped past search parties and, with the help of Richard's friends, fled to France never to return. Michael de la Pole, Earl of Suffolk, once Richard's chancellor, also fled, as did others from Richard's inner circle. Without ceremony, Parliament voted the one noble in its custody, Sir Nicholas Bembre, guilty and ordered his immediate execution. Bembre never had a chance to respond to his accusers, and no witnesses testified to prove his treason. By then we should have understood the mind of the Commons and the London merchants, but my father remained steadfast at Bernersbury.

As the days went by, and the bad news mounted, my mother grew more and more agitated and my father, more and more reassuring. My brother Richard and I sat silent and afraid. I refused to listen to my fears, studying instead my father's calm features and trying to decipher whether they reflected false resolution or true certainty. He would look down into my wide eyes and give my head a pat. "Pay no attention," he would say and send me to bed. When we heard that Parliament indicted my father and the other chamber knights for treason, I knew what I had seen on his face was a courtier's trick.

The true meaning of the signs appeared too late. My father's arrest ended my uneasy complacency. At first confused by the welter of events threatening King Richard and my father, I went through the signs again, but this time detached, without a thought of what I had to lose. In the end I was angry with myself, faulting myself for believing in my father's calming words only because I wanted my life with my family to go on the same as it always had. It would have been easy to excuse myself, for I was young and inexperienced, but I knew in my deepest mind that even at seven I should be keeping my own counsel. Now my father was gone. I could not have changed the course of Parliament nor my father's actions, but at least I could have prepared myself for his arrest and formed plans for the day after he was taken.

The night of my father's arrest, my mother shriveled and fell silent. Her silence caught and froze me. At dawn I beat at her locked door, but no answer came. Weeping, I wandered through the desolate great hall down to the lawns, our ponds, and the shallow, clear stream they fed. Hugging my knees, I sat down by a gravel run. The sun warmed me and dried my tears, and schools of barbel spawned at my feet. They were so resolute and playful, I watched for hours. By evening, coming to myself, I demanded my mother's attention, and she succumbed to my insistent cries.

But she could not comfort me. Instead I supported her, mouthing soft words and hollow optimism. Days later she began to eat again. I never trusted her after that night, and to this day suspect anyone who seeks my sympathy when I am so drained of feeling that I have none to give. I only realized this years later as a novice. By then my family described me as offish.

Over the following weeks, my mother traveled frequently to London with her brother, Sir William Berew, to intercede for my father. During Parliament's April recess, she was in London the whole of the month. When she returned, she retreated to her room and remained secluded for days. She no longer ate with us. Normally slim, weight dropped from her until her gowns hung in folds, and we all worried about her health. No one picked up my father's cause. Parliament wanted to make an example of him, though they had no evidence against him. As my uncle commented to me bitterly one evening, even King Richard would not intervene with Parliament on my father's behalf. He was too preoccupied with keeping his crown.

All that spring, I fixed my mind on the barbel. Their regularity and gravity settled me. Foolishly, I thought I understood them. For the greater part of the day, they fed regularly off the bottom but without energy. They picked at everything. Groups shoaled and tarried in the aquatic weeds hugging the stream. If I crept close, the shoals moved off, leaving huge wakes. If I sat quietly back from the stream edge, the shoals returned and resumed feeding. Toward evening, they took up stations in gravel runs and fed purposefully.

I fed them everything. Our cook, Elizabeth, warned me, "It is a waste of time because I will never—do you understand—never serve barbel. Their meat is poisonous. Everyone knows it."

Nonetheless, Elizabeth gave me bits and pieces of cheese, meat, and bread. I dug worms and scavenged the kitchen's refuse for maggots. In early spring my barbel were partial to cheese cut in small pieces. Later they greedily ate large red worms and white maggots. When the kitchen was exhausted of new baits, I resorted again to cheese pieces and red worms. They became my standbys.

Elizabeth grew fretful. "Why barbel?" And she repeated, "They are useless." Despite her opposition, I kept records of my barbel's behavior. It was exciting. I was writing down events that no one else had ever recorded. Very likely because no one else thought them important enough to record. But I found that when I write down what happens, it becomes real.

Elizabeth was skeptical. "If you weren't a child, I could not explain it to the household. But people forgive children their frivolity."

Angry, I told her, "When my father dies, I will no longer be a child, but I will still fish for barbel."

"You hush. Your mother is doing her best," she whispered.

I had come to believe neither in my mother's best nor in the mercy of the Parliament on which we all waited. But I held my tongue.

Notwithstanding her doubts, Elizabeth called on Robert, the gamekeeper, to help with my tackle. They were thankful to keep me busy. Robert gave me hooks and floats, showed me how to braid lines of horse tail hair, and helped me cut a slim, ten-foot beech sapling for a pole—my first fishing rod. I insisted on grey horse tail hair instead of black for my line. My barbel were smarter than black lines. I knew enough not to insult them. Finally I was ready.

I first tried bits of cheese with a float. Standing back from the stream, all that was needed was a flip of my pole and the cheese and float fell by the weeds' edge. I could see barbel tucked underneath.

It was immediately obvious that a float was unnecessary. The cheese raced down the gravel run a good foot above the nearest fish. The barbel did not even turn for an inspection.

So I removed the float. Flipping the line with my cheese bait back to the head of the run, the current took over again. After it drifted three feet or so, the bait sank to the floor of the stream but then bounced quickly downstream past the barbel. And what was worse, when my line swept past, the current lifted the bait up until it dragged on the surface below me.

Puzzled, I reasoned that the cheese should be pinned to the bottom of the run. I punched the tip of my pole in the gravel and watched while the line and bait sank. But once the line grew taut in the current, the impaled cheese started waving violently up and down. The barbel scattered. It had been so much easier when I threw my baits into the run unattached. Then they found the bottom and slowly, very slowly, rolled along. The line was the problem. I had already proved barbel like cheese. It was not the bait. It was the line.

Investigating our workshops, I found one with materials for patching the hall's windows and roofs. And there, I found thin, flat pieces of lead. With my pole, a bag of cheese, and a strip of lead, I went back to the stream. Cutting what I guessed to be the right amount of lead, I wrapped the strip about a foot above the hook and cheese. Then I swung it all out just beyond the weeds' edge.

A slight splash and the lead anchored the bait in the stream bed. I put my pole down and crept to the edge, peering into the stream. Sure enough, the lead was fixed in the gravel and the cheese trailed a foot back, barely lifting off the bottom. There was only a whisper of movement. Perfect. I crawled back to my pole and sat quietly.

After a while, I lifted up the pole and dropped the bait a yard farther downstream. Again I waited. As I was about to lift my bait again, I felt a gentle pecking. Waiting only an instant, I lifted my pole with a jerk.

Water and weeds churned. Then my line moved deliberately out into the current, carrying weeds and a wake with it. I pulled back again with no effect. My line continued inexorably downstream. Bewildered, I tugged again but only succeeded in enraging the fish. It charged downstream in a rush, pulling the pole from my hands. I ran along the bank, keeping pace with the fish, the pole, the line, and the bait. Sloe thorns plucked at my shift and tunic, and alder branches whipped my arms and face.

The race ended one hundred feet downstream. My barbel dug itself into a weed mass on the opposite bank of the stream, and my rod floated just below it. Yes, my barbel, for it was now more than ever my barbel even if I had not yet held it. The fish not only had my hook in its mouth, but it had also stolen my pole.

A distant ford upstream was out of the question. By the time I crossed it, the fish, pole, line, and hook might be gone. I quickly sat down by the stream's edge and thrust my legs into the current. My shift and tunic, silt, and decaying vegetation billowed up around my waist. The water was frigid, and long, sinuous weeds clung to me when I tried working my legs. Stumbling, I fell on my face. Gasping with the cold and water in my eyes and mouth, I bolted upright, sputtering.

Pushing my legs forward again, I dislodged more silt and uprooted more weeds. They clung tighter as I wrestled to free myself. Finally, with a kick, I made the clear gravel and reached my pole. I lifted it and found the barbel still on.

Teasing the line, I tried to disengage the barbel from the weed mass without tearing the hook out. Water dock and watercress draped my line and the fish. Carefully, plant by plant, I untangled the mass, letting it float piece by piece downstream.

The barbel's back was now visible, so I reached down to grab its tail. But my clumsy probing woke it. It bolted back upstream, pushing a bow wave in front of it. I pulled back on my pole to stop it, but the pole was unforgiving, and my line close to breaking.

The barbel did not slow. I had no choice but to follow. By pulling the fish to one side or the other, I could keep it in the middle of the run. But it was leading me I knew not where. Finally I let the fish have its head, and the barbel dove under a floating weed mass. I was back where I started, but this time, both the barbel and I were tethered together in three feet of water.

The mud and soaking cold sapped my strength. I could not feel my legs. Evening was coming, and a damp mist hung thickly over the meadow. The barbel totally engulfed itself in a thick weed mass. I was losing feeling in my hands, and I did not have the strength nor the patience to pull the weeds off my line again.

So I decided on a reckless course. I threw my pole on the bank. Following the line down into the weed mass with my hands, I determined the barbel's location. Realizing the weeds which slowed me also bound the fish, I dug down with both arms, careful not to provoke it. This great mass of water, weeds, and fish, I picked up and hugged to me. The barbel barely struggled. Neither of us had any fight left. With one last great effort, I threw the weeds, my hook, the line, and my barbel up on the bank and fell exhausted and shivering beside them.

I had become part of the stream, the muck, the slime, and the fish. Strings of weeds clung to my face and arms. My shift and tunic were unrecognizable. But it did not matter. I had crossed over, and a great awe flooded and warmed me. No person, no words, no whispers ever held me again like my barbel.

The barbel was not what I expected. I thought it would be dark. Instead I found it had a green back, golden sides, and a white belly. Scarlet ringed its fins. Gasping, it flopped several times and then lay still so that I could touch it.

It was so, so cold and so, so smooth. But I felt its virtues. The barbel is the bull of the gravel run. It holds its ground against all challengers.

Then I let my barbel go.

the sacristan's bell rings. The night wind dies, and Sopwell's doves stop clapping. I draw on my sandals and take one more look toward the abbey church. A hundred candles light their Matins, and their bells ring the hour over sleeping St. Albans.

Going down to chapel, I listen for ice grating against the Ver River bridge. For three days the south wind blew the moist taste of rotting snow through Sopwell's cloister. Runoff pooled in the cloister where evening and Compline glazed it smooth.

Our sandals skitter across the cloister yard. While I test for balance, my sisters, all younger, skate and giggle past to gain the chapel. Standing at the door waiting for stragglers, I turn back. Spring's constellations etch themselves across the ice. They humble me, and I offer the incense of my breath in gratitude.

Sister Margery follows, trudging slowly. She is in pain, I believe, although she says nothing. Then comes Sister Joan Chapelle, stately and grave but quick with a smile and an encouraging hand. And the last, Sister Carol, our seamstress, hurries past, fighting sleep.

Turning, I listen again for the far-off moan of ice against bridge abutments. I hear a faint scraping. Tonight is the beginning. It is the turn time. Willow buds will begin to swell, leaf, and glow a fragile green. I have missed the voices of bees among our roses and apricot trees. They will return in a few weeks. For several days, the Ver will be high and dark, but after the spate, it will clear and gentle. The Ver's black and red spotted trout now lie motionless under rocks and logs in deep protective pools, but in a few days they will move to riffles and avidly snatch mayflies, stoneflies, and red worms. I could not be happier.

Our bell stops tolling. Pushing the chapel door shut, I find my place in choir, the last to enter the glow of our sweet-smelling candles. Sister Clare, our cantor, stands, and the rustling of Psalters follows. Now it is time for our most important work.

We, the nuns of St. Mary Sopwell, begin reciting the fifteen gradual psalms of Matins for the feast of the Annunciation. Sleep and cold drag on us, but we complete them without error. Our bell tolls a second time, and at my signal falls silent.

I motion to Sister Clare, and she raises her voice for the Deus in adjutorium.

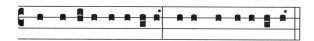

O God, Come to my as-sist-ance, O Lord make haste to help me.

We echo the invocation and then we pray to ourselves:

Our Father, who art in heaven . . .
Hail Mary, full of grace; the Lord is with you . . .

Tonight in the dark, I feel again my father's certain presence, the anxious presence of my mother, and the urgent presence of Edward, the Second Duke of York. But there is more. I feel also the presence of my cousins, Eleanore and Catherine, and more deeply than ever I feel

9

the reassuring presence of my friends, Constance and Isabel, also my sisters-in-law. They have been much on my mind of late.

They surround me in those moments when the border between the living and the dead thins. The odd moment. The unscheduled moment between the end of a task and the beginning of a new one. Those moments when I fall momentarily inward. Turning a page in my Psalter, knotting on my sandals. It is then my earliest memories crowd in on me, confirming my growing sense that I am old.

I have outlived all those I knew in my youth. I have gone from being just old to being ancient. The curious ask me the secret of my long life. The secret, I say, is to ignore the question. In the past, this response brought a smile and a change of subject. But of late it has not been enough. My age has become legendary. They press me harder for an answer. The most truthful answer I offer is that fishing has extended my life, but when I say so, the listeners are never satisfied. So I do not give this answer anymore, although I have stated it in the *Treatyse*, for it is true.

The questions of the curious provoke my own question to myself. It is a question I have entertained for years. It comes to me every night I climb the steps to my cell after Compline, "What will be the sum of my life should I die tonight?" My answers are shallow. They are just the sum of my accomplishments. My books and my devotion to Sopwell and to my sisters. Of course there are my yearnings for the future, for what could be. I know there will not be enough years in my life to realize them all. I do not leave children, but I have loved all my students as if they were my children. And they call me "Mother," a word that quickens my spirits every time I hear it. But these answers are all in the present, where I spend my days.

Lately the question of what sums me up comes with greater urgency. Truly I am very old. I could die in my sleep any night. And so I feel the need to tally for myself the final sum of my life—my whole life. I wish to see it laid out as precise as a column of figures in an account book. Not just what I have done in the present, but also the years before Sopwell, the years I locked away. I have not yet figured them into the sum of myself. A mistake. For years I thought my youthful memories a distraction. While preparing to profess my vows, I took my own special vow: only to look ahead—still my habit of mind. So I carefully rolled up the stories of my youth like so many out-of-date tapestries and stored them away, forgotten, in a dusty cupboard. There they waited for the exploring hands of curious children kept inside on a rainy day to dislodge them. That day has come. I will figure my early years into the sum of who I am. The tapestries thump to the floor and begin to unroll, telling the story of my journey to Sopwell. The colors are intense, more intense than I remember them. They tell of my days at Bernersbury and my visits to Conisbrough and Bodiam, the three tapestries of my youth.

The brilliant scenes capture me, and I feel my family about me. But it is Edward and Isabel I sense most deeply—my guides into the past. Long ago I wove Edward into each tapestry as my mentor, then admirer, and finally as a traitor. I have chosen to best remember him as a hunter, his greatest role.

And it was as a hunter I most often daydreamed about Edward. There was one insistent daydream. It returned again and again to me, then an adolescent girl yearning to relive the old romances of King Arthur and Sir Tristan. It filled many aimless moments. Whenever my mind drifted, it worked its way slowly from the edges of inattention until it rushed to center stage, transfixing me. While in its grip, all I could do was stare into space until it ran its course.

It is a simple enough story, with some basis in fact, even. But it was a story I kept to myself, never relating its details to anyone, not even my cousins. Nothing shameful—just an admission of my strong feelings for Edward, a fact that many guessed. That was more than fifty years ago.

SISTER CLARE ENDS her recitation of the lesson from Proverbs with the verses

She has sent out her maids to call from the high-est tow-ers in the town,

"Who-ev-er is sim-ple, let him turn in here!" To him who lacks judg-ment

she says, "Come, eat of my bread and taste of the wine I have mixed.

"Leave your sim-ple ways, and walk in the way of in-sight."

Edward the Second, the Second Duke of York, was the psalmist's simple man. He never walked in the way of insight. After storing up my memories of Edward, I reviewed them once later upon hearing the news of his death at Agincourt. It was then my adolescent daydream returned to me, coming not as an expression of yearning but as a fitting dirge for a brave warrior.

Tonight my daydream comes again, but this time with the same intense attraction for him I felt as an adolescent girl. While I mouth an antiphon, I stare again, transfixed. A contemplative lost in revelation—the revelation of my own long forgotten yearnings for Edward, yearnings born of days spent working close to him hunting. The poetic romance of Tristan shapes the course of my feelings. But only so far. In the end, my daydream shows I am not like Isolde, who, without reservation, chose Tristan over all else. I found reservations.

My daydream always tells the same story. I am hawking with my mother, my cousins Eleanore and Catherine, my friend Constance, and my sister-in-law Isabel near Hedingham Castle in Essex. In the daydream, Isabel has just wed my brother Richard. My mother chose a high, narrow ridge for us. As we look down its length, Hedingham's massive tower is in the distance to our right, and a broadening valley is close on our left. The valley is pastureland encircled with wooded slopes and a flooded marsh at its far end.

The high vantage point shows off our merlins. They spring off our gauntlets, bells ringing, circling against a pale sky, and then diving. Mother chose well, for by noon, the dogs are tired and only a few young, untested merlins sit in their cadges.

As the pile of dead partridges, rabbits, and pheasants grows, my mother loses interest and manages breakfast. The Earl of Essex has been generous. In a grove of ash trees, his pages roll out a saffron-colored carpet while my mother, cousins, Constance, and Isabel, sitting elegantly straight-backed and blonde, in their green and blue woolen gowns, set out venison pies and aged Gascon red.

They call for me to join them. Adjusting my short blue tunic and sleeved white shift so they rest comfortably on my hips, I beg off for the moment. My mother disapproves of my clothes. Too mannish. My outfit was designed for hawking, more practical dress for sitting a horse astride all day. Catching a golden flash, I stand up on my stirrups and spy a single horseman, riding up the valley toward us.

The horseman is Edward, the Duke of York, unmistakable, even at a distance. His hair and beard are the deepest black, and his complexion a weathered olive, both gifts from his Castilian mother. Deceptively massive, draped in his close-fitting blue and embroidered gold tunic and blue hose, his muscular frame rides deftly with the precision of a practiced dancer keeping time to a familiar beat.

My daydream relates that Edward, his party, and their baying hounds followed the last of their relays chasing a winded hart through the valley and up its wooded slopes. He must have seen our merlins aloft, for moments after the death note sounds, he emerges from the woods and rides in our direction. But his horse is blowing, the race up the steep slope was too exerting, and so Edward's pace slows. I have time to release my last and youngest merlin, a white, brown, and tan acrobat, twisting, turning, and sounding its bells joyfully in the blue.

In the daydream, a hare, the rabbit's larger cousin, bolts from cover to gain its warren below me. My merlin turns, flapping its long, graceful wings, and begins its dive to intercept it. Just before the hare reaches the safety of its warren, the merlin falls on it. Together they trigger a poacher's snare, a wire loop, hung like a hangman's noose at the warren's entrance. Both the predator and the prey are caught, a writhing ball of feather and fur pulling the noose tighter and tighter against its anchor, a deeply driven peg, the merlin caught by its talons and the hare caught by its neck.

Urging my horse downhill, I find the hare and merlin alive. The merlin struggles to fly, but the weight of the hare and the stubborn peg drag it back to earth. Its efforts grow more and more frantic.

Jumping off my horse, I fall to my knees beside the bird and pull at the snare's loop, but the knot is now fully entangled in the hare's ears. I can not work it loose, so I snap the hare's neck and end the melee.

Just then, Edward pulls up. Ragged and bloody from the hunt, he dismounts beside me as I place a hood over the merlin's head and stroke the bird's shoulders to calm it. I can hear Edward's breathing and sense his sure fingers when I hand him the merlin. From my bag, I retrieve a pair of pliers and begin to cut the wire, but my efforts are clumsy. Casting off my gauntlet and pulling my riding gloves away with my teeth, I grasp the wire above the knot and work to shear it.

The wire slackens. With my fingers, I work it loose from the merlin's talons. But as I do so, the now sharpened loose tip whips about and cuts the fleshy tip of my right forefinger. A dull pain arrests me for a moment, but, still kneeling, I gather up the merlin from Edward's hands, remove the hood, and gently toss it aloft so that it can ascend the slope to find refuge among our cadges. I will tend her wounds later.

Sitting back on my thighs, I notice fresh droplets of blood both on the blue of my hose and on the blue of Edward's tunic. Edward also notices. Instinctively I raise my forefinger to my mouth.

But his hand catches mine, and he puts my forefinger in his mouth. Once the bleeding stops, Edward slides my finger from his mouth and deliberately dries it with his tunic, making sure not to reopen the wound. Despite the warm afternoon sun, the wounded finger grows cold. So I place my right arm across my body and rest the injured finger gently next to the skin above my left breast. As the finger warms, I feel it throb in time with my slowly beating heart.

Just then, I look up, and Edward's gaze catches me. His black eyes and my green eyes meet, and the beat of my heart leaps forward. Betrayed by my quickening feelings, I blush and lower my eyes, retreating to gain time and so gather my emotions. To think. Edward has noticed all this, yet he waits.

The space between us turns tactile. Our knees are inches from each other. Our horses grow impatient and stamp the ground nearby. I remain sitting back on my thighs. But my heart continues to race toward what can only be imagined. The daydream never tells me where. Does my heart see me lying down with Edward? Does my imagination see me sharing in all his grace, his mighty heart, and his generosity? It would be such a relief to pour myself out and so, slow my heart.

To find relief, I need only pierce the space between us. A slight smile, a lighthearted laugh, a brush of my fingers. The decision hangs on me. I feel its importance in my deepest self, as a traveler about ready to cross into an unmapped frontier. Curiosity presses me forward, yet I know that if I invade that palpable space between us, memories of my sojourn in that uncharted wilderness will inevitably return and take first place among my thoughts.

My breathing grows ragged and labored. It is then that I and my daydream become one. Do I wish to make more of Edward than a friend? I am uncertain. So I sit, unmoving. Waiting. Thinking.

Neighing, the horses call to us. The urgency of Edward's presence dissipates, and my heartbeat slows. Leaning back, I rise slowly, careful not to cross the threshold between us. Disappointed, Edward rises slowly to mount his horse. Swinging into our saddles, we ride wordlessly toward Hedingham's tower, the space between us intact. No words, no gestures penetrate it.

Such is the story of my daydream. A youthful story, charged with the passions of youth. And as is so often the case with daydreams, it tells the truth of my feelings for Edward.

It was only much later that I asked myself the hard questions. Was my indecision due to my cowardice? Was I waiting for Edward to make the decision for both of us? By then I knew more of him, and the questions became easier to answer.

When the daydream bobbed up tonight during prayers, it towed up with it ancient memories now resting uneasily just below the surface of my mind. It hauled them to the edge of awareness as red and white cork floats haul up fishermen's nets to rest just beneath the surface of a rolling sea. Ancient memories of days spent at Conisbrough Castle, Bodiam Castle, and finally our own Bernersbury Manor lay just out of reach, waiting for the next ocean storm to beach them whole and complete.

Looking down into a blue-green sea, down past the red and white floats, my eyes follow vagrant shafts of light penetrating the heaving sea to glimpse the nets as they fold and unfold in the currents. Ever moving, they tug against their weights. Looking into that shifting murk, I dimly make out events that happened long ago. Their outlines form and re-form in the currents. Turrets, towers, and crenellated walls, fields, rivers, and darkened woods, dogs, horses, and hawks. And I glimpse the faces of my mother, my cousins, and Isabel, as well as the faces of my father, my uncle, Edward, and my brother, Richard, with my friend Constance, and under the lapping waves I hear their garbled voices. More thought than sound.

My eyes return to the tapestries my imagination stretched out on Sopwell's chapel floor. Conisbrough . . . Bodiam . . . Bernersbury. Three castles. Three memories that tell the story of my journey to Sopwell. I thought I was done with them, but I now sense I will not be able to roll them up tonight. They demand my study. In the half light of chapel, besides the voice of Edward, I hear one voice rising above all the others. It is Isabel's clear voice. Her, a wraith, and I, the old nun robed in black wool. Her face and hair are alight, but her manner is grave, and the crisp sweep of her blue gown bespeaks determined purpose.

I stand ready, "You have often been on my mind, Isabel. I am happy to see you."

"And I you, Juliana," she whispers.

"You were my greatest regret." Then tears obscure my sight. Isabel remains silent, impatient, and I begin again, "Why have you come after all these years?"

"To keep an old promise," she says. Then she leans over, whispering in my ear, "I have not come to hear an apology. There is no need. I am here to remind you of our days together and to urge you to find a new path."

"Isabel," I reply, "I spend my days tracing and retracing the geography of my life. My path has been clear for longer than I care to remember. Are you telling me my present path is treacherous?"

"Yes, Juliana," Isabel says, looking anxious.

SISTER CLARE INTONES the familiar first lines of Psalm 95, the introductory psalm for Matins. Her voice is clear as she pushes us to shake off the last of our sleep.

O come, let us sing to the Lord;

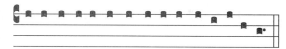

Let us make a joy-ful noise to the bed-rock of our safe-ty!

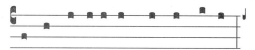

Let us come be-fore him with thanks-gi-ving;

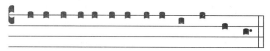

Let us make a mer-ry noise to him with songs of praise.

Sopwell's first business is earnest prayer, our joyful noise. As Psalm 119 counsels, seven times a day, we sing the hours of the divine office, and once at night we keep vigil. The night watch, the eighth hour, we now call Matins. My spiritual father, St. Benedict, cautioned that our minds must be in harmony with the sacred text when we give voice to the hours. At first I took his caution to mean that we must live fully within every word of what we sing. As a novice, this was easy. The psalms, lessons, hymns, responses, and antiphons were new to me. I could sing each word with a single-minded voice.

In time I found my attention shifting while my voice carried forward each word. My mind would periodically retreat to the angle of light on the chapel floor, the fragrance of lavender from the cloister, or my unfinished chores, but then return just as quickly to the words of the office. The problem was that I had completely memorized the office. I not only could recite it in Latin and English by heart, but I could say or sing it without thinking. By the end of my novitiate, the divine office had become second nature.

Yet I redoubled my efforts to remain fully intent on the meaning of each word and every tone. I consciously turned my attention back again and again to the meaning of the prayer only to have my attention wander away again and again. It was exhausting and confusing. Self-discipline, my usual response to personal shortcomings, was for once not enough.

After struggling and failing every day to fix my attention on each word, I reviewed with a new eye holy Benedict's words. It was then I read with new understanding his counsel that the best prayer is short and pure. I began to see the whole of the celebration of the hours as a single exercise. It was not a collection of separate tones and words but one whole. It was not the attention to each word that fostered prayerfulness. Rather it was the singing of the whole. And the sense of the whole of the hours, in succeeding days, deepened my readiness for prayer until it flooded every waking moment. Working, reading, and eating all were buoyed and given purpose through voicing the hours.

Surprisingly, as my prayerfulness grew, I found short and pure prayers surfacing. They detached from the psalms, the antiphons, and the lessons of the hours. Sometimes simple words, like "steadfast" or "measure of life," and sometimes whole phrases, like "they are like a dream, like grass," caught my attention and stayed with me throughout the day, informing my thoughts. And so the enduring side of prayerfulness took shape in my heart. Away from chapel, my mind would turn over the psalms for hours while my hands washed dishes, scrubbed floors, or pruned our roses.

Prayer fragments continue to ascend and float on the surface of my awareness. How they take form, I cannot say. To this day I cannot consciously call them up. I have often tried and just as often failed. They come on their own. When I dive into the depths of prayer, I surface with fragments. Only then the text and the meaning and my voice become one and pure.

Each day now, I eagerly seek to voice the hours because it feeds my soul and propels my spirit through the day. The fragments that surface are unexpected but welcome. Each hour is novel. Each day is novel. And I look ahead with a glad heart.

WE PRESS ON with Psalm 95, an old friend whom we visit almost every night.

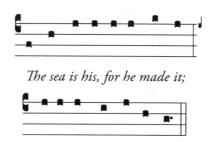

The sea is his, for he made it;

For his hands shaped the dry land.

I went to sleep tonight worried about the abbey's plans to restore St. Alban's shrine. St. Albans's abbot, William Wallingford, has not yet called on Sopwell to contribute to the building fund. All the signs are that he will. As is his practice, he will not consult Sopwell but will simply present us with the bill. And that is what I worry about, the size of his bill.

The abbey owns every square foot of land for miles around. It owns Sopwell. It owns the land on which the town of St. Albans sits. Once the Normans subdued Britain, the town's residents became the abbey's villeins in thrall to the St. Albans abbot, a Norman. It has always been so ever since. No town resident will ever call the property on which he or she has lived for generations their own. For the privilege of residing here, they must support the abbey's monopolies and follow the abbot's laws. The abbey intends to keep it so.

The abbot often governs with a heavy hand. His rule is absolute. St. Albans residents are subject to the abbot in all matters, personal, spiritual, economic, and political. The abbot sets the rules by which the town runs. His court adjudges the accused and punishes the guilty . . . fines, imprisonment, excommunication, even death. His law court sits in Moot Hall. The abbey's great gate serves as the town jail. And the skulls of the executed sit on posts erected at St. Albans's gates.

Of late, the abbey grows poorer. Fewer pilgrims bow before St. Alban's relics. Fewer inns fill up by day's end. Fewer coins circulate in the market. And fewer bushels of grain are ground in the abbey's mills. The abbey plans to reverse its losses by refurbishing the abbey church with more marble and adorning St. Albans's reliquary with more precious stones. The full breadth of the abbot's vision is unknown. He has as yet not revealed his mind.

The signs say the redecorating will be extensive. The town was the first to feel the pinch. A resident of St. Albans must get the abbot's permission to get married, to go to school, even to enter an apprenticeship. Permission is needed to probate a will and to migrate out of town. Each time the abbot grants permission, the resident must pay a fee. Wallingford has raised all such fees. Further, he has raised the portion of grain that goes back to the abbey for grinding the townspeople's grain. It has always been the rule that all grinding must be done at the abbey's mill on the Ver, and the abbey guards its monopoly vigorously. And for centuries, the abbey took a set portion of the grain brought for grinding as its fee. After the recent increase in the portion taken, the abbey's marshals search the town on reports of hand mills. The town is unhappy, but it has no recourse.

Other fees have been raised. The fees for hunting the abbey's warrens and for fishing the Ver are now out of reach for most of St. Albans's residents. The Abbey has raised the fee for setting up a stall in the central market, and its law court has increased its fines for everything from adultery to trespass. The marshals are rewarded for each arrest.

The abbey has not stopped there. It is selling off its great oak forest. This is the most telling sign of the abbey's intentions. Every day we hear chopping and the rustling crash of trees as they fall prone one after another. Magnificent ancient oaks, home to deer and stoat, hare and wild boar, lay still in the sunlight, and the fragrance of freshly cut wood scents the night air. The abbey forest stood unmolested since the time of St. Alban, but now woodcutters cart off to London trees that cannot be replaced. No abbot has worked to so thoroughly eradicate St. Albans's greatest treasure. The townspeople have complained to the bishop of Lincoln, but his loud protests do not move the abbot. Wallingford refuses to even meet with him.

Sopwell will be the last to hear the abbot's demands. I worry that once the abbot assesses his needs after squeezing all other sources of funds, he will present a huge bill to Sopwell to make up the shortfall. His demand will be heavy, I am certain—so heavy it may undo all the progress Sopwell has made toward independence. This is what worries me the most. Our students have been generous to us. Many marry well and remember us with grants of property and income. Sopwell has made steady progress toward the ideal community as envisioned by St. Benedict, a self-sufficient community, making its spiritual decisions as a community and in the full freedom of the spirit. Wallingford is suspicious of Sopwell's motives. Our growing independence concerns him. With an enormous bill, he could begin confiscating our holdings and thereby both end our independence and cure his shortfall.

The most disturbing sign of the abbey's attitude toward Sopwell came to my attention yesterday. Father Joseph, an ordained monk, assigned by the abbey as Sopwell's confessor, took me aside after Mass.

He wished to warn me. "The abbot asked me about your confession. He wanted to know how frequently you disclosed your sins to me."

"I hope you told him. There is nothing to hide," I replied.

"Yes. But that is not all. He wanted to know what you confessed," Father Joseph said, clearly in distress. "The abbot knows that what is said in confession is inviolable."

"No doubt," I said thoughtfully.

"I believe he feels estranged from Sopwell," he said. "It could just be curiosity about your intentions as prioress."

"That may be," I said, "But he need only ask me what my intentions are."

"I am sure he has the warmest feelings toward the community here," he said cheerfully.

"Certainly. I have spoken my mind freely with him and his brother, Prior Thomas. He should have no suspicions about my intentions and the spiritual health of Sopwell," I said emphatically.

"Of course not," he said quickly. "I believe he feels uninformed. It is unorthodox for him to ask about your confession, but I believe it was a harmless question."

"Unorthodox is one way to put it."

"You should spend more time at the abbey conversing not only with the abbot but also with the prior," Father Joseph said. "That will help dispel their doubts."

"I do not believe it is that simple," I said.

"You could be right. He does believe that you are allied with the bishop of Lincoln and are providing him with information that puts Abbot Wallingford in a bad light. There is this business about the forest. All of St. Albans is upset, and the bishop is upset," he said.

"That is none of my doing. The bishop is a distant cousin of mine, but he has better sources of intelligence than the observations of an old nun," I said.

"I will repeat your words to the abbot," Father Joseph said.

"Is that all?" I asked, not wishing to continue a discussion whose subtleties may be reported back to the abbey inaccurately.

"There was one more matter the abbot raised," he said hesitantly and frowned. "He wanted to know whether you or your sisters are opposed to the restoration of the abbey church and St. Alban's reliquary."

"You know best that this subject has not come up," I said with purpose. "You can tell the abbot that we stand ready to help."

"I will carry your message back," Father Joseph said with relief.

SISTER CLARE ANNOUNCES the antiphon of the second nocturn for the feast of the Annunciation:

God shall help her by show-ing her his face.

The office weighs heavily on Sister Margery. She is failing. I have urged her to spend more time in the priory's warming room and have placed a bench there for her. She is losing appetite. Most disappointing, she will not address my suggestion that she retire to the infirmary.

Sister Margery needs trout and salmon to regain her strength. Salmon are now out of season and very expensive in London's markets. The abbey buys them for noble guests, but I could not justify to Wallingford such an expenditure for one who is merely respected as a worthy woman and an exemplary nun.

Tonight Margery's face is set and pale. She sits uncomfortably in her choir stall, drawing her feet up now and again off our rush floor mats. Her night boots appear worn and thin. But Margery makes no complaint during our morning chapter meetings. Exhausted perhaps, she no longer fights the cold. Although I am entrusted with her well-being, I am hesitant to press her. Summer's warmth will help. After Lauds I will speak to Sister Carol about new night boots for Sister Margery. We have three rabbit skins for lining.

What else can I do? Sopwell and the abbey have tried their cures without success. I have searched medical texts and listened to the tales of St. Albans's herbalists.

I stare into the void. Time passes while I fight the conclusion that all I can do is ease her pain. I am losing this fight. I will talk to the herbalists again.

SISTER CLARE CHANTS the lesson for the second nocturn. It is from the Book of Proverbs. I find myself intent on the words:

Bless-ed is the man who hears me, watch-ing dail-y at my gates, wait-ing at

my gate. For he who knows me finds life and shall ob-tain the fa-vor of the

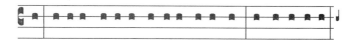

Lord. But he who sins a-gainst me los-es his own soul. Wis-dom has built her

house, she has hewn out her se-ven pil-lars: she has killed her beasts: she has

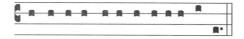

Min-gled her wine; she has fur-nish-ed her tab-le.

Many men have watched at my gates. There have been St. Albans's abbots, five in all since I became prioress. Before Wallingford, there were Abbots Bostock, Stoke, Wheathampstead, and Albone, one a sluggard, one an esthete, and the rest decorators. As with Wallingford, they all called on me with their urgent demands. Shrugging off the rush of words, I carefully examined the abbey's needs, sought the counsel of my sisters, pondered our likely future, and then, when ready, came to a decision. Wallingford does not respect deliberation. It means delay. Yet I know no other way.

The latest man to watch at my gates is Wynken de Worde. He arrived in St. Albans representing Caxton, his master, to negotiate with Wallingford. The abbot wished to purchase one of Caxton's old printing presses. While here, de Worde spoke with the abbey librarian, who mentioned my field sports books including my *Treatyse of Fysshynge wyth an Angle*. He and Caxton were enthused and on de Worde's next visit approached the librarian for copies of all my books to print and sell in London. The librarian informed de Worde that the abbey intended to publish my hunting and hawking books. This leaves only the *Treatyse*, yet Caxton and de Worde remain enthusiastic, for they believe that a fishing book will be very popular among the anglers of London.

Wynken de Worde knows everyone in Westminster and St. Albans . . . and their business. Slight, with darting blue eyes, and a very social, energetic young man, he is enthusiastic about Caxton's new printing press and, as he calls it in his charming French accent, his "new art." Caxton is fortunate to have an apprentice like de Worde.

"Your *Treatyse* should be put out in a single printed edition of all your treatises," de Worde said. "It will be among the first books ever printed in English. And more importantly," he reminds me, "You will be the first English woman to have a book printed and published in English."

"Don't try to flatter an old nun," I said.

"Well, there are the royalties." He was right, and this is where my plan to ensure future income to the priory was leading. "I hear in St. Albans that you're worried about money."

In exasperation, I said, "de Worde, just because I am always looking for a bargain in St. Albans's markets does not mean the priory is pressed beyond its resources." But I hesitated a moment too long. "You are tempting me with my deepest fears. Yes, I do worry about my sisters. But there are other considerations beside the royalties."

"Would it help to discuss them?" he asked.

"Yes, but not with you. Give me some time." And he did.

I am reluctant for Caxton to publish my *Treatyse* because I believe it is dangerous in the wrong hands. This thought assails me ever since I heard of Caxton's interest in it. Some fishermen give no thought to the future. Following the secrets of the *Treatyse*, these profligates will take more perch, grayling, trout, and salmon than a river or lake could ever replace with the generosity on which nature depends. You cannot measure the needs of nature in fractions and decimals.

The loss could be incalculable. Fishing is the surest way to induce a merry spirit . . . to bring the Psalmist's oil of gladness. Far better than hunting. As Solomon said in his wise Proverbs, "A cheerful heart is good medicine, but a downcast spirit dries up the bones." I have studied the old who thrive, and almost without exception they have merry thoughts. They work moderately. And they pursue a healthy diet. Angling supplies all three.

As followers of holy Benedict, we eat fish almost two out of every three days. Pork, beef, and other meats are forbidden. During the winter, Sopwell, like other religious houses, is forced to purchase salted cod. It anchors our supper, our evening meal. But no matter how long we soak them in water, I have noticed thirst, bloat, and lethargy set in. And the discomfort hounds us during the divine office. Earnest prayer becomes a burden. I worry about our diet. I worry about the expense. Fresh fish relieve our prayers and our pocketbook.

I will continue to put de Worde and Caxton off. If I were not concerned for Sopwell's future, I would deny them my *Treatyse* without hesitation.

the words of Psalm 116 intervene, bringing me back to the dark and the cold of Sopwell's chapel.

O Lord, I am your ser-vant, the daught-er of your hand-maid

You have loosed my bonds.

Caxton and de Worde have decided to publish my *Treatyse* without having even read it. They believe there is much interest in its subject, and they are rarely wrong about the London market. If they read the *Treatyse*, they would crave it even more. It does what no other book does. It assures the reader of catching fish with a hook and line so long as the reader faithfully follows its instructions.

Originally I wrote the *Treatyse* for the nun coming after me in the job of Sopwell's angler. I presumed she would know nothing about fishing and had only my prescriptions on which to make a start. The *Treatyse* leads her step by step to competence and then regular success. It is a handbook designed to take the convent's angler by the shortest route from ignorance to regularly supplying fresh fish for Sopwell's table. The book tells her how to make her own equipment, where to fish, the species of fish and their habits and tastes, my twelve patterns of dubbed flies for leaping trout, and finally the moral rules every angler must observe astream.

What makes my *Treatyse* different from every other book about fishing is that it is fully proved. It is similar to the medical texts coming from Salerno. Every proposition set down there I tested over many years. And that is why I can promise the reader that if they follow my advice, they will catch fish. My notes show that I have caught thousands of fish, and I have recorded where each one was caught, when each one was caught, and the baits on which it was caught. And finally I have catalogued the stomach contents of the largest fish I have caught. The *Treatyse* simply summarizes the results of my experience. These summaries are my prescriptions for successful angling.

I, as most anglers, am most concerned with finding the best bait for taking large fish. A few large fish will feed Sopwell for the day. The *Treatyse* gives a list of the best baits for each species of fish. Altogether my book lists dozens of baits, too many for the angler to carry at one time. Nonetheless, when I was determining the best baits for each species, I did carry them all. Everything from worms and minnows to balls of flour laced with blood, honey, different meats, and sheep suet. Every day, I tried all my baits on every sort of fish. I fished with cheese and mutton fat for trout and grayling as well as the baits the *Treatyse* now recommends for them, worms for the most part fished deep. I tried to use as many types of bait each day in the same water over the same fish so I could reliably compare their effectiveness. With cheese, my catches of trout and grayling thinned. But using different larvae—small eels, grub worms, and silk worms, to name a few—my catches increased. I did this day after day.

There was one discordant note. Sometimes the results of the prior day repeated themselves the next. But sometimes they did not. Without a reliable pattern of results from one day to the next or from one month to the next, I could not say with confidence that my prescriptions for fishing were proven. I kept looking for a reliable pattern, but I was stymied. Something was missing. That something was skewing my tests one day to the next.

The something that changed from one day to the next was me. Some days the fish sensed I was nearby. Other days they did not. I knew that my results from comparing baits would remain unreliable until I could remove myself from the fishing of the bait being tested. The worst days were the bright days. The flash of my fishing rod, my shadow creeping along the bank of the river or pond, even the flash of my white hand searching my satchel for fresh bait, all warned the fish, for they could see me or sense my presence nearby.

In the end the solution was simple. I needed to hide in the shadows bordering a river or pond. Until this thought crossed my mind, I never took notice of shadows. My eyes were always drawn toward the light, toward the things I could see clearly. As soon as I started fishing from the shadows, the reliable pattern I sought emerged. The results of one day's test matched the results of the same test the following day. With certainty, I could name the best baits month to month for all eighteen species.

Now when I approach a river, I look for the shadows and mentally mark my path from shadow to shadow. This habit of mind followed me back to town. I began to look into the shadows on St. Albans's busiest streets, Church Street and St. Peter's Street, and it was there

I saw each person the Abbey and Sopwell had forgotten. The hungry mother and her children dressed in rags. The maimed soldiers. The dispossessed elderly. The very ill. I waited for these people to appear at Sopwell's door. But they never came, for what I saw when I looked in the shadows were the newly widowed mother, the self-reliant soldier who maintained his self-respect by hobbling on his own, the newly stricken leper, all those who could not bring themselves to beg. All had too much pride to ask for Sopwell's help, so I went to them. Forever after I have looked into the shadows.

WE PUSH THE pace of our chant to complete Psalm 116 and look ahead to Lauds and then back to our beds.

I will off-er you the sa-cri-fice of thanks-gi-ving

And call on the Lord's name

March is the month for taking stock. It is the month when winter works its cruelest blows, testing the prudence of fall's planning. It is the month for assessing shortages and for making preparations. I check the recesses of our barns for forage. Over winter, our cows and sheep grow thin. Every stray stalk of hay and loose kernel of oats must be collected, for another month will pass before our slowly moving flocks and herds rip and munch new grass in Sopwell's meadows. Only then will we enjoy the play of newly dropped lambs and the fresh, sweet milk of our cows. Our flour, honey, and salt cod are running low. We must conserve until our hens begin to lay, the rivers clear, and ice goes out on nearby lakes and ponds. We look forward to fresh peas.

March is also the month to take stock of my fishing tackle. Soon I will work to catch fresh fish, an encouraging sign to my sisters that the bounty of spring is at hand. Sufficient green- and russet-colored horse tail hair leaders, the colors for spring, hang in my cell. And the blackthorn branch hanging in the rafters of the kitchen is ready to replace last year's frayed rod tip. It comes from the blackthorn bush that stood on a rise above the orchard. It was punished daily by the wind, so the branch is both strong and limber. It has backbone yet will quickly tire a fish testing it with sudden runs. Michaelmas week I cut it and then soaked it, straightened it, and let it dry for six months. I cannot wait for the Ver's trout to strain its supple strength in their splashing rushes for freedom.

Yesterday afternoon, with the light of a pale sunset illuminating the worn oak tables in our workroom, I sorted out my dubbed flies. Few were discarded altogether. The frayed I save for their hooks, but even then I hesitated cutting loose the dangling tatters of wool and feather. They are my relics, whose touch calls up pleasant memories of successful days. They have been my talismans, reaching down into pools and riffles to pull up the miracle of butter-colored trout.

This afternoon I will tie replacements. My fingers have memorized the patterns. A half dozen peacock and brown hackle are the first order. Then more of my dun fly. It will not take long to fill my wallet. In March, I usually fish a dun fly with two upright wings of dark Mallard drake and light Jay under wings. The body is black wool.

Tying flies brings the composure of prayer. It is a composure that begins in the fingertips. The composure of angling is different, where equanimity comes through the eyes, the angler concentrating on her float or her fly, anticipating the take. The composure that comes from tying flies does not begin in sight. It begins in blindness. In tying a fly, the tier's mind migrates to her fingertips and builds composure from their feel.

What the fly tier's mind feels is the tension of the thread. The making of a fly begins and ends in the tying on and tying off of silk thread. In between is the perfect tension of the thread. Too tight and the thread breaks. Too light and the dubbing and wings work loose. The tier's mental task is to stay within her fingertips and keep the perfect tension. At all times. Thus the successful tier works collected.

The anchor of the well-tied fly is the thread, and the anchor of the tranquil mind is the tension in the thread. No matter how scattered my spirit becomes during a day of wayward winds, the tying of flies gathers it together. Tying readies it for prayer. And as I stroke and bind peacock herl to the hook and wind on brown hackle, my imagination looks ahead to April days and flopping trout. This afternoon tying flies will ready me for Vespers. And in my mind I will feel April's breezes and walk by calm pools with rising trout and grayling as far as the eye can see.

WE ARE NEARING the end of Matins. In our black habits, together we sing with swelling hearts,

I am black and come-ly, you daught-ers of Je-ru-sa-lem, Thus the king

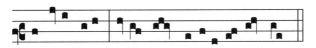

De-lights in me and has brought me in-to his cham-ber.

The last nocturn. Matins for the feast of the Annunciation is almost finished. The lesson from St. Luke is mine to read. I stand in the midst of my sisters chanting the Te Deum. And when we finish, I recite the Gospel selection with upraised arms. We listen to the Collect and pray the Our Father silently. Matins is complete and pure.

Waiting in the dark for the bells announcing Lauds, the same unsettling thought returns. The heavy hand of the abbot will fall on Sopwell soon.

I must stay alert, for without warning what I believed manageable may become exigent. The demands of the abbey could overtake Sopwell, leaving us only the blind choice of the fleeing rabbit jumping either left or right to avoid the hawk's crushing talons. One of the choices will be wrong. Irretrievably so. And the abbey will snatch our hard-won independence away from us.

lauds

Feast of St. George
1:00 a.m.
April 23, 1477

fter a pause, Lauds follows Matins. In the silence of that pause on this day, I think of St. George, the martyred Christian warrior and patron of England who remained steadfast in the face of his own violent death. And I am reminded of those men in my life who remained steadfast in the face of their own violent deaths. The chapel is silent. So, we sit quietly in the cool night air and stare at the chapel's black-and-white checked floor. Flickering candlelight plays across its tiles, exposing a grid. Perfect for hopscotch. My mind skips on one foot and then the other, landing with both feet on two familiar tiles. The first tile belongs to my father and the second to Edward.

And I think of the day my father was lost to us forever. The rider from Tower Hill arrived at noon. Alone. My mother refused to accept his packet of documents, leaving this last reality to my Uncle William. At supper, my uncle announced to the hall that my father was dead, punished for his faithful services to young King Richard. This news was expected.

What was unexpected was my uncle's other announcements. Choosing his words carefully, he said, "Due to the indulgence of the Parliament, Lord Berners's body will be transported here for burial." Weeping was heard coming from the servants and tenants ringing the hall. After a pause, Uncle William then followed up with a hint of relief, "And due also to the indulgence of the Parliament, Lady Berners will retain Bernersbury, its lands, and its tenants." We had all expected complete forfeiture. There was silence and then the sound of muffled clapping. Another polite clapping. My mother sat still as a statue, then stood and swiftly left the hall.

Parliament imprisoned my father in the Tower. From his cell, he could see workmen constructing the scaffolding for his public execution. I learned the details of his death from a monk, Abbot Edmund of St. Dunstan Abbey, who attended my father through his ordeal. With Abbot Edmund's guidance, my father prayed through his last night until detachment took hold. In the morning, his executioners pulled him from his Tower cell and bound his legs to deny him the dignity of walking to his death. He was dragged to the scaffolding. "Nothing," Abbot Edmund related, "shook his serenity. Instead, your father's eyes searched the heavens until they fixed on the swallows flying over the Thames."

At the very end, my father took heart from the swallows' flight. At first I wondered whether he stared heavenward to track their sweeping dive or to watch, instead, their climb upward with flapping wings. I have decided that he watched them working their wings to gain altitude and so grow deaf to the crowd's cries of "Traitor" and blind to their shaking fists. To this day I see him as the climbing swallow who never returned to earth, residing joyfully, at home, forever in the infinite blue of an April sky.

Time proved my father's death meaningless. Young King Richard did not take to heart the lesson Parliament tried to impress on him by executing his friends. Instead of forming a new inner circle with Gaunt, Bolingbroke, and their allies Gloucester, Warwick, and Arundel, Richard refused to form a new inner circle at all. He governed for the next ten years by holding all, even Britain's most powerful men, at a distance. Initially he sat back while Parliament and Gaunt bungled the two projects for which they faulted him and my father, namely, the war with France and the pacification of the northern border. To accomplish their failures, they spent more than the Commons budgeted. London continued to fume.

And all that time, Richard waited. He waited to regain the royal powers Parliament suspended. And once those powers were returned to him, he continued to wait for the day he could avenge the deaths of those like my father who had been close to him.

While Richard waited, Britain's most powerful earls and barons jostled among themselves to gain his favor. At first, he showed no favor to anyone. He spent money on himself alone and kept all estates and fees from wardships and the like for the royal treasury. Rivalries soon developed between York and Lancaster, splitting their old alliance against the king. Denied gifts of land and money from the king, the nobles resorted once again to their old methods to gain power. New manors came from extending the reach of their families. They married their sons and daughters off to each other, spending hours of diplomacy negotiating dowries and rights of inheritances. To win a place at the table of the powerful, minor nobles embraced poverty to provide their daughter with an attractive dowry.

While the nobles competed with each other, Richard plotted against his old enemies for years. Once he felt secure, he struck swiftly. Thomas Woodstock, the First Duke of Gloucester, Richard had assassinated in Calais; another, the Earl of Arundel, was executed on Parliament's vote; and the others he exiled, among them Bolingbroke. It was Bolingbroke, the accomplished military strategist, Richard should not have left alive, for he too knew how to wait and plot for the day he returned from exile.

My eyes return to the floor to the second familiar tile. It belongs to Edward, the Duke of York. Following my father's execution, my mother shuttled us among relatives. During a northern stay, my brother Richard and I first met Edward. We were guests of the Vernon family at Haddon Hall, and together with Edward, we hunted Haddon's great forests. My brother and I were young, hardly adolescents at the time. Almost eight years older than me, Edward became our leader, and his skills were remarkable even then. Later, when Bolingbroke named him Windsor's Master of Game, no one was surprised.

Edward hunted every day, so long as there was light. He reveled in adverse weather. Even on snowy days when the household worked close to its fires, he was running the forests and parks blowing his hunting horn and following his hounds. Each evening, as dark gathered, he appeared, exhausted, in the hall with ripped leggings and jerkin, arms and face cut and bloody from brambles and falls. So long as he was too drowsy to sit through the evening meal, he was happy.

My brother and I hunted with Edward every day of our stay at Haddon Hall. He was our big brother, pounding us up at dawn and driving us until twilight. Edward pursued the old style of hunting, where the risks to the hunter and the hunted are more evenly balanced. The goal of the true hunter, the warrior hunter, was to put himself lightly armed in front of an enraged, charging animal and so test his courage and reflexes. With a few hounds, pikes, and short stag swords, we ranged the forests pursuing deer and boar, sometimes on horseback but more often on foot. We carried only our weapons— no food, no water—drinking only from the streams we came across. Flopping on our stomachs, we inhaled a few mouthfuls and then were off after the hounds.

Edward never stopped. His manner, although frenetic, was not that of a madman. Always disciplined in his language, he was wonderfully skillful in pursuit. And we trusted him, our big brother, to carry us headlong into the thoughtlessness of the hunt, into that physical abandon erasing our fearful past. How often, when the chase ended, he held the quarry at bay until we caught up with him to confront the enraged boar or lunging hart. Encircling the animal, we worked together feinting and thrusting with our spears as Edward taught us until we found an opening for a final stab.

With the blood still running, Edward butchered out the best portions for our hosts. The rest was divided among the dogs. Inevitably, after a brief respite to catch our breaths, Edward grew mournfully silent and then agitated. We recognized the signs, for his uneasiness presaged a new chase. Then the horn blew as the lead hounds picked up a new trail. And soon we were off again, not knowing whether we were chasing a prey of sweet flight or a stoat.

The chase was Edward's remedy for the temptations of idleness. For Edward good hunting made for the good life. This fact he later disclosed in his book, *Master of Game*. What he never did disclose were the thoughts that drove him to keep busy, to charge from one kill to the next. I believed I understood him. Edward fled the thought of reading harsh judgment in a father's eyes. When the last death horn sounded and our hunting party made its way back to manor or castle, Edward's agitation mounted with each step homeward.

Before supper, his father, Lord Edmund Langley, demanded Edward account for his day. His father spoke to him by placing questions like traps, and each question tested for weakness. Idleness brought reproof. "How many kills today, Edward?" Edward's sum always fell short. Invariably his father mocked him by relating his own accounts of great piles of red deer carcasses.

The question Edward most feared was, "Did you break off any chase?" To Lord Langley's mind, a botched chase was inexcusable. It did not matter if the dogs lost the scent or that the horses were staggering with fatigue. Edward was always at fault.

Even one interrupted chase brought Lord Langley's inevitable sermon on preparedness. Incompetence brought early death in battle, for in every battle came the moment when Edward would need to fight back from being overwhelmed. Now was the time to sharpen his skills and build his endurance. For when death sat on his shoulder, Edward needed to dig down within his reserves of strength and store of tricks to overcome his adversaries. Edward's father rode him cruelly as an unruly horse, with kicks and spurs.

To his credit, Edward never cowered before Lord Langley. He listened stoically to his father's reproofs knowing full well that the next day in the field, he would ignore them. His father never gave Edward respect and so never earned Edward's respect. Edward preferred to model himself after the greatest hunter, Tristan, whose legend was sung at night in our halls. It was a good choice.

All I learned about hunting, I learned from hunting with Edward. These lessons I put down in my book on hunting. But for years now, I have not read my hunting treatise, for it was a youthful effort carried along pell-mell by the thoughtless passions of the chase. Those passions no longer excite me. Hunting has its virtues, and it brought me as a youth its best gifts. But I am now repelled by the dying hart when writhing, his copper-smelling blood pools swamping our feet. I no longer enjoy the moment when a boar's eyes turn opaque, staring fixedly beyond the panting hunters into a distant sky. The death horn is no longer the triumphant thrill it once was. Instead it marks the moment when another life passes from nature. My world narrows by degrees with each such death.

The memories of autumn mornings do come back to me. I recollect how the trees turned color and the smoke of our wood fires merged with the ground fog in the meadows. So thick and so pungent. But I no longer think of the circling hounds straining against their leashes to find the scent of a hare or hart. I think instead of the Ver and its riffles shrouded under fog as I have found it so many fall mornings. The bleeding hart is no longer my thought. I think instead of the fog when it shreds into wisps as the morning sun warms the air. And I think of the great trout who, looking up, wonders whether it should fear the fog or take comfort in it.

The weaknesses of hunting, as Edward practiced it, are the weaknesses of the young. These are emotion and impatience. In a word, impulse. As a young woman, I reveled in hunting until I saw the destruction impulse brought. Edward never came to that insight. Rather he remained the captive of his impulses so that in time his character was reduced to them. He was a scattered person.

Fishing brought me integrity. When I started fishing, I fell into my now very familiar rhythm of observing and reflecting. It became as regular as the rocking of a boat on moderate seas. So much of fishing calls for observation—patient observation—and reflection. It is reflection that brought me to Sopwell. It is reflection that healed me and made me one whole.

And yet the hardest fact of all for me to accept was—even now these many years later—that for all his weaknesses, I was drawn to Edward. Let there be no mistake, I had reservations about him, and my reservations only grew as the years passed. But my reservations did not diminish my feelings for him.

One hunt in particular remains my touchstone during adversity. The winter of my sixteenth year, my mother sent Richard and I to Conway Castle on the Welsh border, where Edward and his friends joined us. One morning our party explored wild scrubland laced with ridges and riven with snaking valleys, hardly more than narrow defiles climbing by way of dry creek beds to the ridges above. It was a chill January day. High, featureless, gray clouds stretched to the horizons, and a constant wind encouraged us to sit our horses and share in their heat.

The hounds started few animals. One deer was taken, and that only because it slowed when, in its fright, it blundered into a deep snowdrift. It was dead before it could free its legs. But Edward did not let up. Instead he pushed us from one valley to the next. The hounds and horses slowed, the horses winded and the hounds' bloody footprints giving evidence of their lacerated feet. Finally, when the cold and terrain were near defeating us all, Edward led us into a broad valley through which flowed a thinly iced-over stream. We could hear the water gurgling beneath, and Edward stopped briefly, allowing the horses to break the ice with their hooves and drink freely with the hounds.

Great willows inhabited the valley, strung out like giant sentinels along the stream's winding course. Downed among the living trees lay dead, gray, gnarled trunks and branches. They littered the stream's banks and the borders of the surrounding meadow in heaps. Perfect cover in the cold. Edward recalled the hounds with his horn, directing them to explore the deadfalls for a scent. We riders followed the dogs, gingerly picking our way through the clutter and snowdrifts. Taking a path swept free of snow, I rode the left flank, hard up against a steep slope with few trees, scouting for the sheltering caves and overhangs. Three sniffing hounds accompanied me. With Edward in the lead, the other riders fanned out with the rest of the pack along the stream, crisscrossing the tangle of branches and downed trunks.

One hound bayed, then another. The pack swarmed together, rooting under an ancient, downed willow. Suddenly, three young boar and a sow shot out from under the roots, goring two hounds in their path, forcing the pack to part. Taking advantage of the gap, the sounder plunged up the slope toward me. Immediately, Edward cut them off, forcing them back toward the stream. Edward looked back at me, and I glared at him. In spite of our many hunts together, he had never allowed me to face boar alone.

While Edward, the rest of our party, and the hounds chased the flushed sounder, an old boar, with grizzled snout and long, black hair flowing down the ridge of his spine, crept out from under the roots of the tree and made for the slope.

Edward looked back as one hound broke off from the pack to follow it. He saw me taking chase.

I shouted above the wind, "He's mine."

Edward wrestled his horse about and shouted back, "Take him." He then motioned for the other riders to surround the sounder, shouting, "Stay with them. Bring them to bay."

As I wheeled my horse about to confront the boar, Edward blew one note for my attention. He shouted, pointing upstream, "Push it to the ford, up the valley."

I rode directly at the boar, menacing it with my spear. When it veered off, I turned with it, keeping it between me and the stream, forcing it up the valley. The boar was quick. Baying, several hounds followed, barely able to keep up. I urged my horse on. Rushing headlong, jumping downed trees and flying over snow drifts, the boar and I kept pace, eying each other as we ran full out. The ford was just ahead.

The hounds and the old boar reached the ford together. When they hit the ice, all lost their footing. In a whining, grunting melee, they slid across the ford, hit its overhanging bank, and were flung back. The boar, with its sharp hooves, was first to recover and, swinging its head to the left and right, punished the dogs severely. They retreated to the shore, barking and menacing the boar with halfhearted feints. The boar was not fooled and held the ford.

I pulled my horse up in a swirl of snow and frozen clods of clay. The boar stood deadly still, fixing me with angry red eyes. It was massive. I jumped off my horse, my ash-shafted spear in hand. As the boar looked on, confused, it hesitated as I slipped off my riding boots, the soles worn smooth by my stirrups. My thick wool hose gained purchase on the smooth ice and held me steady.

Just then, the boar stepped toward me, swinging its head, its bloody tusks scarlet in the late afternoon light. I set myself low, leveling the spear at its head. Staring into the sharpened tip, it charged. Undeterred when it broke through the crust of ice, it bulled ahead, breaking off the shelf as it went. The shallow ford was now angry boar, sloshing water, billowing clay silt, and ice fragments.

Wading within a yard, snorting and grunting plumes of vapor, the old boar gathered itself for one last plunge forward. But the ice held firm beneath me. It was then I struck, and the spear point entered its throat just below its jaw. A pumping flood of blood drowned its scream, staining the stream scarlet. In one last great effort, it stood up, shivered, and slowly sank. One more thrust down behind its head, and I withdrew. Putting on my boots, I strung a rope from my horse and dragged it up on the bank. As it lay steaming, I sounded the death horn.

Edward was generous that night when stories of the day's hunt were traded before the hall's fires. He gave me center stage to relate every detail of my kill and, when I finished, praised my skills and courage. After all the stories were told and the wine jugs emptied, the scraping of chairs and benches began. As I pushed out from the table, Edward joined me.

"I have something to tell you," he said, walking beside me for a short distance. Putting a hand on my arm, he stopped me. As his eyes made a slow circuit of the hall, he waited until all were out of earshot.

"What could you possibly say that will add to a perfect day?" I said gaily. Edward frowned. I caught myself and blurted out, "Is it bad news?"

"It is bad news for me," he said, "and I would hope you would also find it bad news."

"Edward, please tell me," I said, concerned.

"Tonight my father informed me that he has concluded all arrangements for a marriage between me and Lady Philippa du Mohun," he said. His darks eyes were alert to any change in my features.

I shuddered within as when hearing the first mournful note of a tolling bell, for his words began the knell of my hopes for a noble marriage. With some struggle, I managed to say, "Your father has done well for you. She inherited the properties of her father, the Second Baron de Mohun, and, as I have heard, they are nearly the equal of your father's."

Deflated, Edward said, "Yes. It is a good match."

"This will be her third marriage, and she will also bring the properties of her first two husbands with her," I said.

"Properties . . . properties. Is that all you can think of?" Edward huffed.

"I did not mean to upset you," I said.

"Have you thought about what I might want?" Edward replied.

I dared not answer the question because I knew what he wanted. He wanted what I had dreamt about. I sensed it every time we hunted together.

"Have you?" he demanded.

"It is late, Edward. I should be getting to bed," I said distantly, avoiding the question.

"But which bed?" he asked, pressing me.

Taken aback, I said smoothly, "Let me answer your first question. It is the talk of properties that ends all discussions of me marrying.

My family has no property for my dowry. Until they do, all discussion of whom I will marry is speculation. My uncle and brother do not speculate."

"You have thought about me then," Edward said.

"I want more than a night with you. I want a life," I said. "Be honest with me now, Edward," I demanded sternly, "Is that possible?"

"No," he said, deflated. "My father would never consider you a match for the house of York. But you know that."

"I wanted to hear it from you. So my pretending for one night that we have a life together would only be a delusion," I said.

Silently, Edward withdrew his hand. "I had hoped your passions for me would be stronger," he said.

I drew back. "They are stronger than yours are for me. You will trade a life with me for one night together. That is a poor bargain. It is I who desire more of you than you desire of me."

"But Juliana, perhaps in the future we might have a life together," he said.

"We will not speak of this again until you realize that I am worth more than a single night," I replied with more certainty than I felt.

There was a part of myself that wanted to surrender to Edward's wishes. That part of me saw us going hand in hand up to his chamber. But silently, facing Edward, I clung instead to that part of me where I found firm footing after my father's execution and my mother's abandonment. It was that part of me that anchored me when the current of daily anxieties so often threatened to sweep me away. And I knew as deeply as the depth of my most secret thoughts that I would never become a party to my own drowning. For the present, I would keep Edward a friend. That was all.

His face turned sad, and he said without emotion, "You can be so cold."

I stood, unmoving and mute.

Then after a moment's thought, he asked, "Will you hunt with me tomorrow?"

I smiled up at him and said warmly, "Of course."

With his booted steps ringing on the stone floor, Edward left the hall. He never looked back. As I made my way up to my room alone in the dark, I realized that I could never let the chaos of ambition and feeling that was Edward rule me. And now that he was marrying Philippa, I decided I would never again entertain the thought of it. But Edward had not signed on as a party to my decision. Nor did my deep feelings of gratitude and admiration for him ever endorse it.

And thus, on this feast day of St. George, sitting here playing mental hopscotch, I can jump from the tile of my father to the tile of Edward, and I think also of noble Tristan and St. George. And I pray they have all found peace.

ST. ALBANS'S BELLS sound for Lauds. Sopwell's quickly join in, and our moment of quiet reflection is over. I motion to Sister Clare, and she announces Deus in adjutorium. Then I give out the antiphon for Psalm 51 and we begin in earnest:

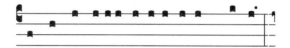

Be-hold, thou de-sir-est truth in the in-ward be-ing:

There-fore teach me wis-dom in my se-cret heart.

YESTERDAY, RETURNING FROM our pasture, I thought of Isabel and her warning as I closed the gate into Sopwell's barnyard. The snap of the latch reminded me of ice snapping under the weight of a horse's hoof, a sound bringing back memories of Isabel and of our cold journey north through the snows to Conisbrough Castle. Edward's father invited my family to spend our Christmas holiday with their family and friends, and my mother and stepfather, Sir Roger Clarendon, brought me; my brother, Richard; and our two young cousins, Eleanore and Catherine. It was on the way to Conisbrough where I first met Isabel.

By October of that year, my eighteenth, we had a new king. Henry Bolingbroke had returned from exile. Bolingbroke's stated intention when he returned from France was to regain what he was owed. Richard promised Bolingbroke he could return from exile on his father's death and receive full title to all his father's lands. After John of Gaunt died, Richard broke his word, refusing to reinstate Bolingbroke and extending his exile. A true leader, Bolingbroke returned from France, raised an army, and won military dominance over Britain while King Richard was fighting the Irish. On Richard's return to Britain, Bolingbroke arrested and deposed him, confining him to the Tower. As winter set in, no word was heard from Richard. The stories multiplied, but Christmas promised a break from royal rumors. We all looked forward to a holiday.

The road to Conisbrough and the heart of York climbed upward to the north. Deep snows clothed the rounded hills in higher and higher ranks, appearing as outstretched chrysalides blanketing all of life in muffled emptiness, and as with a chrysalis, slow pulsing life lay beneath. Blackened chimneys marked crofts and villages, and their thin trails of smoke marked the burrows of huddled families. Few were on the road, and these few appeared as struggling lines of ants on a white salt beach. Men wearing their every rag labored beneath bundles of firewood or led oxen drawing carts of felled trees behind billowing white vapor clouds. It was slow going, even for us on horses. The cold tore at every seam and closed our eyes, freezing our lashes.

On the ridges where the wind swept the road clear of snow, we raced each other to keep warm. In the valleys where the snow was knee deep, my young cousins, Eleanore and Catherine, kept us entertained with their inexhaustible supply of word games. We spent hours competing in turn for all words rhyming with "snow" and "cold." The loser was the first to go silent.

At a crossroads, we caught up with a train of horses and wagons from Kent. It was the family of a knight, Sir Adam Wilstead, who was in service to Thomas de Holland, the Duke of Surrey. He was accompanied by his wife, Agnes, and their daughter, Isabel. They too had accepted Lord Langeley's invitation to celebrate Christmas. While my mother and father made their introductions, my cousins, Richard, and I rode down the line searching for their daughter. Eleanore and Richard discovered a young woman huddled in a wagon. She was bundled in a bulky maroon wool cape lined with wolf fur. Her teeth chattered when she told us her name was Isabel. She stood up to greet us, but when a sudden gust of wind buffeted her, she shrank back. "How far is the castle?" She shouted to me above the wind.

When I said, "One more day," she appeared stricken.

That night, Isabel thawed before the fires of an abbey guesthouse. It was then my cousins and I first came to know her. She was younger than me but older than my cousins. And, as the reflection of the flames played on her pale cheeks and lustrous auburn hair, Richard brought her bowls of warm soups. She was grateful and spoke her gratitude to Richard most forcefully with her sparkling blue eyes. The next day, my cousins and Isabel fell into conversation on any excuse. Even on the road, she happily played their word games rhyming "chattering" and "teeth" to the amusement of our parents.

Just as the sunset dimmed to dark night, we turned into Conisbrough. It was set on a slight incline, and its white walls rose apiece with the snows surrounding it. As the sky turned quickly in evening's last hour from pink to blue to purple to dark, we came before its gate, where the smell of wood fires and hay, and the savory smells of the kitchens, excited our horses. We swept into the courtyard with a clatter, and servants in boots and blue and red tunics scattered among us, helping us to dismount and then leading our willing horses to the stables and warm oats.

It was a week of good cheer. Or so it seemed. Night after night, we sat engulfed in our ermine-lined capes, eating York's delicacies and listening to his minstrels. Then when all were fed and the tables pushed back, we cast off our furs and set to dancing and singing. Pairing off into two circles, men on the outside facing in and women on the inside facing out, we sang and danced our steps and twirls to chorus after chorus of carols into the early morning hours.

Although indulging himself every night, Edward hunted everyday at dawn. He insisted my brother and I accompany him, but I refused, choosing the company of my cousins and Isabel instead. The snow was deep and the weather inclement while my cousins were bursting with news, which they related excitedly sitting beside the hall's great fires. Their eyes danced brilliantly as they chattered, dispelling the cold tedium with a crackling enthusiasm.

On Christmas Eve I found Eleanore and Catherine sitting with Isabel before York's great hearth.

"Juliana, what are you wearing tonight?" Asked Isabel.

"I have not made up my mind, or should I say, my mother has not made up my mind for me. She wants me to wear what I wore last year," I replied. "What are the others wearing?"

"Lady du Mohun, Edward's wife, is wearing a new houpelande of red wool trimmed in ermine and satin with a few golden bells along her cinch," Isabel said. "She follows the latest fashion, wearing her cinch high, well above her waist, and she is wearing jewelry from her first husbands."

Intrigued, I asked, "Why would Lady du Mohun wear her dead husbands' jewelry instead of Edward's?"

"She is telling Edward to be more attentive if he wants an heir. As you know, they have had no children," Catherine said.

"Apparently Edward is never home. His father chose Lady du Mohun, for she brought many estates to the marriage. Edward was given little choice," Eleanore said. She then added in an incredulous voice, "You know that she is older than Edward and has a son from her first husband."

"Yes. I know," I said.

"Edward's father has spoken to him about his absences," Eleanore said, lowering her voice. "You know Edward has two children already."

"Two," I said in disbelief.

"Yes, two, and both boys. Their mother is the daughter of a wealthy London wool merchant. Edward has provided her a small manor outside London to shield her from the nosy, and he lavishes business on her father to keep him quiet. People say she is the reason Edward is spending more time at Windsor than at home.

"Enough. This is not the kind of talk your mother would encourage," I said sternly, and to change the subject I asked, "What is Edward's sister, Blanche, wearing?"

"That is the best story we have," Catherine said excitedly. After looking about her in case anyone was within ear shot, she turned back, certain of our privacy. "Blanche was discussing her dress for Christmas Eve with Edward and Sir Roger."

"Yes," Eleanore broke in, unable to contain herself. "That was when they talked about you."

"What?" I said, shocked. "How did I come up? Did Sir Roger say something?"

"No," said Catherine, now clearly enjoying herself. "It was Edward who brought you up."

"He is probably upset because I refuse to hunt in these snows," I quickly replied.

"No again, Cousin Juliana," Catherine said.

Isabel interjected excitedly, "Blanche was describing the dress she planned to wear Christmas Eve. She plans to outshine Philippa because Edward's father chose Philippa to lead the Peacock Procession, you know."

"I do not mean to throw cold water on your enthusiasm, but what does all this have to do with me?" I asked.

"We are just getting to that," Catherine said, exasperated. "Blanche then said she would be wearing a heavy necklace of Frankish emeralds set in gold. And Sir Roger said he had never seen it."

"It was then that Edward jumped into the conversation and blurted out that the emeralds were a deep green," Eleanore said and then paused for effect. I hung on her words. She smiled slyly at me when she said, "Edward told Sir Roger the emeralds were as deep a green as your eyes, Cousin Juliana."

Stunned, I said, "Why would he say that?"

"There is more. Blanche was clearly unhappy with Edward, and she said that her emeralds were a darker green than your eyes," Catherine said. "Edward then said that your light skin did not show off your eyes to fair advantage."

Short on patience, I asked half to myself, "Why would Edward say that?"

"It is obvious. Edward likes you," Eleanore said and then giggled. Then her sister interjected, "Think about it, cousin! Edward is not attracted to his wife, but he is attracted to you."

"You are wrong. I am just someone to hunt with," I said without conviction. "When we were younger, we hunted together often. Perhaps he misses those days."

"Cousin, you can be so dense," Catherine said, wagging her finger at me. "He yearns for your company. Yesterday we were sitting by this hearth when Edward asked us where you were."

"Yes, he was almost frantic." Then Eleanore looked me full in the face and said in all seriousness, "I have seen that look before in young men's eyes. He is chasing you."

"When we told him, he rushed off without even a thank you," Catherine said.

"You say it was yesterday?" I asked. "I do not remember talking to Edward yesterday." I did not tell my cousins that I did remember seeing Edward nearby speaking with Baron le Despenser, his brother-in-law. When I noticed him, he bowed to me with the most doleful eyes. I sensed his presence during that afternoon, but he never approached me. "It does not matter what his feelings are toward me. Unhappy or not, he is married."

"But Juliana, just imagine. You are his great love, but he is held back from courting you because of his father's demand for a large dowry. His feelings toward you have turned to worship. Just think about it. It is so romantic. The minstrels will sing about you two," Isabel said, waving her arms dramatically.

"Just like he moons and pants for the merchant's daughter," I replied sharply. "How do you three come up with all this?"

"We start early in the morning and go from hearth to hearth. We are slight, so no one notices us," Eleanore said, laughing. "With the suspicious, we smile vacantly."

"You must have noticed that Edward is more restless than usual," Catherine said. "At least that is what everyone says."

"I have not paid attention," I said. My cousins' conversation had gotten beyond me.

"So what are you wearing tonight?" Isabel asked.

"What I wore last year for Christmas, my sage green gown with a satin chartreuse shift. I have nothing better, so I will do what my mother wants," I said. Then, laughing, I continued, "They will deepen the green of my emerald-colored eyes. And set off very nicely the silver chains my father left me."

Gᴜɪᴅᴇᴅ ʙʏ sɪsᴛᴇʀ Clare's firm hand, we begin Psalm 93, a short psalm that we all know by heart. Our eyes have left the psalteries, and with energy we chant:

The Lord reigns; he is robed in ma-jes-ty;

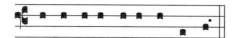

The Lord is robed, he is girded with strength.

FROM TIME TO time during the evening feast, I felt Edward's eyes on me. Once, glancing at the head table with its splashes of Plantagenet reds and blues and its gold lions, I saw him quickly turn away.

That night, as my cousins predicted, Edward's wife, Philippa, took center stage. She led the Peacock Procession. As she stood with her silver platter, Edward rose and to loud acclaim swore his allegiance to the king. He did not name the king, even though we had two kings at the time, Bolingbroke at Windsor enjoying his new crown as Henry IV, and King Richard II imprisoned in the Tower.

While the minstrels sang King Arthur's Christmas stories, servants brought out heaps of roast beef, venison, pork, and every imaginable fowl—ducks, partridge, and heron—their gravies mixing and filling each platter to overflowing. Meat and fish pies with their brown crusts and fragrant, spiced smells—cinnamon, cardamom, and saffron—were set before each guest. Our voices rose, and pitchers of York's red burgundy never emptied.

After the food, we slid the tables back and lined up to dance. It was midnight. My mother was on my right and Isabel on my left. Sir Roger, Edward, and Richard took their places in line opposite us. In the smoky scarlet of the torches and the soft yellow of the candles, my mother was dazzling. She wore our colors—Berners colors, green and gold—a dark green velvet gown over a golden shift. On one sleeve she wore Sir Roger's colors, a blue and gold scarf. Although dancing with vigor, her face remained sober and set. From time to time, I noticed her glance at Edward with annoyance.

Richard, smiling, opposite Isabel, danced with abandon. For once, Isabel left her cape behind, ignoring the draughts sitting in Conisbrough's wood rafters as perched crows waiting for the opportunity to swoop down and chill their prey. She twirled in a rush of maroon and silver, with her long amber hair streaming out behind her, shooting gold and red sparks as an exploding ember falling from the hearth. Her eyes spoke of no reserve. Richard's eyes spoke of adoration.

The last dance was all kicks and turns. The fiddles, drums, and recorders began slowly enough but by degrees increased their tempo, flying toward the climax. Breathing hard, Edward and I grasped each other's hands and swung hard in turns, first to the right and then to the left. Edward was as lithe and nimble a dancer as he was a gifted hunter. I swung him faster and faster, pulling harder and harder to upset his balance. But he was too strong for me, and his feet never strayed from the rhythm of the music. I laughed and pulled even harder to no effect. Once I looked over at my mother and saw her frowning. As the last notes died, the dance called for the male partner to bow on one knee to the female partner. Edward did so, looking up at me over our outstretched clasped hands.

The tableau has stayed with me to this day. With his upturned, flushed face, dark eyes, and black hair, Edward smiles and squeezes my hand. His breathing comes in hard gasps. I am the same, smiling down on him.

Within moments, my mother was beside me. And between her and Sir Roger, we three slowly crossed the hall to the stairs and sleeping chambers above. As we passed, men's eyes searched my face and inspected my person and then, as if satisfied, nodded their approval. Some of the young men bowed. I glanced toward the head table and this time met the smoldering dark eyes of Philippa glowering at me. My mother prodded me on.

At a turning in the stairs, my mother took me aside. She demanded, "What did Edward whisper to you?"

Startled by her intensity, I drew back and said, "Nothing."

"You will not put me off, Juliana," she said sternly. "I saw him whisper something to you. What did he say?"

"O Mother, it was nothing," I said angrily and set my mouth.

Grasping me by the shoulders, she backed me into the wall and said, "There is more going on here than feasting and dancing. You are to find your cousins and stay with them until morning. Let no invitation, no matter how innocent, separate you from them."

Frightened, I nodded.

"We are all at risk. Do you understand?"

There was terror in her eyes. I nodded again.

Slowly she and I climbed the stairs to find my cousins. As we turned into their sleeping chamber, my mother kissed me. Just then Eleanore and Catherine clambered up the stairs behind us. In high spirits, they dragged me away, and I waved weakly to my mother as we disappeared into our room.

Barring the door, we stripped naked and crawled under our down blanket. In the dark, we clung to each other's warmth, snug in the smell of spiced wine and wood smoke. Of course they had questions about Edward and what he said to me. When I told them Edward called me "his Diana," they shrieked and kissed me. We fell asleep while I was listing the young knights who nodded to me when I passed through them. It was a long list, and I forgot some of the names.

After that evening, I was more alert. I noticed the men in deep and sometimes heated discussions. The Earl of Salisbury and the Earl of Kent cornered Sir Roger several times, but my mother rescued him on the excuse of family business. Mother was polite to Edward, thanking him for his hospitality, but refused to allow Sir Roger any extended discussions with him. Once I heard her say angrily to Sir Roger, "I lost one husband to royal politics. I will not lose another."

But it was not only Sir Roger that Mother guided about. She kept me in her orbit also until I grew more irritated with her than usual. Spitting out the cruel words, "Leave me alone," I put distance between us whenever I sensed her presence. She ignored me, and by the end of our stay, we were no longer speaking. Again. More festering of the old wound opened by my father's death.

All the way back home, wrapped deep within my wool traveling cloak, I mused on Conisbrough. Along the frozen, rutted roads and at the slippery ferries, I sat apart from my cousins, pensive. I enjoyed the hunger I awakened in men's eyes. Yet I wondered what emptiness within me needed their appreciation. Had I grown up to find a new loneliness? More alarming, I wondered how deep my emptiness, my loneliness, went. And then the most difficult question: How could I plumb that depth without getting caught in its subterranean currents? I had no answers.

SISTER CLARE LAUNCHED us into Psalm 52 without pause. Its first lines remind me of the tenor of our time. It feeds my fears.

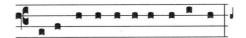

All the day you are plot-ting de-struc-tion.

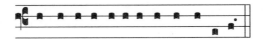

Your ton-gue is like a sharp ra-zor, you trai-tor

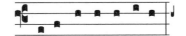

You love e-vil more than good,

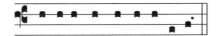

And ly-ing more than speak-ing the truth.

the days following Christmas confirmed my reservations about Edward. The opulence of the celebration hid its true purpose. During the feasting and dancing, Edward plotted with Salisbury, Kent, le Despenser, and others, some our closest kinsmen, to kidnap and kill Bolingbroke during the Epiphany tournament at Windsor. Edward had no love for Bolingbroke. He and many others were committed to returning Richard to the throne, restoring the true order as my father would have wanted. Bolingbroke alone, they mistakenly believed, stood in their way. At Conisbrough, Edward was firming alliances, seeking recruits, and planning strategy.

To our dismay, King Richard and all the conspirators were dead by the second week of January. Most beheaded for their treason. All, that is, except Edward. We waited for word of his death, but he was left untouched. Disbelieving, we later learned that Edward had betrayed all. The rightful king; the earls of Salisbury, Somerset, Kent, and Huntingdon; and even le Despenser, his brother-in-law—all eminent men, all our kinsmen, with whom we had just danced, eaten, and sung—were dead due to his treachery. We later learned the reason for his change of heart. When Edward's father heard of the plot, he threatened to settle his title and estates on Edward's younger brother. Upon his father's insistence and without a qualm, Edward rode hastily for Windsor and Bolingbroke's forgiveness.

Once again, my mother lived in fear, becoming a recluse and eating little. Memories of my father's imprisonment returned and struck her dumb. Again I could not reassure her, nor she me. This time I knew enough not to expect it. Left alone in January's cold, my apprehension uncovered a new well of anxiety. The faces of those now dead occupied my stray thoughts. I saw them fixed at Conisbrough forever, joyful in the midst of singing carols, exhilarated returning from the hunt.

And yet, to my own disgust, I found that my kindly feelings toward Edward lived on. And it was then I knew that my feelings for him would not die even at the hands of his monstrous treachery. No matter how frequently I read fear in my mother's eyes, I still remembered those morning hunts with Edward. Even today I remember the days alongside him, the grace with which he held to his horse come what may, and his mighty, undaunted heart when on the hardest days, he continued on when all others dropped off from exhaustion.

For only with Edward's help did I win what renews me every morning. Daily I recall the hunt at Conway Castle where I confronted my immediate death. I saw it in the boar's angry eyes, and by fighting to the death, I believed ever after in my own survival. No matter how heated the confrontation, no matter how threatening the circumstances, and no matter how risky the endeavor, I never again trembled before any threat nor doubted the outcome of my intent. I will survive, and at my center is that calm that tells me so.

WE START PSALM 50. I am always struck by the novelty of its thought.

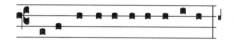

"If I were hun-gry, I would not tell you;

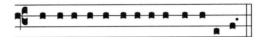

For the world and all that is in it is mine.

Last week, I called once again on hunting's gift, that calm I learned at Edward's side. Abbot Wallingford summoned me to St. Albans Abbey to attend their parliament, a business meeting. As I expected, it proved to be the meeting where the abbey finally ordered Sopwell to share in the renovation costs.

The walk to the abbey is a familiar one, filled with familiar feelings and thoughts. Every time I leave Sopwell's front gate, I am reminded of the town's animosity toward us Benedictines. That animosity is born of the daily struggle between the abbey's demands for regular income and the town's aspirations for independence. The abbey's milling monopoly and game laws remind the townspeople daily of their powerlessness, and that daily reminder fosters the daily commitment of the townspeople to frustrate the abbey's purposes.

But there is also the town's personal animosity toward my family. From my first day at St. Albans, I felt it. The town revolted in 1381, the year of my birth, breaking for a brief time the abbey's hold on them. Violence in St. Albans erupted as a side show to the general peasant uprising begun in Kent by Wat Tyler and his followers. Within the month, the abbey fought back, forcing the town fathers to recognize its absolute rule over them. It was a brutal end, backed by Richard II and his troops. In St. Albans, the king personally approved the execution of William Grindcobbe, the town's own firebrand, and the hedge priest, John Ball, a friend of Wat Tyler. And my father stood at Richard's side all the while, watching and smiling with the king as the two rebels were led to their deaths. Their heads were later fixed atop poles at the town gates. No one alive that day will forget the cruel end to a good neighbor.

I think of Grindcobbe every time I pass his house on the Salipath. Before his execution, he was allowed to speak, and his last words burned themselves into the memories of St. Albans residents. "Friends, who after so long an age of oppression, have won yourselves a short breath of freedom . . . I die for the cause of the liberty . . . I shall think myself happy to end my life as a martyr." It is plain to me that the town is simply biding its time until the next episode of unrest when they will flock to any force opposing the abbey.

I am sympathetic to Grindcobbe's words. Long hours I have pondered how to avoid reminding the townspeople of the abbey's, and so Sopwell's, privilege. But my downcast eyes are not enough. The abbey takes no notice of the town's animosity, believing in the strength of its spiritual authority. But as prioress, I have decided that Sopwell must take notice of the town's feelings and will foster healthy change by making common purpose with our townspeople.

With these thoughts, I began my trek to the abbey. Sitting in the center of St. Albans, the Abbey is a few miles east of Sopwell. The most direct route crosses over the Ver to Sopwell Lane, leaving only a short walk into town. From Sopwell Lane, I go right, following Halliwell Hill, and walk to Church Street and the Waxhouse Gate, a heavily guarded abbey entrance.

Everywhere are signs of wool and pilgrims. The smell of wet wool dominates my walk down Sopwell Lane, for directly west is the tenterground, where row after row of fulled broadcloth dry on lines. On windy days, the cloth sails and flaps, waiting, once bone dry, for shipment to the Netherlands. Not today, for all is still, and there is the threat of rain. Nonetheless the smell of wet wool lingers.

St. Albans caters to its pilgrims. Many inns line its street, growing denser on Sopwell Lane and Halliwell Hill as the traveler draws nearer to the abbey. Most are of timber frame construction, and shoulder to shoulder, crowd the very edge of the street. On bright days, as far as the eye can see is the geometry of the architect, dark timbers framing whitewashed wattle and daub. Freshly limed, bright squares, rectangles, triangles, and so on. It is the same for all the inns and most of the shops I pass as I walk north down Halliwell Hill. Some have second stories overhanging the street, protection from rain and snow and either living quarters for the shopkeeper or extra rooms for pilgrims. Others are a single story, with entrances opening to yards at their back. Early morning is a dangerous time to be a pedestrian in St. Albans, especially one as short and nondescript as I am. The streets are crowded with butchers' carts, hay wagons, and carts carrying hogsheads of ale and wine, every manner of saleable good heading to the marketplace.

By the time I turn into Church Street, the carts have grown even thicker. And many smells mingle with the smell of wet wool: new rope, planed wood, bread, ale, and butchered meat. Church Street is the boundary between the abbey and the marketplace. The great clock erected by the abbey and the Eleanor Cross erected by King Edward stand to my left. And I see Sopwell's two inns, the George and the Swan—more timber frame and white plaster—to the west, just ahead on the north side of the street. They discharge our obligation as Benedictines to shelter the traveler. As a novice, I edged sheets and curtains for our inns, personally delivering my finished work. I will visit our inns later and then search for the market for my friend, the vendor of sewing needles. My supply of hooks dwindles, and I need the finer needles for my small caddis flies. But for now, I need to attend the abbot, so I do as I have so often done before, turned into the Waxhouse Gate, that impregnable monument of stone the surest sign of the abbey's rejection of the town's aspirations.

For months now, I have heard muttering against the abbey. It is the burden of the new fees. The abbey commands the allegiance of all the townspeople. They are its tenants and its parishioners. The new fees remind the townspeople they are tenants before they are parishioners. We are now at the point where performance of their obligations, what the law requires, is all that can be expected by church authority.

At the Waxgate, the gatekeeper waves me through. The abbey's helmeted marshals hardly notice my passing, but before long a young monk falls in beside me and leads me to the chapter house with a smile and the words, "I am Brother Simon. The Abbot is expecting you." All is correct—swept halls and the pleasant smell of waxed paneling. The young monk opens the chapter house door, and with great ceremony leads me to the head table, gesturing toward a bench at its lower end. Then Brother Simon takes a stool to my right, where he sharpens a quill pen and opens a log book. This was an official meeting.

Sitting with his brother, Prior Thomas, on his right hand, Abbot Wallingford, tall and ascetic in his black habit, begins slowly.

"Peace be with you, Mother. I hope all is well at Sopwell," He said somberly.

"And peace to you, my abbot. Yes, all is well," I replied guardedly.

"To get right to our business," he paused.

"That would be best, your Excellency," I said.

"The abbey is embarking on a rebuilding program to return the abbey church to its historic preeminence among the churches of Britain," he began. "We have the relics of Britain's first martyr, but we do not have a church befitting them.

"We plan a new altar screen and a massive, silver cross decorated with precious jewels."

"A more dramatic show," I said.

"Yes," the abbot replied tersely.

Then Prior Thomas intoned, "And we are building a new chapel dedicated to my brother. It will hold a carved marble sarcophagus for his final resting place."

Wallingford sat waiting for my reaction, and I responded out of politeness, "Your plans are ambitious. The altar will be a memorable sight for our pilgrims."

"You have caught my purpose." He added, "This brings me to the agenda for this meeting. I am counting on Sopwell to support us."

"The Priory will do whatever it can," I said firmly.

After a long silence, he fixed me, enunciating carefully, "I will test your willingness." Casting his eyes momentarily upward, he said, "Transfer to us immediately the farm left you by Lady Alice Westby."

Lady Alice Westby had recently bequeathed me a small farm on two parcels. The farm's income is negligible but enough to include her name daily in our prayers and to celebrate a Mass for her family annually.

Not anticipating this demand, I fell silent. The signs were even direr than I divined. I needed to reassess my plans to placate the abbey. If Sopwell was no less autonomous next year than it is this year, it will be a victory. It is time to hold the line.

All the while the abbot was talking, Prior Thomas repeatedly smoothed his meticulously tailored black robes as his brother spoke. With my lengthening silence, he smiled to himself, then looked up, letting his hands drop to his lap.

"We must have your response today, Dame Juliana," Prior Thomas said.

I looked over to the abbot and said, "Lady Alice left the farm to me understanding that I would transfer it to Sopwell. That was her intent, and I am obliged in law and conscience to follow her wishes."

"You are putting us off," Thomas said, looking over at his brother, "as we expected."

Abbot Wallingford was growing impatient. In irritation, he rose slightly from his chair, looked at Brother Simon with upraised pen, caught himself, and then sat back down. Carefully adjusting his black cowl, he said, emphasizing each word, "Sopwell must not obstruct our plans for the abbey church."

"Forgive me, Abbot. Lady Westby's estate was distributed just this last month. I received the title documents recently and intend to follow the dying wishes of a pious, noble woman when disposing of the property. In fairness to her family, I should first visit the farm, and then make my decision," I offered apologetically, adding in a hushed voice, "in consultation with both of you . . . of course."

Somewhat relieved, Abbot Wallingford said, "When can you make your inspection?"

"I will go as soon as the roads are dry," I said with bowed head and lowered eyes.

"If you delay," Prior Thomas reminded me, "the abbey will intervene."

After a moment's hesitation, Abbot Wallingford glanced over at his brother, who met his glance and nodded. "It is our judgment that you manage Sopwell's affairs with too light a hand. That is why Prior Thomas and I believe the abbey should take over management of Sopwell's properties. With the expenses the abbey is taking on, expenses that will add luster also to Sopwell's name, it is only fair that the convent contribute more generously than it has in the past." Pausing for effect, he glared at me and said, as if I had missed his intent, "More income can be demanded of your tenants. You are too lenient.

"Thus I am directing my brother, Thomas, to supervise you closely. At your age, you are not the manager you once were. You must see the need to make Sopwell more profitable, and I will expect you to obey my brother as you would me. He will be meeting with you to detail what the abbey needs from Sopwell."

"Detail," I asked.

"Yes, detail. Sopwell's cooperation is needed if the abbey is to succeed with our renovations," he said. "In the next few days, Thomas will detail what Sopwell must do for the abbey."

"Your words sound ominous," I said.

Prior Thomas came alert, cleared his throat, and signaled to Brother Simon. The clerk's scratching abruptly ceased.

"Yes. We will exact what we need from Sopwell one way or another." Wallingford spoke, an edge in his voice.

"What building expenses do you see coming from Sopwell?" I asked.

"Sopwell will pay for the chapel dedicated to me as well as my marble sarcophagus, which will be the chapel's centerpiece," he shot back. "Italian sculptors are expensive. It will cost one hundred pounds. We expect payment in coin."

Prior Thomas folded his hands and was smiling again.

The meeting ended with Wallingford adding, "The office of sub-prioress has been vacant too long. You need provide for your successor. At your age, there is no telling when your replacement will be needed." Drawing himself up, he said tonelessly, "See to your successor's election before the abbey appoints her. Once one is in place, the abbey can move more quickly . . . if need be." Then he chuckled to himself and added, "Do not bother your cousin, the bishop of Lincoln, with this latest news, his words mean nothing to me." His brother gazed in admiration.

I protested but quickly saw my words, as my earlier conversation with Father Joseph, had no effect on the Wallingfords.

Prior Thomas then gestured for Brother Simon to lead me out. The official meeting was over, and Brother Simon's account would become an entry in the Abbey's Annals to satisfy the critics, like the bishop of Lincoln, of Wallingford's administration of Sopwell.

What I thought but did not tell Wallingford was that the cure for the abbey's money problems was a score of miracles before St. Alban's relics. The lame walking; the leper cured; the infertile young wife with child. That will bring pilgrims.

Wallingford's words, "one way or another," hung on me all day. The brutal face of the abbey would come when Prior Thomas "detailed" Sopwell's obligations.

WE PRESS AHEAD with Psalm 50.

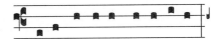

You sit and speak a-gainst your si-ster;

You slan-der your own fa-ther's daugh-ter.

That was last week. Yesterday I received word that Prior Thomas demanded my appearance that morning in the abbey's chapter house again. As the note said, he summoned me to the abbey to "detail" the terms of Sopwell's support for the abbey's renovations. With the smell of incense from Mass sweetening the chapter hall's wood fires, Thomas sat bristling in the abbot's chair.

As I looked about for a bench, he said, "Remain standing. This meeting will not take long." Shuffling through Sopwell's account books, which lay before him, he said, "You lack any sense of rigor. Your bookkeeping is sloppy, and you go for days without balancing your accounts. There is no way to determine where Sopwell stands from one day to the next."

"Do you wish me to balance our accounts daily?" I asked, on guard now for what might follow.

"It does not matter, for you will soon have no need of keeping accounts," he said sternly. "It is time to stop this charade that you call managing Sopwell. My brother and I are in agreement that Sopwell must be stripped of all its properties . . . the sooner the better. There will be no excuses and no delays."

I said resolutely, "I will not agree to that." At last, the true intent of the Wallingford brothers was spoken out loud.

"My brother has sat by and watched you maneuver his predecessors into allowing Sopwell to increase its holdings. You own and take profits from two inns and many farm properties up and down the Ver Valley. You have been very clever, but no longer," he hissed. "My brother is in full agreement with me that it must end, and today I am putting you on notice it will end."

"If you do it, you will do it without my consent," I said deliberately. "What you propose is theft."

"I have drawn up sales agreements for each of your properties," he said, gesturing to a stack of papers before him. He offered a quill dripping with ink.

"I will not sign away the independence of our community," I said adamantly, crossing my arms.

"Nothing will stand in the way of our renovations. Certainly not you," he said with a sneer. "You will not thwart the abbey's plans for my brother's chapel and the everlasting acclaim he deserves."

"There is nothing more to be said."

"There is one more thing to be said. My brother and I anticipated your stubbornness," he shot back with his chin jutting out in anger. He waited for effect.

"And that is," I said, prompting him.

"We are raising the abbey's fees for mass and confession," he hissed. "The new fees will pay for my brother's chapel and his marble sarcophagus. One hundred pounds. By five o'clock, the last day of September, you will pay ahead for the whole of next year. The fee must be paid in gold coin. So on or before September 30th, you will put in my hands enough gold to pay our priests. If you fail to do so, Sopwell will be a community beyond the sacraments and will be disbanded. Then all your properties will fall to us without the need to challenge your title in court," he crowed, pointing a shaking finger at me.

"Will you put your request in writing?" I said, "I want to enter it into our daily accounts."

At first Thomas flinched and then reddened. "You have failed to take my measure. There will come a day where you will be begging me to take Sopwell's properties off your less than capable hands. And that includes the Westby farm."

"I believe I have your measure." Then I added, "If you make out a reminder of the new fees now, I can save your messenger a trip."

Pulling back the proffered pen, he scratched out the onerous terms for the sacraments, the one service we women could not provide for ourselves. He asked without looking up, "Two more questions. Have you inspected the Westby farm?"

"No," I said.

Smugly smiling, Prior Thomas let my answer pass without comment. "Has Sopwell elected a subprioress?"

"Yes, Sister Joan Chapelle," I replied.

"Send her to me," he ordered. "I wish to assess her fitness."

Before five o'clock, September 30, 1477 . . . before Vespers of Michaelmas this year of Our Lord. One more preparation for this winter.

The abbey had its plans. I now made mine. I will not be Sopwell's last prioress. That will not be the final tally in the sum of my life.

WE PRESS AHEAD with Psalm 50, comforting in all these memories of yesterday.

Mark this, then, you who for-get God;

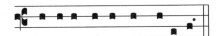

And there will be none to de-liv-er.

I am the spiritual daughter of Letitia Wyttenham, the prioress who preceded me in office. She was Sopwell's finest seamstress, gifted in embroidery. The Abbey sent her copes and chasubles to the Vatican to increase their good name in Rome. Her predecessor, Matilda de Flamstead, urged me to work at fishing. She assigned me to spend long hours on the Ver and nearby ponds and streams, emphasizing the value of fresh fish in our diet. She had discussed the idea with my mother after my mother praised to her my fishing skills. At my suggestion, Matilda enlarged Sopwell's ponds and allowed me time to experiment with reproducing bream and tench. Prioress Letitia concurred with Matilda, and she had me continue angling to fill Sopwell's larder when Matilda retired.

On most days, I provided fish for the convent. But from time to time, my angling was unsuccessful, leaving the priory short an entree. This happened often during the leaping season. On days of heavy mayfly or caddis hatches, very few trout were served from our kitchen.

One June day over forty years ago, Prioress Letitia invited me to sit with her in the work room. She was finishing the border stitching on an alb. Looking up as I entered, she dropped her work and gestured for me to sit next to her. She began by complimenting my angling skills and the success I enjoyed over the years. "Sopwell is healthier for your work.

"I do not wish to seem ungrateful, but as the summer approaches each year, the number of trout you bring to our table diminishes," she said and then was quick to add, "This is not a criticism. You supply us with all the fish we need. But I wondered if I could be of help to you?"

"We are in the middle of what I call the leaping time. With the onset of spring weather, countless insects appear on the surface of the river, and the trout will have nothing else," I started. "I find it useless to even try for them with my baits, so I try for other fish. Other species do not become as fixed on insects as trout do."

"Is there any way to catch these insects and use them?" She asked.

"I have tried, but they are too delicate. My hooks mutilate them and drag them under the surface, where the trout ignore them."

"How delicate are they?" Letitia asked, picking up some red silk thread she had been using. "Are they thinner than this thread?"

"No. Their bodies are several times thicker. This month, a fly with tan wings and a thick tan body will appear. It is a type of caddis fly, a fly whose worm encases itself in tubes of pebbles or bits and pieces of vegetation while living under water," I answered, bending forward and rolling the thread between my fingers. "It is a tawny color, tan with highlights of orange."

Sorting through other thread on the worktable, Prioress Letitia picked up another roll of thread, "Is it this color?"

"No. A little darker," I said, now intrigued.

After sorting through other silk threads on the table, she found another roll and held it up to me. "Would this color match?"

"Yes." I was now at full attention, my mind excited. I knew where she was going.

"In my embroidery, I have found that with patience and the right materials, my sewn butterflies look like real butterflies. My sewn peacocks look like real peacocks. Perhaps using silk thread and other materials, you can fashion insects that look like real insects."

I nodded, surveying the table, "The silk thread is a start."

"Of course you are welcome to any materials we keep here. You have worked as a seamstress and are very familiar with the qualities of silk, wool, linen, and gold and silver threads," she said. "My suggestion is that you spend some time testing which materials best imitate your insects of the leaping time. Do not be afraid to try feathers, which I have seen sewn into hats and cloaks with great effect."

And that is just what I did. I cut snippets of different-colored wools from our sheep. A young jay fell into the cloister yard with a broken neck. I saved the skin with its feathers. Partridge and ducks were delivered to our kitchen. I saved their skins. I visited our barns, where I plucked feathers from our chickens and geese, leaving them to run clucking and honking from me.

The leaping time was no longer a mystery. My flies imitating the Ver's bugs met with success month after month. Tying dubbed flies took me over. Besides mayflies and caddis, I dreamt up hundreds of dubbed creations to substitute for beetles, crickets, leafhoppers, minnows, worms, maggots, cheese, bread, and so on. I had visions of my fly book holding imitations of every possible bait for every possible fish. Some creations even worked sometimes, but my many failures drove me to even more elaborate concoctions and days of fewer fish.

Nature's materials captivated me. The iridescent greens, blues, and bronzy browns of peacock tails, the gray flight feathers and subtly shaded breast feathers of the drake, the marked tans and browns of partridge feathers, the whole gamut of hair from deer to sheep, all held me in their power and beauty. As I worked with nature's everyday dress, I was smitten.

I lost sight of my purpose. I believed the striking beauty of partridge and hawk, deer and sheep, and all the other creatures that flourished around Sopwell could not but mesmerize the Ver's trout, as they mesmerized me. My concoctions took off from my tying vise as a pent up horse let loose from its corral. They were beautiful, attractive to the human eye, flaunting nature's most flamboyant colors and shapes. Sometimes they caught fish that rose, I now believe, more out of boredom or anger than hunger.

My fly book became bulky—too bulky. It was then a new vision struck me: a fly book with one fly. I prospected for a universal fly, one that caught every species of fish under every circumstance. My mind grew feverish with combinations of the most beautiful and rare feathers. One pattern showed promise, especially with trout, perch, and salmon, and I tweaked it day after day to increase my catches.

But my experiments with my universal fly ended one afternoon. I was working at the sewing table with Sister Joan Chapelle and Prioress Letitia. Sister Joan inquired about my universal dubbed fly, a white silk ribbon laced with silver thread, topped with black hair from a stoat, and a dash of red. It resembled a wounded minnow.

Holding my artificial minnow up, I said with conviction, "No trout could resist this fly."

Sister Joan fingered it, admiring its colors. She knew enough about small chub and roach to say admiringly, "Very nice. Be careful the small fry do not adopt it and convince it to swim home with them."

Sister Letitia motioned to Sister Joan to look at the minnow fly. She turned it over in her fingers. "Will this work better than your natural baits?"

Her question brought me up short. Struggling with the truth of the question, I colored and then said, "Probably not."

Prioress Letitia then said, "If your minnow fly will do no better than a real one, wouldn't your day be better spent on the river than cooped up in here. Full sunlight and clear air would be my wishes after a day spent at Sopwell's sewing tables." She then smiled broadly at me and said, "Your angling needs little improvement. Certainly your dubbed flies have brought us trout when they are leaping, and your natural baits never seem to fail for pike, bream, tench, perch, and flounder. You even bring us salmon when you are able to dangle worms in front of their noses."

She was right. It took me time to accept her kindly wisdom, but I did and limited my dubbed flies to the twelve I have listed in the *Treatyse* and then only after I proved them effective.

SISTER CLARE'S VOICE moves us ahead to complete Psalm 50.

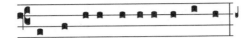

Make thanks-giv-ing your sa-cri-fice to God."

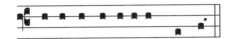

And pay your vows un-to the Most High.

Being an ardent observer of holy Benedict's poverty, I fixed myself in this place by the Ver, avoiding all ownership. It is as it should be. Thank you. I have nothing. Living by the river, I utter "thank you" every time I glimpse the Ver from a window, every time I hear its music, indeed, every time I catch its musky fragrance.

So it was yesterday morning. I planned to catch a trout for Sister Margery before Prime. She continues to fail and did not protest when I directed her removal to the infirmary. With only a spotty run of salmon expected for the fall, trout must be her summer diet. During the leaping time, the best time to angle is between four and eight o'clock in the morning. For me, that is during the hours of Prime and Terce.

Overnight the wind shifted to the west, the sky dawned gray and overcast, and the air felt chill. All to the good. After netting out several minnows from our ponds and dropping them into a small canteen, I followed the Ver upstream past Sopwell's mill to where I knew of a pool home to several good trout.

The pool, long and deep, collects when the Ver drops several feet after clearing a gravel-bottomed riffle. Picking up speed, the river bounces off an ancient crack willow tree exposing its tangle of roots. Then it turns into the far bank, sculpting a crescent. Its work done, the Ver then slows its pace, becoming a deep, placid pool with only a hint of current and with a deep, uncertain sand and silt bottom.

When I reached it, a cold breeze ruffled the pool. Most of the Ver's waters were frigid, so its trout were lethargic. But the pool I had chosen was different from most reaches of the river. It was the very first to warm and the very last to cool. During a drought years earlier, the Ver fell and exposed its banks. The crescent-shaped, undercut far bank was not only a refuge from herons but also the well head for a seam of underground springs. The springs seeped generously all year long. Their waters were warmer than April's cold floods and cooler than August's tepid flow.

But the pool was not as I expected. Instead of featureless, lead-gray water fringed with stark, leafless alder and barely budding hawthorn bushes, the head of the pool was awash with rings of rising trout. Graceful March Brown and dark olive mayflies floated its surface, as did wind-sown hawthorn flies, bulky and black. Dislodged from their bushes, they floated flush in the surface. The rises brought slashing sprays.

I would rather fish for trout with bait. Usually there is nothing better than a minnow for large trout, and one large trout was all Sister Margery needed. After rigging up my rod, I hooked a fair-sized, silver-sided, black-backed minnow just behind its cheek. Taking up a position back from the river's edge on the far bank opposite the old willow, I dropped the minnow into the pool at the point where the current slowed. The minnow dove down to the bottom. I waited. And I waited. Not a twitch. In stages I crept farther down the pool dragging the minnow, fishing as I went. Still no strike.

Trout continued to rise at the head of the pool. I surveyed them again. When feeding, a hover of trout usually sorts itself out with the largest trout up front and the smaller behind in descending size. At the very head of the hover, near the tangle of willow roots, two large fish fed leisurely, displacing a great heaving of water each time they rose. They were fixed on floating mayflies emerging from the riffle above. Choppy water. Returning to the head of the pool for a closer inspection, I quietly peered into the riffle. A glimpse of large, dark, struggling mayflies here and there confirmed the trout were feeding on March Brown duns. The cold and wind kept the flies on the surface longer than usual, and with little effort, the trout steadily scooped them up.

Searching my fly wallet, I picked out my dun fly with partridge wings. It holds first place among my twelve dubbed flies, my twelve apostles of the leaping time. Attaching a new green-colored leader woven of nine hairs, I fluffed the fly and was ready.

The one discordant note was the wind. It was proving unpredictable. Time was passing, and Prime's bell was due to ring shortly.

I would need to work quickly, if only the wind would cooperate. Waiting motionless, I guessed at the timing and luckily made a passable cast into the riffle. But the thread of current carried my dun fly away from the main current sweeping past the willow roots, and my fly floated a good foot away from the sipping trout. No takers.

Another such cast was too chancy. More importantly, I doubted I could cast my dun fly safely to the thread of current that hugged the willow roots. My line would straddle two diverging currents, and eventually it and my fly would be dragged across the river. No large trout would mistake a dragging fly for a natural March Brown. Further, a brief gust could slap a second cast down, making them suspicious or, worse, put them down. I did not have the time to experiment. My place was in chapel when Prime started.

Perhaps the wind could be useful. With my time short, I invented. Adding another length of leader to my line, I undid my sandals, slipped off my socks, and hitched the hem of my habit up in my belt. Stepping into the riffle, I stood upstream from the willow tree, my back to the wind. The cold water jolted me. Instead of keeping my fifteen-foot rod low, as I had on my first cast, I raised it into the breeze.

My dun fly became a kite. Edging further into the riffle, gauging the collection point for the current hugging the willow, I began testing the wind. When it dropped, my fly alighted and bounced on the Ver's surface. When it gusted, the fly rose and wavered in the air. As I raised my rod tip even higher, the fly sailed even higher.

With my rod extended at waist level, the dun fly danced several feet upstream aloft the willow roots. For a few moments, a gust held it there. Deliberately, I lowered the rod tip until the fly floated a bare foot above the river and no more than a foot or so upstream from the trout. Now I waited for the gust to die. I did not need to wait long. It died, and the dun fly landed as thistle down. But the wind was not finished. In a last gasp, a stray puff undulated down my line, briefly picked up the dun fly once again, and just as quickly dropped it inches from the snout of the first of the two trout. The fly vibrated when it settled.

Immediately, a trout struck, throwing up a geyser of water. I pulled back on my rod. Stung by the hook, the fish jumped twice and ran downstream toward the broad reaches of the pool, throwing off sprays of gold, brown, and red as it went. This was fortunate. Holding my rod tip over the fish, I worked it toward the undercut bank away from the willow roots. Leaping onto the bank and fighting the alders, I followed the fish downstream to slower water.

Here the fight ended. Luckily the fish was hooked in the roof of its mouth. By keeping it under my rod tip and simply maintaining upward pressure, I was able to exhaust it. By degrees, as the fish weakened, I led it closer and closer to the bank. It was a good fish. Searching for a level place, I walked the now docile, great fish downstream as on a leash to a shallow sand shelf at the foot of the pool. Here I slid it up over a bed of watercress onto the clear, grassy bank, where the hook fell out. I fell on my knees between the flopping fish and the river, subduing it with a rock.

Sister Margery will have several healthy meals. The fish was beautiful, as all trout are beautiful. Retrieving my socks and sandals and stowing my rod, I wrapped the trout in grass and slipped it in my satchel. After leaving the fish with the infirmarian with the instruction to cook it as Sister Margery wished, I crossed the cloister for chapel just as our bells rang for Prime.

The fish smell on my hands was a wondrous distraction. No one seemed to mind.

We have reached the Our Father, and I wholeheartedly repeat with my sisters the words. As I recite, I think of my father and Edward and of course Tristan, and finally St. George. In my youth, all were my protectors and teachers, and I thank them again this morning.

> . . . your will be done
> On earth as it is in heaven.
> Give us this day our daily bread
> And forgive us our trespasses
> As we forgive those who
> Trespass against us.

So many years have passed and so many trespasses, so many murders to forgive. Parliament, John of Gaunt, and the rest responsible for my father's death were the first—and the hardest—to forgive. Then there was Bolingbroke, who ordered Sir Roger's execution. And there was Edward and his treachery. Through tearful prayers, I forgave them all. I take comfort now in the thought that my father is in the company of Tristan and St. George.

Lauds is finished. Out the darkened chapel and through the cloister yard, we return to our beds and sleep.

My dream of Isabel and her warning remains on my mind as I drop off. At Conisbrough, Isabel impressed me as just another pretty girl interested in clothes and gossip. The person whom I later discovered was a remarkable woman I first believed a shallow, privileged girl with a generous dowry that she took for granted.

It occurred to me that Isabel's dowry was no more valuable than the Westby property. My belated dowry perhaps. But the question is, how long will I keep my dowry?

Prior Thomas reminds me of a greyhound in pursuit. He will stay on Sopwell's heels, prodding me daily until I fall to the ground like the winded hart, too exhausted to flee the snarling pack. Then the abbey will replace me, and in the confusion of transition, extinguish our hold on the spiritual security it took years to achieve.

From Edward, I learned the hart cannot outrun the greyhound. Its only hope is to set false trails. This is not in my nature. But in hunting, Edward was always right. I have seen hart die on their feet, running in circles. Prior Thomas has studied my habits and believes he can push me to circle back on myself. He believes I will dither because I am old and have no stamina for the long cross-country chase he has planned.

Prior Thomas does not know me. He hopes I will panic as the foolish hart panics with a pack of greyhounds snapping at its hind legs. There will be no panic. I come from people who faced the worst—their own deaths, as my father and St. George did—composed. I will not invest my feelings yearning for an outcome. That is beside the point. What is important is how I face the abbey's challenge. Calm and steadfast.

Indirection. A false trail. I must reflect on it.

"No excuses and no delays." Prior Thomas will be watching.

prime

Feast of St. Monica
6:45 a.m.
May 4, 1477

BIRDSONG, ST. ALBANS'S bells, and first light on the ceiling of my room woke me with a jolt. Swinging my legs out of bed, I found my hand bell and, murmuring a Miserere, rang the dormitory awake. With quiet purpose, my sisters stretched and dressed. Then we all hurried across the cloister yard to chapel for Prime, the first hour. The day had begun.

As I was climbing the chapel steps for Prime, Sister Joan handed me a note. It was from the abbey. She was plainly disturbed. "Prior Thomas enlists me as his go-between. I resent the role," she said, narrowing her eyes. "He even questioned me about what you say about him and his brother."

"Would you like to hear the message?" I asked, breaking the seal. Sister Joan nodded. I read, "For Sopwell's protection, the abbot has instructed his marshals to lock the outside doors of the convent for the period between seven o'clock in the evening and six o'clock in the morning. Marshals shall be stationed at the priory doors throughout the night."

"I suppose we should feel safer," Sister Joan said in disgust.

"Such precautions are lost on me also," I said thoughtfully.

"I surmise from Prior Thomas's hints that the abbey intends great changes for Sopwell," she said. "This will be the first but surely not the last."

"Your read him correctly. I fear the abbey will methodically eliminate our privileges one by one until it gets what it wants—our properties and the surrender of Sopwell's independence," I replied.

"Prior Thomas asked me about the Westby farm." Sister Joan said quizzically. "I could tell him nothing because I know so little about it."

"The abbey wants the farm," I replied. "My guess is Wallingford will sell it immediately. I have delayed giving it up because the Westby property by itself will not satisfy the abbey's need for funds. If it could, I would gladly give it up today. But as you know, the renovations the abbey plans are expensive—very expensive. Sopwell would need to sell many of its properties on short notice to raise the hundred pounds the abbey demands."

"Many?" Sister Joan exclaimed.

"The buyers will have heard that our sales are forced. We would need to put more properties on the market to raise the same amount of money we could realize if we sold them gradually to our own advantage," I said.

"I understand," she said.

"For the present, as to the Westby farm, I choose to stand in the abbey's way," I said.

She asked tentatively, "Is there a way to avoid selling off so many properties at once?"

"I am not sure. The Westby property has unique features. I believe it has rich potential for a healthy income," I said. "But we need time to reshape its operations. Prior Thomas will refuse to give Sopwell that time," I replied, refusing to reassure her. I knew of no good reason to offer reassurance.

Thoughtfully, Sister Joan mounted the steps and disappeared into chapel for Prime.

After visiting the Westby croft a week earlier, I decided that Wallingford would never receive it from my hands. It was really two properties. The farm's cropland was a virgate in area, about thirty acres. Its yield from year to year was unremarkable. Set about a half mile down from the cropland on a spur surrounded by fenland, the other property, another virgate, was populated with mature oaks and larch.

On my visit, the tenants, Will Marsh, his wife, Mary, and teenage son, Edward, greeted me politely. Tanned, with calloused hands, they moved precisely and answered my questions soberly. Mary offered a bench and brought me a little ale kept cool in a nearby spring. I did not protest.

The Westby croft was charming. We sat in the close formed by the Marsh house and two barns. A whole oak tree dragged from the woodlot and laced together after being split down the middle framed the tenants' toft, their farmhouse. The roof of the toft was thatch, and the walls were wattle and daub and freshly limed. The barns were sturdy buildings also. One barn housed oxen, the other, Will's carpenter shop. In the shop, he kept ornate chests, chairs, and tables that he manufactured and offered for sale at St. Albans's Saturday market. Finally, set apart from the close, Will kept a small forge, where he worked the iron and steel parts for his chests.

From Will's description, the woodlot would satisfy Sopwell's fuel needs and leave a surplus for many years to come. A great saving to Sopwell. While prices of agricultural goods stagnated, firewood prices climbed. I pressed Will only for a verbal description of the woodlot. I had no time to inspect it. Now past noon, I needed two hours for the walk back to St. Albans. Promising to return on Michaelmas to inspect the firewood set aside for the priory, I assured Will I would personally inspect the woodlot then. With Mary's prompting, Will said, "The woodlot is a sight—ancient trees with a large spring at its heart." I promised to see it when I returned in the fall.

As I turned to leave, I told Will, "Leave the cropland fallow this summer. I will find a better use for it."

Will and Mary looked at each other in dismay. "Do not worry. I will make certain there is sufficient income for your family from the woodlot," I said.

ONCE THE CONFITEOR ends, Sister Clare immediately begins the Deus in adjutorium, and we join her in reciting the morning prayer:

> O Lord God Almighty, who has brought us to the beginning of this day, aid us with your grace that we may not fall this day into sin, but that our words may be spoken and our thoughts and deeds directed according to your just commands.

The hymn for St. Monica's feast day follows, and we sing:

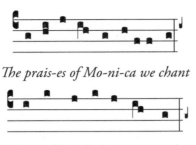

The prais-es of Mo-ni-ca we chant

To whom all lands their treasure bring

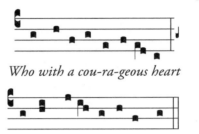

Who with a cou-ra-geous heart

Be-spoke in her life true wo-man's worth.

St. Monica, the mother of St. Augustine, being neither a martyr nor a virgin, is a rarity on the liturgical calendar. As a widow, she won her place by converting her wayward son to Christian belief. Only our kitchener, Sister Anicia, has been a mother. Most of the rest of us have ordered our lives so that our burial Mass will be celebrated from the Common for a Virgin.

On this day, my mother is in my thoughts. The deaths of her two husbands shaped her life and thus my life and the life of my brother, Richard. The first death, my father's death, drove my mother and me apart. My brother and I spent months away from Bernersbury Manor. While my mother looked for a new husband, we made the circuit of our relatives.

The geographical separation fostered an emotional one. But it could not be helped. Her brother, my Uncle William, impressed on my mother the family's need for additional estates. My mother, a beautiful woman, made the circuit of every festival and celebration where unwed noblemen crowded. My mother found a new husband, Sir Roger Clarendon, King Richard's half brother.

They were a good match; Sir Roger was well known at court. And it was to court Sir Roger, my mother, and my uncle brought their list of requests. First on the list was Bernersbury. Richard was due to inherit Bernersbury once he attained his majority, years off. My mother pled the term be shortened. For the term of Richard's minority, however, Bernersbury Manor was managed by Robert Braybrook, Bishop of London. After deducting the cost of management, he directed a small income to my mother. Second, my mother pressed for an estate to fill out my dowry. Simple addition and subtraction proved Bernersbury, even back in the family's hands, could never provide one. Without a substantial dowry, I could not expect to marry nobly. My mother continued to press for more manors, but the matter was put off. Third on the list was my mother's need for more income. This request alone was granted. Eventually she was allowed income from two of my father's forfeited estates, but on her death, this additional income by law ceased and so could never be pledged as a dowry.

Sir Roger survived the Epiphany plot only to be lost to us two years later. Refusing to believe Bolingbroke secretly assassinated his half-brother, Richard, in the Tower after the Epiphany plot failed, Sir Roger encouraged itinerant Franciscan monks to spread the news on Britain's northern border that King Richard still lived. Bolingbroke saw the rumors as treason. In May of 1402, he ordered the arrest of Sir Roger and his sympathetic clerics and shortly afterward saw to their execution.

My prospects for marriage died with Sir Roger's execution. I turned twenty-one that year and became a realist. Were it not for Sir Roger's treason, my mother and uncle may have eventually convinced the king to grant our family additional estates. But it was not to be. And I gave up any hope of a dowry. Bolingbroke's preoccupation with the persistent rumors of King Richard living in Scotland made our family unwelcome at Windsor and thus made any further plea for additional estates hopeless. Edward was one of our few friends at Court, but even he, later Bolingbroke's Master of Game, could not count on the king's generosity. All signs pointed toward me living out my days as a spinster residing with my brother, Richard, and his wife, Isabel, or worse, serving as handmaiden to my mother nursing her during her last years.

Sir Roger's death left an ever deepening chasm between my

mother and me. She refused to give up her plans to have me married. Her hopes confounded me, and I became, in her eyes, a vacillating coward. I, in turn, could not believe she did not see the inevitable consequences of the hard facts staring us in the face. Even though it was clear to me that I would never marry, I still felt guilty for questioning my mother's plans. She resolutely pushed forward as if a husband were on the near horizon. I know she felt betrayed by my obstinacy, but I was convinced her resolution was a delusion, and a painful one for both of us.

It was Edward that raised her hopes.

SISTER CLARE GIVES out the antiphon for Prime's three psalms and we listen:

This wo-man is beau-ti-ful a-mong the daugh-ters of Je-ru-sa-lem.

Then we take up Psalm 118 singing:

Out of my dis-tress I called on the Lord;

The Lord an-swered me and set me free.

Last night, as I arranged my sandals together on the floor within reach of my feet, I thought of Isabel's cautious preparations. To greet guests, to ride out hawking, to pray. Coming as the surprise of a lone, clattering gust rushing down a wooded ravine, I heard her say out of the dark to me, "You were flourishing when you first visited Bodiam." And I was.

St. Albans sat silent, and Sopwell's meadows and ponds lay still. No breeze disturbed our fruit trees. Only the memory of Isabel's words filled my ears. Bodiam is where I first came to understand her worth. So much happened there.

Then the memory of her voice trailed off, and I heard a barn owl shriek in the orchard. Another foolish, wandering rabbit impaled after it stopped to listen for the flapping of an owl's silent wings.

The Bodiam story begins in hope. My reputation for training and keeping hawks spread among our neighbors, and invitations multiplied, one from Sir John Dalyngrigge, Lord of Bodiam Castle. According to his note, he wished to consult me regarding his hawks and falcons. Many were sickly, and a few had died. Fewer females laid fewer eggs. For he and his falconers, the cause was a mystery.

Bernersbury stood on the cusp of death and hope. Sir Roger's absence dragged on our spirits. His death put my mother into a second mourning deeper than convention dictated. She remained in mourning even after my brother Richard's marriage to Isabel. The wedding interrupted but did not dispel her grief, and she went into seclusion again immediately following the last guest's farewell. This changed when Sir John's urgent request arrived, and my mother, my brother, Richard, Isabel, and I made the trip to Bodiam the very next day. Sir John's note was directed to me, but the messenger was careful to add that Sir John believed travel would also be good for my mother's spirits.

Bodiam mimics the castles praised in our romances. Sir John Dalyngrigge's father was a veteran of the French wars and a trusted friend of King Edward III. He married well, and near his wife's family manor, he built a moated castle set on a mound circled by the Rother River. Bodiam's walls rise shimmering from the Rother's blue waters as if they were born of the river itself. Sir John's favor with the king is proclaimed in its many massive towers and tall crenellated battlements. As his father before him, Sir John found his greatest pleasure in entertaining his neighbors, and he was well liked throughout Sussex.

My first introduction to Bodiam began in light and shadow. Immediately after arriving, I spent my afternoon inspecting Sir John's hawks and falcons. A single stone building of gray limestone, Bodiam's mews sat long and squat. With small windows rowed on one side, it backed onto the battlements. The windows threw much light into the front side of the mews while leaving in restful shadow the cages set in the back. I sat on a stool just inside the door looking down the aisle of light, smelling newly scattered sweet hay. All was quiet but for the rustle of an occasional bird preening its feathers or briefly fluttering its wings. Waiting unconcerned on their perches, silent in their creams, ambers, grays, and browns, they stood as chained stoics.

The falconers were gentle but correct. Sunset came too quickly with me concluding only that the mews and the falconers were not the cause. One of the ill birds visibly weakened during the afternoon, needing help to stand, and I feared another fatality by morning. I took my stool to the yard in front of the mews, and Sir John, stooped and white haired, sat beside me. Once a large man, old age had been unkind to him. His breath came in rasps, and he was forever rubbing his cold hands for warmth. Before long, he retired to the hall's fires to entertain my mother, Richard, and Isabel.

And so it was, one of his hawks died during the night. Sir John was deeply affected, his pale pallor lightened a shade. More disturbing was the news that several more birds had grown ill. Anxious over breakfast, he brusquely prompted me for my thoughts. There was nothing to reveal, and I told him so. I made my way to the mews, but this time without Sir John. Fighting time and the unknown took its toll on all of us. The falconers grew more solemn as the morning dragged on. Another bird died. The falconers kept glancing in my direction, but I sat silent, following the best course, sitting and observing.

Finally, about noon, I called to Thomas, the head falconer. "Thomas, I see you are feeding your birds doves, chickens, and ducks. Where did you get them?"

"Lady, we collect them from our tenants. These were the birds that hardly survived the winter. Of late, some died of old age and some were too weak to lay. They are of no use now except for the hawks," he said.

"How long have you been feeding your hawks the tenants' discards?" I pressed him.

"About three months now."

Pausing for a moment, I then asked, "How often have you hunted your hawks of late?"

"Less now, Lady Juliana. As they have weakened, we exercise them less and less. Perhaps once every two days," he said. "We lost a few on windy days. Others had difficulty climbing and refused to leave their cadges when they returned. These birds we do not exercise at all, but, as you can see, they die anyway."

"So, during this winter, you fed your hawks desiccated carcasses and did not exercise them. Sir John must be upset, denied his hawking," I said tactfully.

"Not so, Lady. Sir John went through a bad spell, coughing mightily, not leaving his bed for weeks at a time. During the winter, he hardly visited the hall."

"Thomas, does the manor have any cows ready for slaughter?"

"Yes, Lady."

"Then I suggest you lead one here." Thomas turned to go, but I called him back. "Thomas, I strongly suggest you throw out the remaining bird carcasses. The hawks are dehydrated."

"Yes, Lady." While I headed toward the hall, Thomas gruffly called to a pair of younger falconers, and with much waving of arms, he set them in motion toward Bodiam's gate. The two set off at a trot.

Now, for Sir John. In the hall, I found him sitting with my mother and his wife, Joan, finishing a plate of sliced meats and roast partridge. He gestured for me to sit down. There was hope in his eyes.

"Can I call you some food?" he asked, surveying me expectantly.

Bowing to my mother and Lady Joan, a hearty, ever-smiling woman, I said, "Thank you. Some bread, custard, and one of those partridge, please."

Then drawing himself up to his most imperious, Sir John demanded, "Well, what is it?"

"The trouble is, Sir John, you love your birds too well," I said.

Taken aback, with a wry smile he said, "No one has ever accused me of being too kindly."

"Your hawks need to share in your diet. And," I said, pausing for effect. "And," I repeated, "they need to be worked."

"They need to be worked?" he asked incredulously.

"Is there anyone at Bodiam who does not work?" I asked. "You and your birds need to work harder." My mother gasped, and Lady Joan laughed.

"Are you always this blunt?" Sir John roared, slapping his open hand down on the table. "No wonder your mother, Lady Anne, is worried about ever finding you a husband."

I looked over at my mother. "Of course I worry about marrying you off," she said. Then retreating, she added, "Do not fault me in front of my friends."

Turning back to Sir John, I said, "Thomas, your head falconer, is bringing in a cow for slaughter. Your birds will need a regimen of beef with the blood still running and live mice. Also after a day of this diet, they will need to be exercised once a day for a week and then the normal twice a day for the weeks following. I am sorry to be so curt, but your mews are in crisis."

Just then, Sir John's daughter, Constance, entered the hall and took a seat next to me. She was my brother's age, a smaller version of her mother, with deep blue, mischievous eyes and ashen blonde hair.

Sir John turned to her, beaming, "Juliana has been here for a day, and she is already running my life. She has ordered me to hawk every day."

"It is about time someone does," Constance said gently. "We are all so relieved you are feeling better now, father. With the warm weather, it is time to spend your days outdoors as you once did." She was clearly Sir John's favorite.

Turning to his wife, Sir John asked, "Do you think you could teach Juliana some manners while she is here?"

Before she could answer, my mother interjected, "It will take more than one visit. I have given up."

Lady Joan said, "Juliana is always welcome, Lady Anne." Constance laughed and squeezed my arm.

"I had better see to the cow's slaughter and the feeding of my beauties," Sir John said, rising. "Edward was right about you," he said.

"Edward?" I asked.

"Edward, the Duke of York. Last time I was at Windsor, he told me that there was no one better than you for hawks and their problems."

Confused, I replied, "But we have not spoken for years." I glanced at my mother. The memory of Edward's part in the Epiphany plot was still fresh. Our Christmas celebration at Conisbrough was only three years before. She frowned.

"That may be. He must trust the reports he receives about you,"

Sir John said and then added, "He will be here tomorrow with his wife, Philippa, the new Duchess of York."

My mother gasped while I, speechless, turned to Constance. To cover my confusion, Constance chattered about bathing in the Rother that afternoon. "I have not had a full bath since last September," she said. "I am told the Rother has warmed." With a twinkle in her eye, she added, "We should take advantage of it on a comfortable day like today."

We spent the afternoon up to our waists in a slack section of the Rother. Wearing nothing but our shifts, the three of us, Constance, Isabel, and I, splashed and bathed over a warm, sandy bottom, our privacy protected by a screen of high banks. As the sun set, we brushed each other's hair. And that night in the hall, we ate bare headed, adorned only with dancing flickers of candlelight. We were beautiful.

That night Constance and I shared a bed chamber. We went to sleep smelling of the Rother and woke in the morning to the sun spilling its rosy light over our white linen comforter.

psalm 118 approaches its last verses. The light in the chapel grows as we hurry to savor each verse.

I shall not die, but I shall live,

And re-count the deeds of the Lord.

the next morning found me in Bodiam's mews. The hawks and falcons were improving. The sides from the slaughtered cow hung nearby, still dripping blood. The carcass was much diminished and the meat hung in shreds, but no birds weakened during the night.

With Sir John's raptors improving, Constance, Richard, Isabel, and I gathered a hunting party. But Edward arrived earlier than expected, and we were not there to meet him. As we breakfasted on the edge of a dense wood of oak and beech, Edward and Philippa rode up, followed by their servants. Edward made a show of good cheer, bowing to Isabel, Constance, and me. Philippa hung back, stiff and unsmiling, with her hands folded in front of her. Both wore the red and blue of York with gaudily dagged surcotes and gold embroidery everywhere.

Bodiam's kitchen provided cider and fried loaves for the hunt. As the dogs annoyed each other on their leashes, we toasted the loaves on an open fire. Bodiam's cooks had mixed in bits of pork and cheese with ginger for taste and saffron for color. Philippa refused all but a taste of cider. We munched heartily, coating the toast with honey, while Philippa watched in strained silence. In an attempt to overcome our reserve, Edward grew voluble with news from the royal court. He went on cheerfully with lengthy stories of our kinsmen. By the end of the cider, we had assumed a polite reticence, masking our distrust with free-flowing, albeit meaningless, conversation.

Finally Philippa broke in and said to Edward, "We are not here to spread gossip. Get to the point, Edward. Our time is short." She read accurately the meaning of our reserve.

Edward's face darkened. "We should be enjoying this day. Hear the song thrush. Smell the air with its tang of spring rains and sweet odor of meadow flowers. And we have delightful friends for company. We should take our cue from the languid morning and make our proposals leisurely. We have all afternoon and evening for business."

Philippa replied sharply, "What you plan to put forward has a short life. The queen may have already made her choices in our absence. This matter must be addressed immediately."

"Edward, perhaps Philippa is right. Your visit is short, and we can hunt together another day," my brother, Richard, ever the conciliator, said.

Philippa's impatience aroused my curiosity, so I added my voice to Richard's, "Edward, we are not put off. What better atmosphere in which to discuss your proposal?"

Edward fell silent. Without looking at her husband, Philippa took his hesitation as a sign for her to proceed. "Queen Joanna will be inviting ladies of suitable education and background to join her at

court. She will be extending several invitations, and she will personally test the qualities of the candidates. Every courtier, noble, and
court hanger on is whispering in her ear naming their relatives."

Pausing for emphasis, Philippa continued, "Edward believes you,
Juliana, would make a good candidate, and with his influence, you
could very likely be chosen." Pausing again, she narrowed her eyes
and looked directly at me. "I believe his idea is foolish. Edward has an
endless store of them. I believe I know my queen, and you, Juliana,
are not suited to her."

Before I could blurt out an emphatic refusal out of annoyance,
Constance spoke up first, "And why would Juliana not be acceptable?"

This was a subject Philippa was prepared to discuss with relish.
Addressing me, she said, "In a word, Juliana, you lack discretion."

"Is that all?" I asked.

"You have proved my point. Need I say more? Discretion is essential for the royal court, and I do not believe you will ever learn it,"
Philippa said vehemently. "You fail to comprehend that as members
of the queen's court, we are expected to use our beauty to educate the
men of the King's court. By remaining aloof, we can enforce the finest
of manners. Juliana, you carry the odor of the woods and fields, not
the perfume of the sophisticated lady."

"You take great delight in pointing out Juliana's shortcomings,"
Constance said.

Philippa shot back. "Our queen is very sophisticated. Juliana will
not get far at court as the plainspoken huntress. Queen Joanna takes
no pleasure in the hunt. She is never found in camp when the hunt is
with hounds, par force, because she dreads hacking her way through
an untamed forest. She will accompany her husband only when he
hunts with coursing greyhounds or when, as in bow and stable, she
need only shoot a crossbow into an enclosure crowded with deer."

"I do not call that hunting." I said under my breath.

Ignoring my remark, Constance went on, "Could you be jealous
of her beauty and people's good opinion of her?"

"Jealous of an untutored, awkward girl!" she exclaimed. "Never.
She will add nothing to court, and she will not learn its ways because
she does not appreciate the importance of our court."

In my defense, Richard and Isabel interjected, "But Juliana is well read. She studies Chaucer, Beroul, and Chretien de Troyes. This winter she translated Tibor and Clara d'Anduza of Languedoc. And she writes well. I am sure the queen would enjoy conversing with her."

Unswayed, Philippa said definitively, "Those are popular works. For people like you, Juliana's accomplishments may seem extraordinary, but in the queen's court, they are quite mediocre. We read every day and together discuss what we read. Chaucer wrote for us, as you may have heard."

Isabel was offended. "Richard reads very well."

"But not much, if he is like the men at court, and I believe he is no better than them," Philippa said. "The queen and her ladies set the standards for male behavior. We teach the young men manners, and we punish any man, earl or duke, who ignores them. They must be trained like dogs with treats and whippings."

Standing up, Constance motioned to Sir John's master of game to lead the dogs back to the castle. As they moved off, a field of waving white tails, she asked, "What would you have Juliana do at court?"

"There is not much she could do. Constance, you say Juliana is beautiful. Look at yourselves," Philippa barked. "Your clothes are out of fashion. If Juliana were at court as she is now dressed, she would be laughed at by us and scorned by the young men. No matter her personal beauty."

Isabel looked at Richard. "I have been telling you that we should have our clothes done in London by tailors who serve the court." Turning to Philippa, she asked, "Could you recommend one who is familiar with current court fashion?"

"Of course. But he must be paid before he starts on a wardrobe," Philippa replied. Richard was about to open his mouth but went silent as if slapped. Philippa must have heard of Bernersbury's meager income.

"And after I have the right wardrobe, then what? Do I start whipping any knight who comes near me?" I asked.

"Juliana, Philippa is making attendance at court more daunting than it is," Edward said, glancing at Philippa, who scowled at him. "You are known for your skill in hawking and hunting. Except for a few gowns suitable for the king's feasts, your day to day wardrobe need only be suited for the field, sturdy wool gowns and cloaks. Your reputation for training hawks will add luster to the court."

"But it will not endear her to the queen," Philippa interjected. "Perhaps you should convince the king to hire her as a falconer."

"Philippa, you are not making this any easier," Edward said, his impatience showing. "Juliana belongs at court. We must find a way to bring her there."

"A new wardrobe would be a start. She will need one new gown just for the queen to interview her," Philippa said, bending forward to finger my gown. "She will need new chemises to show off her bosom such as it is. And she will need several new, bejeweled girdles to cinch her waist. And she must have her sleeves tapered at her wrist with buttons. Above all, she must show more color. Look at this drab gown. Is that what you call beige? It will never do."

"I was educated at the court school," Constance began.

But before she could say more, Philippa shot back, "Then you have no excuse. Your gown is cinched at your hips and is unlined. I hesitate to guess at the color. Is it forest green?"

"Yes," said Constance curtly.

Not finished, Philippa added, "Your most backward habit is leaving your hair hang freely. At court we are now tying up and covering our hair, wearing jeweled nets and hats of our own design. It is best if no hair shows."

Cowed, Isabel sat quietly with Richard. Her beautiful auburn hair was often complimented.

"Could you lend Juliana more fashionable gowns and girdles for her interview?" Edward asked.

"It will do no good. The queen remembers all our wardrobes. What she does not remember, her ladies will," Philippa said. "Besides, my gowns will not fit her because they are cut to show off my figure. Juliana is slimmer. Too many hours outdoors, running down grunting boar. No, it serves no purpose to lend Juliana my gowns."

"But you will try to find one for her," Edward said sternly.

"Yes, I will try," Philippa said reluctantly, stamping her foot and throwing up her hands in surrender. "Perhaps I will find an old one that my seamstress could make over. Presently I have no arguments for the queen in Juliana's favor, but I will find some even if I need to lie." The she added sarcastically, "I do it only for you, dear husband."

His point made, Edward asked abruptly, "How large is this forest behind us?"

Constance answered, "It extends more than three miles west. Do you see those limestone cliffs toward the south?"

"Yes," Edward said.

"The forest extends well beyond them."

"How often does your father hunt it?" Edward asked.

"Rarely," Constance said. "His health is not as robust as it once was."

Philippa broke in, "Husband, you have often said that in hawking, women are superior to men. And you have said that some women, Juliana was such a one, you said, are superior to yourself."

"Yes, that is true," Edward answered, clearly puzzled with this turn in the conversation.

"Will you tell us the reason you believe women are superior in hawking?" Philippa asked and then added condescendingly, "Please give us the reason you give your friends at court."

"I am not sure to what conversations you are referring," Edward said, clearly reluctant to answer his wife.

"Edward, you know very well to what I am referring. Do not play word games with me," Philippa demanded.

"I have said that women are better at hawking because they are more like their birds, rapacious. Now are you happy, Philippa?" He said, turning to his wife, who was gazing at me triumphantly.

"Does that make men better at boar hunting because they are gluttons like their prey?" Constance shot back, pushed well beyond the limits of her good manners.

"There are times I do see the resemblance," I added, laughing. Edward glared at his wife and then looked into the distance, avoiding my eyes.

Constance stood up and directed the servants to prepare for our return to Bodiam. "It is getting late, and my father plans an early supper."

On the way back, Edward rode next to me. At one point, he said, "Do not take offence at Philippa. Her venom is reserved for any woman of beauty and good report. Her jealousy is a sure sign of your worth."

"Thank you Edward. But I do not plan to spend what remains of the day reflecting on her spiteful comments," I said. "My guess is that there are others like her at court. They enjoy deflating young women's confidence."

Edward remained silent. I took it as an affirmation.

My mind was made up. There would be no interview with the queen. The bickering between Edward and his wife was a foretaste of Windsor's witty conversation. It was not to be endured.

But I had not counted on Edward's resourcefulness.

the community has moved well into Psalm 116. The words have always been a great comfort to me.

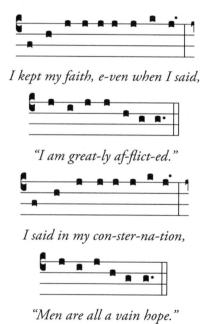

I kept my faith, e-ven when I said,

"I am great-ly af-flict-ed."

I said in my con-ster-na-tion,

"Men are all a vain hope."

dismounting in Bodiam's courtyard, we interrupted Sir John returning from the mews. He was beaming. After greeting Edward and Philippa cordially, he directed his servants to care for their horses and lead them to their chambers. He held me back from following Philippa and Constance inside. "Will you help me exercise my beauties tomorrow, Juliana?" He asked. "I believe I could learn a thing or two from watching you."

"Of course, Sir John," I said. "Have you thought of asking Constance to join us? I think you should, so when I am gone she can help you."

"Thank you for the suggestion," Sir John said. "It is time you ready yourself for the feast, so I will not delay you further."

Washing my face and arms and changing my shift and gown, I descended to the hall. My girdle still rode low on my hips, and my black hair was defiantly uncovered. Looking for Constance, I found instead Isabel, my brother, mother, and Edward huddled together conversing at one end of the massive head table. Richard motioned to me, making a place on the bench beside him.

He smiled at me and said, "Edward has opened a very attractive prospect for you."

I looked at my mother, and she smiled back neutrally. "Is someone offering me a dowry?" I said with mock cheer. Isabel sat silent without expression. Her eyes spoke concern.

Edward and Richard laughed. "And so we shall get right down to business," Edward said. "Not a dowry. I am offering a way to a dowry. I have always been fond of you and your brother. What better hunting companions than you two? No, I am offering you the opportunity to gain a dowry."

My mother looked at me hopefully. The hope in her eyes, however, was tempered with suspicion. The memory of Conisbrough had not faded. She would never trust Edward. "What must I do?" I asked.

"Try to win the queen's approval for a position in her court. Perhaps not as a lady in waiting but in some other court office," Richard said. "Edward will pay for your wardrobe until we are able to make other arrangements. Once you gain a dowry, we can pay him back."

Looking to my mother, Edward was quick to say, "This arrangement will be formalized by a written contract, thus protecting you and Juliana from gossip."

My mother remained silent. "Where will this dowry come from?" I asked.

"Perhaps the queen. She has been known to use her influence with King Henry to settle estates on her favorites," said Edward.

Discounting his enthusiasm by half, I replied, "That could take years, and the passage of time is my enemy."

"You will win over many young knights at court," Edward said brightly. "They will become your advocates."

"You are foolishly optimistic. If I had estates, I might win a few hearts," I replied quickly. "I accept your flattery for what it is. Thank you, but taking a position at court will put me in the dreary round of those women who spend their days reminding the young men not to belch, not to wipe their mouths with their sleeves, to clean their blackened fingernails, and not to add another morsel to an already full mouth. Did you not hear your wife? My disposition is too simple and my dress too plain for court intrigue. Your wife for all her testiness is right."

"It was a mistake to bring my wife today," Edward said. "I apologize to both you and your brother."

I looked over at Isabel and my mother. Isabel's pained manner spoke her distress, but all she could do was glance over to her husband and remain silent. This was a matter between me and the men at the table. My mother looked down, refusing to meet my eyes. Again I was left on my own in this decision. I refused to allow it. "What say you, mother?"

She looked up, "I wish it was more straightforward." And then she fell silent and looked away.

"Just think, Juliana," my brother began, "you would be at court and could help our family win favor with Bolingbroke. I need not say how bad a start we have made with him."

"I would be just one of hundreds of people, mostly men, who bow and scrape to him every day. For the queen, I would be just one of a few dozen women who tend to her needs. The king and queen owe us nothing. I do not see myself as an effective emissary for our family," I said.

"I think you should make the attempt," Edward said. "Hope for the best. Opportunities will come your way, but you cannot take advantage of them unless you are there, at court."

"Let me think about it," I replied. Edward and Richard expected me to say more. Repeating myself, I said, "Thank you. I will give you my answer in the morning. I do not want to hear any more of it tonight."

With an uneasy laugh, Edward poured wine for himself and my

brother, and both toasted me with upraised cups. My brother wanted estates, my mother a married daughter, but what did Edward want? A friend, a lover . . . an heir. Niggling thoughts that I could not quiet. I stood and looked down at Edward, and his toothy smile reminded me of a rapacious wolf, or even a pike, the wolf of the waters.

SISTER CLARE BEGINS Psalm 22, truly a comfort. Its opening passage captures my feelings of that evening so long ago at Bodiam.

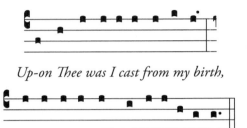

Up-on Thee was I cast from my birth,

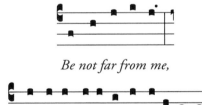

And since my moth-er bore me, thou hast been my God.

Be not far from me,

For trou-ble is near and there is none to help.

Last night we had pike for dinner. I had not planned it that way.

Every day we visit Sister Margery in the infirmary. Yesterday after Terce, I took her for a walk in the meadow surrounding our two fish ponds. In truth the ponds are spring holes dug out and widened to several acres each. Their overflow empties into the Ver just upstream from Sopwell Bridge. In one is tench; in the other, bream.

Sister Margery is gaining strength, but not quickly enough to withstand another winter. Last week she was feverish. Priory work is too much for her. She pesters me to allow her to tend the cloister garden, but I refuse her requests, remembering her the day she entered Sopwell's two-year novitiate, vigorous and inquisitive. Now, forty-five years later, she is seventy-two and in constant pain. Her vigor is but a memory, her questions come less frequently.

As we were walking, I noticed a disturbance among the reeds fringing the little stream connecting our ponds with the Ver. The rivulet is hardly more than a yard wide. I keep a few German carp in it. My plan is to increase their numbers, another dish for Sopwell.

The disturbance was a large swirl that shook the reeds. I have seen such swirls before. A large pike was feeding, and I mentally marked the location.

The first time I saw such a swirl was as a child in the millpond near Bernersbury Manor. Following my father's funeral, while we were still at home, I avoided the incessant political talk that filled our hall by fishing. As I have related, by then I had caught my first fish, a barbel. One afternoon, bored, I wandered down to our mill and its pond.

The midmorning sun burnished the pond's surface into a silvery sheet of glare. Sitting in a patch of mint and forget-me-nots back from the pond's edge, I waited patiently, resting my chin on my knees. The only movement was a moorhen swimming with her young, seven in all. In single file, they made a circuit of the pond searching out breakfast. Except for the mother's occasional quacks, directing strays to close ranks, not so much as a rise ring from a fish disturbed their progress.

This changed when a vortex formed under the last duckling in line. It was lost to view and did not reappear. I jumped up. Rocked by the ripples from the vortex, the mother turned. In an instant, she let out a string of shrieking quacks, which threw her brood into a panic and scrambling for the shore. The survivors made it to the bank shivering at my feet.

No doubt, a large fish was the culprit. Running back to the hall, I tracked down Robert and breathlessly related my saga of the moorhens. He showed no concern until I came to the part of my story where I demanded something be done. He protested that he had more pressing chores. I insisted that something be done and now. He left to confer with my uncle, and when he returned, headed toward his workshop, signaling me to follow.

After sorting through an overflowing box atop a workbench, he retrieved from the jumble a large hook, a ball of twine, and a small net. No rod, no float, and no lead. I reminded him of his oversight, but he ignored me. Before leaving, he threw a loop from the twine over a goose wandering in the yard and led it complaining down to the millpond. On the way, he netted a roach from a small feeder stream.

Brusquely, he turned aside my questions until the three of us settled by the pond. He informed me the fish that ate the duckling was a large pike. As Robert laid out his plan to catch the fish, I sat attentive while the goose muttered continuously, straining against its leash. Robert's plan was to impale the roach on the large hook and then tie it with about a foot of twine to the leg of the goose. Then the goose would be released into the pond for a swim. All was made ready and the goose coaxed into the pond. Looking back at us from time to time, the goose was plainly mystified at this change in its routine, yet it took advantage of its swim, occasionally shaking its leg trying to slip the twine and roach.

Passing a section of reeds, the goose suddenly dipped almost totally from view. Regaining the surface, it screamed. Again it was dragged down. But this time it could not fully regain the surface. Angrily it flapped its wings and began to lift, only to be dragged down again. The fight was on: the goose screaming and flapping, the great fish pulling and diving.

The fight ended in a draw. The goose regained the surface with a foot of twine trailing from his leg. No hook and no roach. Frantically it paddled to shore where Robert collected it and placed the leash back around its neck. Explaining that my Uncle William did not allow him any more time for my problems, Robert headed back to the hall with me and the goose in tow.

It was an odd trio. There was Robert, twice my size, quiet and determined, and me, excitedly waving my arms, flinging questions at him. But the oddest of all was the goose, limping and muttering angrily. Occasionally, looking up at us, it let out a vicious stream of honks.

I stopped and tugged on Robert's sleeve. He turned and looked down at me. Sternly fixing an eye on him, as I had seen my father do when he was dissatisfied, I drew myself up as tall as I could and announced, "We need a bigger goose."

SISTER CLARE CARRIES us well into Psalm 22. I become aware of the words:

I am poured out like wa-ter, and all my bones are out of joint;

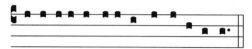

my heart is like wax, it is mel-ted with-in my breast;

My strength is dried up like a pot-sherd, and my tongue cleaves to my jaws.

I worry about Sister Margery. I worry. . . .

I worry about Sopwell's independence. I worry. . . .

After walking Sister Margery back to the infirmary, I collected my rod and fishing satchel and ran toward the reeds where I first saw the swirl. Visions of young carp disappearing down the pike's gullet filled my imagination. On the way, I scooped out a small bream and unfurled my rod. Rummaging in my satchel for a leader made of brown dyed plumber's cord lapped round with metal wire, I knotted it to my line, attaching a medium-sized float and a lump of lead.

Pike attack from below. Where a trout will eagerly take a minnow resting on the bottom of a river, a pike is not so willing. For hours they sit hidden, poised for ambush. With their eyes set on the top of their broad, flat head, they are designed to look up. They take their prey from beneath. They wait for a trout sipping mayfly duns or the unwary, kicking frog or the swimming mouse above them. Thus the angler's bait itself must be lifted just above pike. I do this by means of a float. For pike, the float is placed on the line just above the baited hook, and a lead weight is placed on the line above the float. The effect of this rig is to raise the bait fish and leave it floundering just above the pike, all the while anchored to the stream bottom by the lead weight.

Hurrying across the meadow, I stationed myself on the bank where I first saw the swirl. The current was quick but smooth and only two feet deep. I swung out the bream and saw it twisting just under the rivulet's surface, where it kept trying to right itself. But the current flung it this way and that.

Suddenly, a swirl and the forest green back of the pike churned the surface. Waiting momentarily for the great fish to engorge the bream fully, I struck, planting the bottom spike of my rod in the bank and pulling back with all my strength. Because a pike's mouth is bony, extra force is needed to set the hook. Constricted by the narrow rivulet, the pike jumped, arcing and throwing spray, which flashed light green, white, and yellow. It fell back with a great splash, digging up silt, sand, and weeds from the bottom of the run.

Then the pike ran, and ran toward the Ver. Keeping my rod tip over the fish, I ran with it. Straining the leader, I pulled back every few yards to slow it. The fish did not slow. Steps from the Ver, the pike stopped. I could feel it shaking its head as it rubbed the wired cord between its teeth. To distract the fish, I planted the spike again and yanked sharply on the rod. This stopped his sawing on the line but brought another twisting, head-shaking jump. The mangled bream flew skyward, but the hook held.

Then the pike sulked. I could feel sawing again. Success hung on the wired leader. I have seen pike stretch the protective wire to expose the cord below. Sometimes in such cases, the pike's teeth will cut the unprotected line and compromise the leader entirely. These pike go free. I needed to land this fish soon.

My best chance to end this fight was to provoke another jump. Softly creeping downstream below the fish, I gently pulled it toward the Ver. The fish moved again, quickly picking up speed. I watched it run past me and out from under my rod tip. Giving him a few more yards of line, I lowered my rod and then pulled back, yanking as hard as I could.

In a great leap, the pike came out of the water, tail and all. Just as it cleared the surface, I shifted my stance and yanked again, but this time toward the meadow. In midair the pike cartwheeled end over end, landing just up the grassy bank. But the pike was not done. Squirming like a snake, his long body slithered for the safety of the stream. Frantically, I backed into the meadow, dragging the great fish farther and farther away from the water. He flopped for minutes.

Sister Anicia baked the pike in olive oil, butter, parsley, and thyme. Its bones were so soft we hardly noticed them. And the sauce made a feast of our dripping morsels of bread.

I RECITE FOR the community the collect for St. Monica as the morning sun floods the chapel with its warmth, and then we chant the last antiphon of Prime.

She stretch-es out her hand to the poor; yes she reach-es forth her hands

to the nee-dy; she does not eat the bread of i-dle-ness.

Bodiam remained on my mind as Prime ended. Leaving chapel, our place of serenity, I followed Sister Anicia down to the kitchen. There I collected loaves of warm bread for the convent's breakfast. Closely gathered in my arms, their fragrance flooded my mind and brought back the smells of Bodiam's kitchens that last night. The reverie stunned me like a blow from a sword's flat side, and I stared into the dim rafters of the refectory.

There I pictured Isabel in Bodiam's great hall. And heeding her words, I searched my mind for the new path she counseled. But I saw only what I had seen so often before, myself as a young woman trying to set a course for her life. That course led me to Sopwell and St. Benedict's Rule. I could not shake the inevitability of that picture. But my sense of Isabel's nearness pushed me to try again, harder, to penetrate the meaning of my youth. I felt her urging me to search for my real self, as though breaking into a rigid eggshell to find the meat beneath.

I could sense her say, "I am simply asking you to go deeper. Discard your settled conclusions. View the woman you were before you professed your vows."

As I made the circuit of Sopwell's refectory table, setting out a loaf of bread at each place, I called to mind Bodiam's crenellated walls and its great hall. At first they did not speak to me, and I fell back upon myself, the prioress of Sopwell. My vows have been the hard facts of my inner life for almost as long as I can remember.

I concentrated harder, calling up the last night of our visit. I saw Isabel's smiling face. And I saw the faces of my family and the faces of Edward and his wife, Philippa, and the Dalyngrigges. All of us were seated at the head table. Supper went into the evening. The warmth of the day hung on the hall's gray walls beside the family's heavy blue shields and crossed pikes. As a summer sunset's glow died slowly in the hall's windows, Sir John lavished on us platters of fresh roasted meats, doves, and ducks. Yellow lilies and pink roses adorned the head table, where my mother, my brother, and Isabel wearing Berners's green and gold chatted with enthusiasm amid laughs and smiles. Our trenchers grew soggy.

Lady Alice honored me by seating me on her right. And at her mother's direction, Constance took up the seat on my right. With supper well under way, Sir John toasted me, expressing his gratitude. And with great show and an elegant introduction, Edward seconded the toast, thanking me for confirming his trust in my skills. Sir John's minstrels sang of Griselda, and his spiced wine brought tranquility and repose to our spirits. Even Philippa's incessant scolding could not disturb our sense of well being.

I drank little and held Constance's arm back when she went to take a last cup of wine. She flashed a startled look at me. "I need your best thoughts tonight," I whispered.

She laughed aloud, disturbing the minstrels, and was hardly able in her mirth to whisper, "Of course. And why?"

Laughing now myself, I whispered, "My own mind has flown off to the mews to hide with your father's hawks."

When we had undressed and slipped under our linen comforter, I lay on my back on my side of the bed, staring up into its dark canopy. The dark of the night closed in on us and the fertile smells from Bodiam's stables and kitchen carried through our window on sweet breezes from the meadow. "Constance, I promised I would give Edward an answer tomorrow. I am of two minds. Do I follow my own lights or seek to further my family's fortunes?"

Lying on her back on her side of the bed staring up into the dark, Constance said, "Speaking as one rustic to another, I suffered through two years of court school. From my memory of those days, Philippa has overstated the influence of the women at court. This is Britain, and men own the land and so, in the end, it is men who make the final decisions."

"What are the young men at court like?" I asked.

"Just like their fathers," Constance said. "Obsessed with property, women, and hunting. They hardly distinguish the last two. I have no doubt some would find you interesting, but after they have learned their manners, accomplished their quests, and carried your colors at jousts, they will expect a reward for their devotion, a graduation gift, a liaison with you. That is what they work for—you. It is one of the unspoken rules of the court."

"Need it always be true?" I gasped, repelled by Constance's blunt talk.

"Think of Philippa's position and many properties," Constance said. "Nonetheless, she must play the same game all court ladies play. Even she cannot avoid the inevitable physical liaison. Some ladies proudly call court the School of Love"

"I did not know," I said. Waiting for a moment, I returned to Constance's words. "So I would be expected to have liaisons with the young men I train."

"Eventually. Or their fathers. You have no property and so are vulnerable. You would be an easy mark for their false promises," Constance said. "Should you become too many men's favorite that way, the queen will dismiss you, for when the games become prevalent, they no longer draw men to culture. The queen will step in to ensure the lure remains potent. Otherwise she will have no hold over the men at court."

"No wonder my mother did not press me to accept Edward's proposal," I said thoughtfully.

"Your mother is torn," Constance agreed.

"Thank you, Constance, for your candor. You have given me much to think about," I said, yawning. "So the question remains, should I or should I not take Edward's proposal?"

"From what I have seen of you over the last few days, I can say without reservation the court would destroy you," Constance said emphatically. Looking up into the dark canopy, she then said after a moment, "You have not asked me about Edward."

"No. That is too complicated at this late hour," I said.

"He has strong feelings for you," Constance said, yawning.

"He has strong feelings for many things. That is what he is— strong feelings," I said. "He cannot be counted on in love nor, for that matter, in friendship." I thought of the snows of Conisbrough.

"I have heard that. I have also heard that he ended his affair with a London woman whom he pampered with estates and jewelry," she said. "Perhaps he is ready to find a more permanent love."

"Edward does not decide to end relationships. He just tires of them and seeks new ones as he would look for a new forest bursting with game," I said, trying not to sound too cynical. "Need I add, he is married?"

"Philippa is a shrew," Constance spit out.

"I might behave like her if I were married to Edward and he was spending more time with the London merchant's daughter than with me," I said.

After a long silence, Constance asked, "So what are you going to do about Edward's offer?"

"I will not burden you with my musings," I said. "I will sleep on them."

In the dark, I heard the rustle of fresh linen as Constance turned her face toward me and said, "I am beginning to wonder if you think too much."

I giggled.

"But I trust your good sense, Juliana," she added quickly.

Sleep came quickly but was of little help.

I dreamt of hunting a lowland forest with Edward. It was all underbrush and marsh. Game was scarce, and there were few chases. Nevertheless I followed Edward jump for jump.

It left me wrung out and spent in the morning.

terce

Feast of St. William of York
9:00 a.m.
June 8, 1477

Today, a gray, overcast day, I stand at Sopwell's chapel door greeting my sisters assembling to celebrate Terce, the third and last hour of morning. Yesterday's chapter meeting was still on their minds, and the turmoil it brought lingered as they glanced questioningly at me, hoping for better news. The meeting was unsettling, for the agenda was unpleasant: the Westby gift and the abbey's demands. The agenda was my doing, but I had no choice, for I needed my sisters' questions and even their protests and criticism.

Passing one by one into the chapel, their eyes fell from mine when I refused their silent entreaties. It was a somber procession. Sister Carol, the most disturbed by the chapter meeting and the last through the chapel door, glanced at me, plainly flustered, and slid into her place in choir. We could now begin. Sister Clare pulled the chapel bell one last time, leaving its final note to die drowsily in our meadows and ponds, the pools of the Ver, and the streets of St. Albans.

SISTER CLARE NERVOUSLY fingers her Psalter, then finds her place and begins the invitatory in a tentative voice. Today the prayer we needed in order to collect ourselves was as always our opening prayer, the Adjutorium.

Lord, reach out as a help-er to me, hur-ry as a help-er to me.

She follows with the hymn for a confessor bishop, for it is the feast of England's own, St. William of York, a relative of mine whom I have always kept close to my heart.

Thus to the meek, from his high sta-tion,

Strong in vir-tue, he was generous to sup-pli-cants;

YESTERDAY I OPENED the chapter meeting by revealing Wallingford's demand for the Westby farm. "Abbot Wallingford has asked me to transfer the Westby farm to the abbey. I have refused even though the farm may not, as it presently operates, be of any great benefit to Sopwell."

"Scutage is the problem," I said. I need not have explained, for everyone at Sopwell came from a family that owed scutage to the crown. "There are substantial taxes due on the property." The Westby family owes allegiance to Henry, the Duke of Buckingham. The Duke and ultimately the king expected the fee to be paid either by the Westby family or by Sopwell should we accept the bequest. It would do no good for Sopwell to arrange with the Westby family to extinguish the knight's service fee. It followed the land. Centuries of rulings by royal judges protected the king's rights to scutage. Any challenge by Sopwell through the king's courts was futile, no matter how the language of the gift read.

"Is it certain the king will seek his scutage fees?" Sister Anicia asked.

"I have no doubt the king will enforce his rights to the fees from the Westby farmstead," I said.

The fee for a knight's service increased during our war with France and continued to rise during our more recent civil war. The taxes on wool, a significant source of income to Sopwell, became oppressive. Balancing our income with our expenses was a worrisome prospect.

Each year it became a more and more daunting business.

It was then Sister Carol raised her hand. "So you suggest we refuse the gift?"

"Not just yet," I said. "My plan is to approach the Chancellor, point out the history of the farm's poor harvests, and ask for a reduction in the tax. At the same time, I suggest that we move the tenants away from farming to some more profitable pursuit."

Sister Clare looked skeptical. She was listening intently, and I chose to read the trace of anxiety on her face as a question.

"Yes, Sister Clare," I said, "the king may not reduce the scutage fee."

"What then?" Sister Clare demanded.

"Then we are left to the mercy of Abbot Wallingford," I said. "He will take the farm and sell it to support his renovation plans. He will then argue that the proceeds of the sale are abbey property, not subject to the Crown. Thus the abbey owes no taxes on it. There is precedent for the Abbey's position where there is none supporting us."

"So perhaps we should honor Wallingford's demand, transfer the Westby farm to the Abbey now, and avoid the controversy," Sister Clare whimpered.

Sister Joan, solicitous of Sister Clare's anxiety, shrugged off her passivity and leaned forward waiting for an opening in the conversation.

"That is one course," I said, "but by taking that path, we will break faith with Lady Alice and her wishes, and what is worse, we will be shrinking from taking one more step toward the day that Sopwell secures its full independence once and for all. In that independence, where we need rely on no one but our community, we will then be able to achieve true spiritual autonomy. No more detours from our own spiritual path."

"But what if we keep the farm but fail to make it more profitable? What good is it then? We have made our point, but why risk antagonizing the abbot?" Sister Joan asked, bringing us back to the most vulnerable part of my plan. Sister Joan was the most astute of our community.

"Ah," I said, "One more matter I should add to our discussion. The abbot and his brother are totally committed to adorning the Abbey church with all the silver and gems they can afford. They hope to remove any doubt that St. Albans is the foremost church in Britain. Wallingford has chosen Sopwell for the dubious honor of paying for the chapel dedicated to him. Central to the chapel will be a carved marble sarcophagus showing his likeness.

"The Abbot proposes to erect a chapel to himself," Sister Clare said in disbelief.

"Yes," I said. "The renovation of the Abbey church is all that matters to the brothers. To finance their plans, they even suggested I transfer not just the Westby farm but also all our properties to the abbey for their management."

There was a gasp. Then silence.

I looked about the circle of faces and saw all feared the prospect. "Yes," I said. "The abbey does not believe we should be taking care of ourselves any longer. No more kitchen, no more gardening, no more bees, no more herbs . . . and no more fishing. They would support us with what they decide we need. All that would be left for us is sewing the altar cloths and such that the abbey orders."

I added, "You may have already heard the rumors in town. Prior Thomas is criticizing my bookkeeping. He blames the Abbey's lack of money on Sopwell and my negligence."

"They have always blamed us for their problems," Sister Anicia blurted out in disgust.

The meeting went silent again, all remembering the Abbey's past criticisms. They were unfair. The war with France and the war for royal succession that followed were not our doing. The war with France brought increased taxes on wool and closed many continental markets. When Sopwell was sacked in the aftermath of the Second Battle of St. Albans, we lost not only our provisions but also all our silver altar vessels and some silver plates. During the years of grinding financial hardship that followed, the abbey added to Sopwell's misery by confiscating and selling off Sopwell's silver and gold thread and even our finished embroidered fabrics. In one instance, the abbey even burned our gold vestments to retrieve the gold thread, which it sold, keeping the proceeds for itself. It was of little matter to the abbey that the work of a generation of our highly accomplished seamstresses was lost forever. Woman's work was cheap. It took years of scrimping for Sopwell to make up these losses.

"That is intolerable," broke in Sister Joan. "But, and this is difficult for me to say, we really have no choice," she said somberly. "They are practiced at litigation and have powerful friends in London and Rome."

"They are vulnerable on one point," I said. "Should the courts take up the Abbey's confiscation of Sopwell's properties, I do not believe the Abbey wants it known that we have lost all simply to glorify Wallingford's name. He does have his enemies, the powerful Bishop of Lincoln, for one. And he knows it."

"But why should Sopwell take that risk now? Why jeopardize our future? I did not join our community to spend my final days litigating against St. Albans." Sister Joan said, glaring at me.

"You read the risks correctly, Sister Joan," I said. "Let me also say that Prior Thomas mentioned disbanding the convent should we press our rights."

More silence. Then Sister Clare wailed, "There is no other place for me."

"I suppose we could join other convents," Sister Joan suggested. "If we could make arrangements with them."

"That may be possible for you, but my family is not wealthy. The civil war has impoverished them," Sister Clare said. Sister Anicia and Sister Carol nodded at her words.

"Let me add," I said. "The abbey is gambling on one audacious gambit to achieve a swift victory. Prior Thomas has increased the cost of the sacraments. They demand a hundred pounds paid in advance beginning this fall. Without the sacraments, we cannot exist."

Aghast, Sister Carol sputtered, "That is exorbitant. How do they expect us to come up with such an outrageous sum."

"Why do you challenge the abbey?" Sister Joan queried. "Our goal should be to reestablish amicable relations with the abbey. As we grow more independent, the abbey grows more suspicious. We need allay their suspicions. If it means giving up our properties, then we should do it to show our goodwill toward the abbot."

"You see the problem, Sister Joan," I replied. "Even if Sopwell makes its own arrangements for the Westby farm and is able to meet their price for mass and confession, the abbey will read it as another act of rebellion. And before you ask, let me say that I believe Wallingford and his brother, Thomas, have decided to take Sopwell's properties and have led us into this dispute to give themselves an excuse for disbanding us now."

"Then why challenge the abbey now?" The question came out more bluntly than Sister Joan had intended, and she added, "I do not want to be a nuisance. I am sure you have prayed over this question."

"I have. As you know, I work continually to make Sopwell independent of the abbey." I replied carefully. "My prayers have led me to believe that the abbey has stagnated. It is of the old order, and the old order is passing. You know that the towns owned by our secular leaders have steadily gained rights of self-government while St. Albans and other great abbeys, such as Bury St. Dunstan, continue to oppose any change in their tenants' status. Our townspeople enjoy no more rights today than they did two centuries ago, yet they know full well what rights Londoners and others have won."

"You want us to strike out alone?" she asked. "The abbey will never allow it. Our fate is linked to the abbey's future."

"I cannot see blindly handing over our fate to this abbot," I said. "Once the change comes, perhaps the town will view us differently from the abbey and so treat us more kindly."

"I am worried about the timing," Sister Joan said. "Why now?"

"At some point, we need stand on our own feet," I replied. "You may be right that this may not be the moment. But even if we fail this time, our community must keep pushing for full autonomy as St. Benedict counseled. A day will come when we will succeed."

Sister Joan said, "I fear it is suicidal, Dame Juliana. You know I respect the wise counsel you have provided for so many years. If there is an upheaval, we will need powerful friends. Who better than fellow Benedictines? No matter what, the abbey will necessarily be our friend."

"Perhaps. I have pondered my tepid obedience in this matter, but I no longer see us as subject to the dictates of the abbey. I see Sopwell as a separate community under St. Benedict's rule. I now doubt that this abbot is our true and wise superior. I came to this conclusion some years ago and have been working, since, to loosen the abbey's hold on Sopwell."

"I share your vision, but I think to step away from the abbey now will only generate more friction." Sister Joan then added, "I need not tell you how grateful we all are to have our own kitchen and infirmary as well as our own flocks of sheep and cattle. We have grown more confident about our future."

"To return to our most immediate problem. The Westby bequest has provided another opportunity to increase our autonomy. I believe now is the time for Sopwell to start thinking about partnering with our tenants in new ventures," I said in conclusion. "The Marsh family, the tenants of the Westby property, could be our first real partners. How we might join with them I do not know. I would appreciate your ideas."

"Is there any decision we must make today?" Sister Anicia asked, clearly confused.

"No, I am asking for your help in reforming the Westby gift, thus making it more valuable to Sopwell. Who knows? If we are successful, the abbey may take a lesson from what we do.

"Is there any other business to discuss?" I asked. "If not, let me raise one more matter. The abbey is now locking us in at night. They do it, as you have probably guessed by now, to remind us of our dependence on them. There will be more reminders in the days ahead.

"As Prioress it is my duty to give the following advice. It is not too early to start making plans for the day the Abbey disbands Sopwell," I said.

Another sober silence and then I added, "Old nuns are always an inconvenience."

"And they rarely win," said Sister Joan gravely.

"Rarely," I agreed.

The meeting closed with the reading of the names of the nuns who had gone before us. We filed out, each consulting her own fears.

PSALM 24 CARRIES my thoughts away from the chapter meeting. Sister Clare's quick hands direct us to rush forward with our chant. She increases the tempo as morning fills the chapel with its glow.

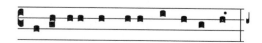

The earth is the Lord's and the full-ness of it,

103

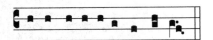

The world and those who dwell in it;

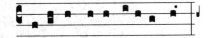

For he has found-ed it up-on the seas,

And es-tab-lished it up-on the riv-ers.

On this, his feast day, I reflect on the life of St. William, an early relative of mine. It was the Cistercians, spiritual relatives of the Benedictines, who tested his holiness. Elected the Archbishop of York and confirmed in that office by the Vatican, St. William was denied his office at the last minute. Church politics intervened. The pope who confirmed him died, and the new pope, Eugenius III, a Cistercian, deposed St. William. Through argument and gentle persistence, however, St. William won back his archbishopric.

The Cistercians are a sister order to the Benedictines. Their founders were Benedictine monks who retained Holy Benedict's Rule as part of their governing charter. They claimed to reform Benedictine practices by returning to the Rule's original simplicity. But they eventually lost direction, miscalculating the importance of the one element of community life that has confounded monastic leaders for centuries. And to this day it confounds us here at St. Albans. The snag on which all perfect societies founder is manual work—grinding, exhausting manual labor. The community cannot exist without it, but it tears the community apart.

St. Benedict's genius is the inclusion of work—all types of work—in the monastic's daily routine. He made work a part of the monastic's day by regularizing it. For six to seven hours a day, each day, Benedict's Rule originally obligated monks and nuns to engage in work. In his day, St. Benedict suggested that monastics work between Prime and Vespers, between the morning chapter meeting and the onset of evening. There were short breaks for singing the hours and for partaking of lunch, but work consumed all day and part of the evening. Today our monasteries disregard this schedule. Work is performed principally in the afternoon.

St. Benedict believed that his monks won their spiritual independence through work. To Benedict's mind, his followers must share all the work necessary to achieve the community's autonomous well-being. This included all forms of manual labor. His first monks drained swamps, prepared fields for planting, herded and milked cattle, planted crops, and harvested them. This was and is mind-numbing, difficult labor. He also expected his monks to be masons, carpenters, plumbers, glaziers, and smiths, and to become artists, bee-keepers, physicians, teachers, hoteliers, administrators, veterinarians, bookbinders, herbalists, millers, brewers, and bakers.

As St. Benedict foresaw, with the economic independence of each Benedictine monastery, the community could pursue on its own the great work, namely, devoted worship expressed in the chanting of the hours. Thus each Benedictine community was freed from all outside interference. Independent Benedictine monasteries owed nothing to secular or ecclesiastical princes. They were not beholden to local politicians, and they were not even beholden to the Vatican. Each Benedictine monastery was thus free to follow its own spiritual path, with no other guidance than the decisions it made in its chapter meetings. Majority vote and the concurrence of its abbot made it official.

Independence is my fondest wish for Sopwell. But every City of God, every Republic, and every Benedictine monastery carries within itself the latent forces of its own corruption. This is true also for Sopwell. For us, these forces reared up from the very work meant to liberate us. Days of sweltering field work and back-breaking building construction warred with the regularity of the monastic's day. Tired monks and nuns fell asleep at Matins and Lauds, the night-time hours, and were physically corrected. They could not concentrate during study time, confessed their failings in chapter meetings, and were physically corrected. Typically their corrections or punishments were canings and denial of meals. The pain of punishment was minor compared to the pain of knowing their own failures to celebrate the hours perfectly. Their true horror was that they saw their spiritual life slipping away. Heavy, demanding labor sapped the spiritual strength of each community in its striving for independence.

As the centuries passed, manual labor became a greater and greater problem. Chanting the hours became a more engrossing task, for monastery liturgy increased in length and complexity. At some point it became clear that the laboring monk or nun could never keep up with the liturgy. In Britain, the Benedictines were blessed with royal patrons. The foremost were the Plantagenets. William the Conqueror handed over lands to his Norman Benedictine abbots, and with the lands came the villeins who were tied to the land by law. Thus Britain's Benedictines became principally administrators supervising peasants who worked the land, harvested the crops, herded and sheared sheep, repaired abbey buildings, erected new ones, and more. The Benedictines who manage St. Albans are hardly distinguishable from Norman lords.

The Cistercians took a different road. The Cistercian monks chose the obvious solution. Create a lower order within their communities, the conversi: lay brothers who ran their mills, tended their flocks, and farmed their fields. The conversi prayed but did not keep the hours in full. When the conversi disappeared last century principally due to the labor shortage brought on by the Black Death, Cistercian monasteries too were forced to hire outside workers, and from the largesse of their noble patrons, they also in some instances gained peasants.

And so it has been with all reforms of the Benedictine Rule. On the rocks of exhausting manual labor, the reforms of Cluny and the many other reforms coming afterward foundered. On those same rocks, Plato's many Republics fell and Augustine's City of God never rose. Philosophers and theologians never really understand the demands of manual labor.

In the days to come, I believe we at Sopwell must earn our keep by finding work and running businesses outside the convent. Holy Benedict reminds us that true monastics "live by the labor of their hands." But life-sustaining labor can just as easily be achieved through new, successful businesses that do not detract from the demands of the Rule and our spiritual life.

And so I remain a Benedictine. The flaw in the Rule remains, and each day I work to circumvent it.

psalm 24 and Sister Clare call us to answer the question that the contemplative must answer every day.

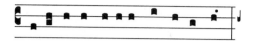

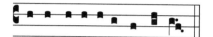

Who may as-cend on-to the hill of the Lord

Or who may stand in his ho-ly place

He who has clean hands and a pure heart

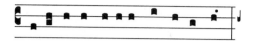

Who has not sworn de-ceit-ful-ly

There is a secret in the *Treatyse*. Only the most dedicated angler will discover it. The secret is that the most uninviting day, the day promising rain, is the best for angling. Today is such a day. The serious angler looks forward to such days, days I call dark, lowering days. For me, these are the gray, overcast days where glowering clouds softly roll in, gathering themselves above the Ver. It is the same dark I felt as a teenager when my hawks leapt from my hand, beating their broad, powerful wings for altitude, and then again when they glided back above me with wings fully extended, braking onto my leather gauntlet and blotting out the sun. So on the days where the clouds mimic the shadows of my hawks, I thrill at the prospect of angling.

Meager light makes fish vulnerable. On dark, lowering days, the light is spectral. Its waning strength leaves anemic shadows and turns the surface of the river the color of molten lead. Certainly there is glare, but it lies ponderously on the water, only to be enlivened occasionally when shafts of sunlight work their way through holes in the clouds. Then the sunlight becomes dense and palpable. Then we see the light for what it is and not for its reflection.

On such days I have made my best catches. It does not matter whether I angled early or late. If the cloud cover remains thick enough throughout the day, the angler is offered a full day of that magic hour of half light usually found just before sunup and just after sundown. It is that pervasive light that colors all it touches a single color. On dark, lowering days, the atmosphere colors all flies, natural and dubbed, the same gray. Even my colorful yellow dubbed fly for May assumes a dingy cast. During the leaping time, the angler need only tie on a dubbed fly that approximates the size of the natural. The heavens will take care of the rest.

Ordinarily the angler should concern herself with the color of her dubbed fly. Sometimes after reading my *Treatyse*, visitors have remarked on the number of my dubbed flies requiring black wool for their bodies. I use black wool for fully half of the dubbed flies described in the *Treatyse*. As my experience with sunlight grew, I came to rely more and more on raw black wool. True black wool is rare. The fleece of our Rylands carries many colors. That is why we must dye our wools black for our habits. On close inspection, most black-appearing wool is truly a mix of colors, with a dark reddish brown predominating. To prepare my black wool, I do nothing more than comb it out and wash it in cold water, thereby preserving its oils.

One day I realized this fact when inspecting a flock of our sheep. I found myself in a low meadow north of Sopwell, looking up toward the ridgeline, where some of our colored Rylands were grazing. It was midmorning, and the slanting morning sun had just climbed from behind the ridge. The sheep were grazing between me and the sun. Its powerful rays caught the sheep from behind. Those which first appeared black now bore a halo. For some the halo colored reddish brown. For others the halo colored a golden dark tan. Even some white sheep gave off an olive cast.

Once the sun climbed above the sheep, their aspect changed. The blacks appeared a flat black, and the whites appeared a flat white. Never was I so aware of the difference between what trout see and what the angler sees. Trout see floating natural flies against the sky. They are back lit. My dubbed flies, too, appear to the trout set against the sunlight. Most anglers, however, see dubbed flies away from the light, from above, either as they rest on the water's surface or as they sit pinched in her fingers. The angler rarely sees dubbed flies above her lit from behind. To do so, she must hold the flies above her eyes and against the sky.

With this insight, I began to tie my dubbed flies from the viewpoint of the trout. Thus I began to use more and more black wool. The blackest wools I reserved for my stonefly imitations. The reddish brown colors found in lighter black wools I tied into my March dun fly and August drake fly.

My black dubbed flies show well in full sunlight due to their natural oils. The light transforms the blacks to meet the expectations of the trout. As the light changes, the oily dubbed wools reflect the change, assuming the color most advantageous for the angler. On bright days when brown mayflies are on the water, I cast my typical black wool dun and drake flies between the trout and the sun. Looking up into the sun, the trout sees a burst of brown and red, the same color displayed by the natural fly when set against the light. The truly black wool dubbed stoneflies appear against the light a charcoal color, closely representative of the actual insect. At worst, the oiled wool reflects many overtones of color, which mix with its general hue and so imitate the complex shades of the natural insect.

On dark, lowering days, the oils in my black dubbing soak up the gray light. Casting them between the gray sky and the trout, they appear gray yet keep their definition, an easy mark for feeding trout. On dark, lowering days, definition is critical. The trout looking up from below against the gray, overcast sky is looking for the outline of a mayfly in clear relief. When they see it, they are more apt to chase and strike it. This is especially true for trout feeding in faster water, for they get the briefest glimpse of the fly before it passes over them. The stark definition of the fly makes it more vulnerable because the trout is sure of its location and confident that its rush will intercept it.

Once I started seeing my dubbed flies through a trout's eyes, my catches increased.

SISTER CLARE PRESSES forward, beginning Psalm 26. It speaks so well of my feelings that last morning at Bodiam.

I do not sit with false men,

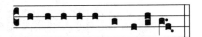

Nor do I con-sort with hyp-o-crites.

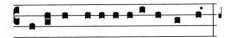

I hate the com-pa-ny of e-vil-do-ers,

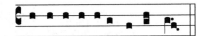

And I will not sit with the wick-ed.

Sister Anicia requested trout for supper. And trusting in my skills, she has already set out thyme sprigs in the kitchen. Time to go to work. I collected my fishing equipment from the kitchen and heard a "Good luck" from Sister Anicia as I headed toward the Ver. But it was not the Ver I saw once through Sopwell's front gate. Rather the slow waters of the Rother appeared before me. And it was then I realized that I had never fished with Isabel. We did so much together. I could have invited her to fish the Rother with me when we visited the Dalyngrigges that summer. But I could not be bothered. For sure, that last day, Edward was on my mind, but I could not blame him for my bad manners. They rose simply from wayward feelings, feelings fed by the tale of Grizelda that last night at Bodiam. No excuse for ignoring another, especially another like Isabel. The plain truth was that I could not be bothered.

That last morning at Bodiam, I woke carefully, not wanting to disturb Constance, and went alone to the mews. They were still. Sir John had not yet arisen, and only his falconers were moving about the kitchen and workshops.

While in any mews, my mind consciously guides my every glance and gesture. I move gravely as if dancing a bassadanza. The gaze of every hawk, of every falcon, fixes each intruder. To this day, their gaze arrests me even though a frequent and experienced visitor. My demeanor stiffens to alert. My eyes flash from bird to bird. As their eyes fix me, I fix on them, not wishing to dominate but merely to acknowledge their worth. Everything hangs on that first gaze. That first step into the mews, that first effort at silent dialogue, must acknowledge each bird's importance. Unblinking, I take each step with confidence and find the eyes of each bird with appreciation.

I fixed the yellow eyes and the orange eyes of the young hawks. The red eyes and brown eyes of the adults. The blue-black eyes of the falcons. They all fixed on my steady green eyes. Respect. Satisfied, they retreated into themselves, grave and upright.

Movement in the stables. The mews were again alert to intruders. Edward's servants had entered the courtyard to saddle horses and assemble Philippa's baggage train. Heads swiveled and yellow, orange, red, and black eyes concentrated on the bustle. Once the servants retreated to the hall for a scrap of breakfast, the hawks and falcons discerned the end of the commotion and their eyes went blank . . . waiting. With fixed eyes, I returned to the hall for the farewells.

Edward tracked my arrival. Deciding against the empty place on Edward's right, I sat next to Constance, nodding to my mother, my brother, and Isabel. Constance's and Sir John's presence postponed the announcement of my decision. It was a Berners family matter. Yet, I did not doubt that everyone at the table wondered about my decision while politely discussing the weather and the roads. From time to time, they glanced in my direction and measured my features, looking for an answer. I could only smile.

I had decided to talk to Edward alone. And so, when everyone rose, leaving the table for the courtyard, I asked, "Edward, could you stay behind for a moment? I need to speak with you," gesturing toward a corner of the hall.

Once out of earshot, he asked hopefully, "What will it be, the court or spinsterhood?"

Smiling, I said, "My choices are not that limited."

"Perhaps you have not thought deeply enough. Your family has never recovered from your father's impeachment," he said.

"Let us not go over that ground again. You and my brother were explicit on the family's needs. I am not a dunce," I replied, making no attempt to mask my irritation.

"I do not mean to upset you, but your family has a stake in your success at court," he said soothingly. "So what will it be? Are you coming to Windsor?"

"No," I said in a subdued voice.

"You are making a mistake," Edward barked. Clearly angry, he repeated, "A mistake. A grave mistake. You will have no future."

As if physically struck, I rocked back but recovered in time to utter almost vehemently, "You are fickle, Edward. I cannot believe knowing you as I do that repayment of my debt will not include other demands. A written document alone will surely not bind you. My guess is that you will ask more, should I follow you to court."

"You are not following me to court," Edward shot back.

"Everyone at court would know I am," I said and then, narrowing my eyes, added, "No matter. It is what I believe."

Edward glared at me. "What you believe? What you believe? You are so often wrong. Listing your shortcomings would delay our return to London."

I replied firmly, "The heart of it, Edward, is that I am not interested."

"How can you not be interested in the court and my company? You would meet Britain's most eminent men and women. I hunt with the king and his son every day, and you would come to know them," Edward pleaded.

At first confused by Edward's response, I reconsidered my words and then said, "I misspoke, Edward. I did not mean to say that I am not interested in the court and your company. Forgive my imprecision. What I meant to say was that I am not interested in the person I will become should I spend my time at court. You have many strengths, but they are not the ones that will work to strengthen my character."

"You will regret your decision," Edward said, first in defense and then in anger, "You have no future."

"We have nothing further to discuss, Edward," I said.

Edward strode out of the hall, nearly colliding with his wife as she descended from a final search of her sleeping chamber. Philippa halted to intercept me.

"Apparently Edward did not get the answer he expected," Philippa said.

My humor wearing thin, I replied grimly, "Apparently."

Philippa surveyed me. Satisfied, she then said, "You have made the right decision. I did not expect it from you."

"I seem to be surprising everyone this morning," I said. Slowly the tension from confronting Edward dropped away. To my own surprise, Philippa's approval reassured me. "Then we are of one mind on the subject, and you need not sort through your cast off gowns when you return home."

I was about to leave when Philippa caught me by my girdle and drew me close. "You are not the silly girl I remember that Christmas at Conisbrough," She said deliberately.

"I was swept up," I said.

Philippa went on, "Perhaps. But what I see now is a young woman with a great talent for self-criticism."

"I work at it," I said candidly.

Philippa smiled to herself, "I can see why Edward is drawn to you. You have an abundance of what he most lacks." Then she dropped my girdle, leaving it low on my hips, stepped back, and left the hall.

WITH SISTER CLARE in the lead, we finish Psalm 26. More than ever I feel Isabel's presence as I with my sisters chant.

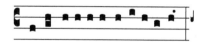

But as for me I walk in in-teg-ri-ty;

Re-deem me and be gra-cious to me.

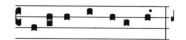

My foot stands on le-vel ground;

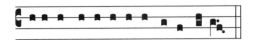

In the great con-gre-ga-tion I will bless the Lord.

following philippa out, I stood on the level ground of Bodiam's great paved courtyard. I turned to join my mother and brother but retreated when I saw their distress. I did not need to inform them of my decision. Edward's impatience to get away already told them.

My mother stood deflated, my brother distant. Not ready to discuss their disapproval, I stood apart, gathering my thoughts, planning what promised to be an empty day alone. My mind was firm, yet I felt a part of myself depart with Edward for Windsor.

Lost in thought, I was startled to find Isabel beside me. As Philippa's retinue clattered toward the gate, she grasped my left hand firmly and brought it up between her breasts and then I felt her right arm encircle my waist and pull me close so that our shoulders touched side by side. We both stood looking toward the last riders leaving the courtyard.

It was then I sensed Constance on my other side. She grasped my right hand and brought it up between her breasts, and then she encircled my waist with her left arm. We three stood shoulder to shoulder, watching the last man at arms leave the courtyard. For a time we stood together without conversation. Isabel, my new confidant, Constance, my new friend. When we finally turned back toward the hall, the courtyard was empty.

I then remember saying to Constance, "Why don't we kidnap your father and take him hawking?" And hugging Isabel, I said, "I will not take any excuses from you. You are coming with us."

Both laughed. "I will need to tie up my hair and dress appropriately," Isabel said.

"I would expect no less," I said with a broad smile.

"It might rain," Isabel added.

"Let's chance it," I replied, laughing now.

The memory began to dissolve. I vaguely heard my sisters assembling in the refectory for breakfast. Their bustle warned me to dispel Isabel and the story of Bodiam.

In that moment of reverie, between the dead and the living, the thought struck me that my rejection of the royal court freed me to live fully in the countryside. Fishing and hunting became my excuse, my disguise, to take up the everyday. In my freedom, I could consider in great depth the trivial: the flitting brown warbler, the dithering bee, the recalcitrant trout. How fortunate I had become.

In that thought I felt Isabel's approval. At Bodiam, my youth took on direction. Field sports—hunting, hawking, and fishing. My memories of Isabel's talents began there, and I feel that strong, warm presence . . . as strong and warm . . . and familiar . . . as the embrace of my black wool habit. In my thoughtlessness, I did not realize her virtues until too late. She so often hung back, leaving her husband . . . leaving others to fill the quiet with their opinions. What a fool I was. I should have drawn her out.

OUR CONFIDENCE BUILDS as Sister Clare chants the final passages of Psalm 112 to end Terce. The golden light of a clear June day penetrates every corner of the chapel, falling with a glare on the open pages of our Psalters. The candles and the cold of winter seem so long ago. We are spurred to complete the hour.

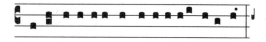

He has dis-tri-bu-ted free-ly, he pro-vid-ed for the poor;

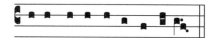

His righ-teous-ness en-dures for-ev-er . . .

The memories of Bodiam and the slow-working Rother slip away, and I am on the banks of the sparkling Ver again. Today, on the feast day of St. William of York, the Ver swarms with the tandy fly, tawny-colored caddis flies. Every year the day of St. William's feast is the first day of their emergence. For the rest of June and part of July, this insect will hover and dance over the Ver's riffles and pools every day. The trout begin feeding midmorning, ravenously jumping out of the water to snatch insects from the air.

It was on a St. William's day more than forty years ago I tied my first dubbed fly. And so it is also a day I call to mind Mother Matilda de Flamstead, my guide to living the Benedictine life. At her urging, I brought a box filled with feathers and colored wools and silk threads to the Ver. Sitting on the bank near Sopwell Lane bridge, I chose an orangey-tan wool for the body and the dark drake breast feathers for the wings. The wool I rolled between my fingers until it formed a yarn, which I wound round the hook and reinforced with silk thread. The wings I attached faced each other and lay across the back.

The first wings I tied for the tandy fly were dark. Later I would use light mallard drake breast feathers for the tandy fly's wings. I have noted this change in the *Treatyse*. The reason for the change was plainly visible as I sat by the Ver tying my first dubbed fly. But in my excitement with trout leaping about me, I observed but did not notice it. After they emerged from the water, the insects were always in flight above the river. I had tied my first fly to resemble in color the tandy fly at rest. I caught a few and tied my first fly to resemble the ones held in my hand. In fact, for most of its life near the river, the tandy fly is in flight. The trout see it as it shoots up from the river's depths, taking wing once it breaks through the surface. And they see it later when it dances above the Ver's riffles, dropping here and there, touching the surface with its abdomen. They never see it at rest on the surface.

The difference between the tandy fly at rest and the tandy fly in flight is the wing color. At rest the wings are darker to the eye. In flight they are several shades lighter, almost white. With this realization, I tied motion into my flies, fluttering wings. My catches improved. Thus for forty years, I have kept tandy flies in my wallet. It never fails.

The tandy fly emerges most heavily in a gravel riffle just below the Prae mill. The Prae riffle is two miles due west of Sopwell and just southwest of St. Albans, a long hike through the dense Eywood and then a rambling walk across Deerfold meadow. I follow the deer trails and cowpaths skirting the edges of town. On days I fish, I avoid the eyes of the townspeople if at all possible. As Sopwell's prioress, I have little concern over where to fish. As a Benedictine, there are miles of the Ver open to me to fish without permission. St. Albans's residents must purchase a license from the abbey. Without a license, the angler becomes a poacher and, if caught, can be hauled before the abbey's court, where he is fined or imprisoned. If the fish he poaches is a salmon, then the fine is heavy. I have none of these concerns.

Nonetheless I resort to a subterfuge to avoid giving offense by reminding other anglers of my privilege and their jeopardy. My subterfuge is to disguise my fishing rod as a walking staff. When I walk to the Ver or other waters owned by the Benedictines, passersby see me as a doddering old nun relying on her great staff for support. The trick works.

The invention was born the year I became prioress. It is very simple and is perhaps my greatest invention. The best rods have three sections. The lowest section is the longest. My angling rods have a lower section of six feet at least, as is my preference. The perfect size for a walking staff. Because of my small stature and increasing age, I have fashioned longer and longer rods. The longer rods allow me to cast farther off, and they give me more leverage when playing a fish. The upper section of the rod is two parts that, when lashed together, I make slightly shorter than the lower section, for I store them in the lower section and then fashion the lower section to look like a staff.

The bottom section takes the most work. It must be hollowed out so that the two upper parts can be lashed together and inserted within it. Usually, I make the bottom section of hazel, willow, or aspen. The middle section, I make of hazel. For the very top section, I have many choices: blackthorn, which I prefer, but also crabapple and juniper.

The wood for all three sections is cut between Michaelmas and Candlemas, namely the end of September and the beginning of February. By then the sap has dropped to the roots, and the wood dries quickly. The three sections are then soaked, straightened, and baked. I store them in the rafters of our kitchen to dry.

Both ends of the bottom section are bound with iron ferrules. A spike can be inserted in the very bottom end, as is the case with most walking staffs. The spike is handy for walking up hills as well as for grounding your rod to keep your hands free. The two upper sections are lashed together with cord from six horse tail hairs. And the top section is then bound up entirely with the cord, with a loop left at the very top where the fishing line is attached. Before the spike is inserted to plug the bottom end, the two top sections are inserted into the bottom section.

When all sections have been properly prepared, the rod can be shaken out to its full length within seconds. The top section will emerge with a single shake. Then it is possible for the angler to extend the rod to its full length by grasping the top loop and smoothly pulling it until the upper parts of the rod slide snugly into the ferrule of the bottom section.

The rod can be returned to a walking stick just as quickly with another shake. I untie the line and bounce the base of the rod on the ground. It retracts instantly. Thus by disguising my fishing rod as a walking staff, I avoid affront. It is my triumph of diplomacy.

Today, a dark lowering day, the tandy fly hatch has every trout hovering snout up just under the Ver's surface. The Prae riffle is a broad one, running one hundred yards in length. Today dozens of trout have collected and thousands of tandy flies dance above them. Trout after trout leaps for the whirling orange caddis, timing their lunges to intercept the dancing orange blurs as they wing upward or then drop downward again and again. The trout will jump a foot and more for them. Bright and yellow, they flash their brilliant red and black spots as they snare the tandy fly. Then they fall back, quickly righting themselves, fixing their eyes again quickly toward the sky. It is the day when the trout are at home both in the water and the air. It is the day Ver's trout make air and water one element. It is the perfect day to celebrate St. William's feast and my first success with the dubbed fly.

A half dozen trout in hand, I walk quickly, making my coming back across Deerfold and Eywood quicker than my going out. Sister Anicia's thyme was waiting.

It was a lucky walk. A brilliant blue kingfisher scolded me, and as I neared Sopwell, I heard the croak of a heron returning to its rookery.

I so wish I could have shared one day of fishing with Isabel.

chapter five

sext

Feast of St. Thomas of Canterbury
July 7, 1477
12:00 p.m.

Sopwell works between Sext and Vespers, noon and sundown. For this reason Sext has always dragged for me. I am anxious to start work and, once started, to finish without interruption. The short hour of Sext follows dinner, where the reading for today was from the life of St. Thomas of Canterbury.

finally we begin. We say our Hail Marys and Our Fathers and chant through the Adjutorium, hymn, and the antiphon from the Common for a Martyr Bishop. Sister Clare senses my impatience and presses us to complete Psalm 19, but it catches and holds me, calling to mind my last meeting with Prior Thomas.

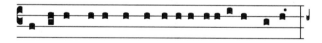

Let the words of my mouth and the con-tem-pla-tion of my soul

Be acceptable in your sight, O Lord, my rock and re-deem-er.

Weekly the abbey's marshals appear at Sopwell's gate, prodding us for records, reminding us of our jeopardy. Last week they demanded my records of Sopwell's flocks and livestock, and after securing them, wandered our pastures to check my count of our sheep against their own. They found what I already knew. Our pastures were full.

119

Another summons from Prior Thomas, this time for St. Albans's Moot Hall, a conference after the morning court call. It was the day of the week set aside for prosecuting tenants late with their rents. Any plea for delay awoke Prior Thomas's wintry smile, and the words froze on the debtor's lips. Waiting until the end of the call, an object lesson not lost on me, I approached the high bench after the last delinquent debtor was taken into custody.

"Good morning, Mother. There were more profligates today than usual and I am a trifle late," he boomed. "Just take your place before me, and I will be brief."

"As you wish, Prior," I said humbly, standing where debtors stood just minutes before making their futile pleas for mercy.

"My brother and I want to make plain that you may not meet your new obligations to the abbey by selling any of Sopwell's sheep or their wool off any Sopwell properties," he said gravely as though rendering harsh judgment on me and Sopwell.

"I understand," I said. "And I am in full agreement with you." The coursing greyhound was gaining ground.

Taken aback, he surveyed me for a moment and then proceeded ahead with his next topic. "You have been grazing more sheep than I believe Sopwell's pastures will carry," he said, fixing me sternly.

"Yes. We have allowed a few more of our young Rylands to mature this season," I said without showing any great concern. "But now that you have raised the matter, I will keep a close eye out and shift them to other pastures as the need arises."

I paused, aware that my docility had caught Thomas off guard.

"There is a trick here," he said.

"None," I said. "I will follow your directives to the letter. Will that be all?"

Thomas hesitated and then, flicking his fingers, he dismissed me saying, "You may go."

I left Moot Hall knowing that Sopwell needed to lay a false scent. And it occurred to me that the crafty hart could just as easily mislead by laying many false trails. Being too open and too predictable, providing too many clues could be just as misleading. Prior Thomas would be looking for only one. Indirection in the many.

During my meeting with Prior Thomas, a heavy rain had begun

thrumming loudly on the Hall roof. As I stepped out into St. Albans's marketplace, the downpour drove me to John the fishmonger's shop, which stood in the marketplace between Moot Hall and the bull ring. This week the ring featured a fight between a bear and three dogs. As the dogs struggled in the mud, the bear, rain streaming down its black coat, sat down, waiting to dismember the first who worked its way free.

"Welcome, Mother," John said as I entered.

"A blessing on you and your family," I said. The rain had cleared the shop of customers.

"How can I serve you?" he asked. "I see you so infrequently during the leaping season."

"I understand you received a shipment of flounder," I said.

"Yes, they were caught yesterday in the Thames," John said cheerfully.

"I'll take enough for our sick. The infirmary needs a little variety," I said.

As John wrapped the fish, shouts from the street interrupted him, making me turn and look out the shop door. The abbey's marshals were harrying an old man. They had ripped off his traveling cloak and were shoving him toward the London Road. Stumbling in front of the shop, he arose fully drenched and muddy.

I turned back to John and said, "Show mercy on this poor traveler."

"As you say, Mother." Running out into the rain, he grabbed the old stranger and dragged him, dripping, into the shop. One of the marshals followed, and in an angry voice screamed at us, "This is a Lombard, here to buy wool. Neither the abbey nor the guilds welcome his presence. The abbot has ordered the inns shut to him."

"I sympathize. But let me show him St. Benedict's hospitality by leading him out of town more gently," I said. "You are risking a murder charge."

"Very well. Just make sure he is gone from here today," the marshal said.

After the marshal left, I asked John to find the stranger's cloak and horse. Alone with the old man, I said, "You are wearing the clothes of an Italian."

With a slight accent, the stranger said, "Grazie, Mother. At my age I could not have withstood their kicks much longer." Shaking the water off, he said, "I just hope I do not become ill."

"Who are you?"

Drawing up his thin frame, he said with great dignity, "I am Laurentio, a wool buyer for his excellency, the great Gerard Canizani of Firenze, a true friend of your king and the Pope." Then shaking his head in disbelief, he said, "Such facts were lost on your marshals."

"The fullers and weavers are worried about their jobs, and the abbey is worried about its fees from the fulling mill," I said.

Just then John returned with Laurentio's horse and cloak. "Thank you, sir," said Laurentio.

"It is time we leave. The rain is letting up. The convent has a few empty guest rooms. I believe that that will be the best you can hope for in St. Albans. You are welcome to stay."

"Per favore, Mother," Laurentio said. "I need to sit in front of a hot fire with some warm ale."

"When you are back to your old self, I believe we have much to discuss."

AS WE END Psalm 19 with its antiphon, Sister Clare launches us into Psalm 18, and its words recall a memory of Bernersbury in its awful clarity.

The cords of death en-com-passed me;

The tor-rents of per-di-tion as-sailed me.

An intense dream brought back Bernersbury last night. It was suggested during an afternoon among Sopwell's barns. Oxen returning to Sopwell from plowing jangled their chains and thudded to their stalls. These sounds reminded me of Uncle William, and I felt his strong presence all evening. Often as children we watched him and his men practicing for battle with mock charges and swordplay.

He and his jangling, armored horse sounded his menacing strength.

That same sound stayed with me through Compline and accompanied me to bed, where in a dream I saw far off, on the infinitely bending horizon of my imagination, a silent, determined figure trudging toward me. It was the helmeted man I had seen at Bernersbury so often as a child, my mother's brother, Uncle William. He was dressed in a dazzling silver and embroidered gold surcote over a suit of burnished mail.

Watching him take off his helmet, I could almost hear him say, as he had so often said, "We should get down to business."

Uncle William's words fueled memories of my last full year at Bernersbury. They carry me to the first months after Isabel and Richard's wedding and begin at the head table in Bernersbury's hall.

It was in the hall, where Isabel came to mean so much to us. Candle glow and the smell of savory partridge pies drove away evening shadows and past desperate memories of my father and Sir Roger to create a new present, a new start for our family. At first I did not believe Isabel could supply the missing ingredient to our new start. I had inventoried her accomplishments and found very few. A very ordinary person. Thus at first I dismissed her as a shallow, pleasant girl, an ornament to Richard's life. But I was wrong. As I later realized, the list of virtues I judged her against did not go deep enough.

Even now I see within the warm circle of candlelight, Isabel sitting next to Richard, with my mother and me on a bench opposite, all smiling and chatting. Always careful in her dress, from her first night in the hall, Isabel made our evening meal an occasion, wearing her best gowns and jewelry, and she did so without pretense. And we and the kitchen joined her with our own careful preparations. It was all cheer and then joy when she showed the first signs of pregnancy. I see her blue eyes studying our faces in the bright candlelight and dancing with the flames in rhythm to the rise and fall of sweet evening breezes.

At first I faulted her, in my mind, for having no strong opinions. She took no position on any issue nor would she argue even when it was plain she disagreed with us. Instead she asked questions, turning our answers over in her mind as she smiled, digesting our response.

What I began to understand was that Isabel took no delight in contention. Her interests lay elsewhere, and she was single-minded in pursuing that interest. She believed in one thing: a family celebrating itself. And she never lost track of this goal for us, her new family. She worked to shift us away from past disputes and injustices to the pleasantries of the day. What she wanted to hear were the good moments of our day. The moments of beauty we experienced in the countryside. The good smells of a spring meadow, of planed wood, and of the roaring forge. The grace of timid woodland flowers, of a bird's undulating flight, and of a soaring horse. She always praised the best parts of the meal within earshot of the serving maids. It was she who always questioned me about my angling. And it was through her questioning I found the vocabulary to speak of my best days angling and was thereby able to expand my day-to-day notes into what became my *Treatyse*. Perusing the *Treatyse* today, I read terms she pushed me to coin, terms for the art of angling, terms I found within myself during those lighthearted evenings in Bernersbury Hall. The leaping time. The drake. The water knot. And so many more.

In time I began to appreciate her wisdom. With the winding down of the day, I began to look forward to our family meals. And I know my mother and brother did also. None of us came late, and conversation began immediately. No guile, no agenda. We just began to talk together, sharing our day, a gift to each other we all accepted joyfully. She endorsed our cheerfulness and became absent with the dour, choosing by her questions to point us to a bright moment or perhaps an overlooked joyous happening. We hardly knew she was doing it, but, in time, I began to understand her and to appreciate her. Each evening she worked to draw out our disparate, small joys into the circle of candlelight, where they became the meat of our conversation.

While I do not believe anyone should avoid the hard facts of life, I learned from Isabel that for a few hours a day, the celebration of simply being together was as substantial a truth as my hard facts. It is a skill she taught me, which I employ every day to transform Sopwell into a joyous family, the celebration of us being together one more day, experiencing the small joys of our existence one more day. I have taught all my sisters to put names on our joys, and we have become eloquent on the subject of good cheer. And for that reason, we look eagerly ahead to the next day of our lives, carried along by the shared prospect of recounting our joys that evening.

That year Isabel was my most favored hawking companion. And I have never ridden with anyone like her since, for no one matched her genius for recognizing the luminous present. I remember our last day hawking together. Her pregnancy was far advanced, and she went into confinement the next day. While skirting one of Bernersbury's forests, we came on a display of rooks. The overwhelming din transfixed us in our saddles. We watched them as they flocked for the winter, on the wing, looping and wheeling in great gouts of black, folding in on one another and then landing by the hundreds in the upper stories of great oaks. I appreciated that, without prompting, she held tight to the jesses of our flapping falcons lest they get loose and disperse the rooks and end the wonder.

Truly I appreciated in our rides how all the signs of nature affected both of us. The musical song of the lark, of the brook rushing over gravel shallows, of the sudden rattling windstorm in the birch. The earthy smells of the barnyards, the sweet smells of a new rain in a parched meadow, and the insistent smells of the pines. The thrill of our merlins ascending, of the sun's heat intimately touching our faces, of the kitchen's exclamations when, on our return to the hall, we handed over bags loaded with partridge and rabbits.

At no time did her presence detract from my own sense of nature. On the contrary, her presence only deepened it. She never grew impatient with my joys but felt them as I felt them. Just a glance over to her after a stunning show of beauty told me that she and I were one in feeling. And she knew, for she would smile back at me, waiting selflessly for me to break the spell. I have not experienced complete oneness in nature with anyone else since those days spent out with her. But to my great regret, I held back from telling her.

During that winter, she accompanied me on my visits to the crofts of our tenants. It was a duty I took over from my mother. When Isabel and I visited Bernersbury's tenants, we made the usual inquiries about their food supplies and their health. To us women, the tenants always put the best face on their hardships. As we stood in their drafty, smoky tofts, I accepted their words, as I had so often in the past, as the representative of the hall. But not Isabel. She saw, and, over time in our visits together, especially to the poorest of our tenants, I began to see what she saw: the truth of their condition. I needed only follow her eyes and have mine alight where hers had.

Holy Benedict teaches us to care for the poor. But it was Isabel who first taught me to recognize poverty, the true poverty which I, as prioress, now work against. She saw the poor's meager bran bread and their thin pea soup without bacon, where I saw only bread and soup. She saw the children's oat porridge swimming in water instead of milk, and so much more. She saw the chickens that were not laying and the dry milk cows, where I saw barnyard fowl and livestock. The tenants truly loved her because her questions to them came from one who truly sensed, on the most elemental level, their deepest concerns. Her unspoken lessons make me a better prioress to this day.

But the most lasting lesson Isabel taught me was that poverty was not confined to the lowest stations. Want was only one sign of poverty. Poverty, she taught me, was found not only in the croft but also in the house and the hall. How often we had entered the lowliest toft and found children whose eyes spoke of curiosity, who formed their questions thoughtfully, and who respected one another. In those tofts, there was always . . . always a selfless woman whom Isabel sought out for praise. And just as frequently, we entered lofty houses and halls where the eyes of the children were frantic with need, children who could not put a word to their feelings, children who were contentious with their brothers and sisters. Those homes, no matter how high their station, suffered poverty as deep and grinding as physical want. This was the greatest lesson Isabel taught me.

How many more lessons she had to teach, I will never know. Isabel's last day came too soon. It began in Isabel and Richard's bed chamber the day she was due to deliver their first child. It was a room of whites. I see the white sheets on their bed, the white shift Isabel wore, and the white aprons and caps of the midwives.

Looking down, I saw Isabel lying in pain. Although occasionally flinching as the pain sharpened, her eyes remained a steady reflection of joyful anticipation. The long months of waiting were over. Just a little more pain before her great joy would be born. Resolutely, she endured the hours as the waves of pain began to cycle more frequently.

Finally the child began to emerge. One of the midwives gasped. The umbilical cord was wrapped about the child's neck, and the child emerged a deep blue. Perfectly formed, but a deep blue. His mouth, yes it was a boy, was cleared, and triumphantly, Isabel extended her arms for the baby. One of the midwives stared over to me in warning, and I told Isabel, "Wait until the midwives have cleaned him." The midwives took the boy aside, and I could see that he did not move, even after the cord was removed and cut. They poured cold water on him and bathed him, but he remained still and blue. They then moved quickly, clearing its mouth again and probing for obstructions. They found none. They slapped its back, but the child remained still. More cold water. Isabel's eyes grew frantic as she looked to me and said, "Please, I want to hold him." I soothed her by running my hand across her brow. "Just wait a little longer," I said.

"He is not crying," Isabel said.

"Yes. Let us wait a little longer," I replied hesitantly. But no amount of waiting would end with the child's cry. Her son, the son she and Richard would never know, was dead, and the midwives' sorrowful look told us that nothing more could be done. They wrapped the child fully in a piece of white linen and placed it on a side table.

It was then one of the midwives noticed the gush of scarlet blood following the purple afterbirth. As Isabel lost all color in her face, the midwives tried with towels to staunch the flow. They looked at me gravely and shook their heads. I gestured forcefully for them to renew their efforts. But it was not long before Isabel fainted.

I shouted for her to keep breathing, and her eyes opened to smile at me, saying softly, "Yes." And she tried to breathe, but her breath was erratic and shallow. I caught her hand and found her pulse thin. She was dying.

A midwife went to call for a priest. Isabel understood. At first I saw a flicker of panic and disappointment, then she turned her head to look directly into my eyes. Sitting next to her, I gripped her hand more tightly in mine as she had done for me months earlier in Bodiam's courtyard.

A slight smile formed on her pale lips, and she said, "We will talk again, Juliana." As her eyes closed and her hand grew colder, I felt my racing pulse and fevered skin quickly and irreversibly losing ground to the cold of her retreating life. No matter how hard I willed it, I could not impart my pulsing life and strength to her. The harder I tried, the faster she drifted away.

I have read that the last of the senses to die is the sense of hearing. So as Isabel's pulse stopped and her hand grew icy, I gave up the race for her life. Instead I thanked her. I told her that she had that rare quality to take other's feelings as they came, without question and without judgment. I thanked her for our rides last fall, our only fall together. I told her how such experiences seeped into the lowermost caverns of my mind, emerging later unbidden to lighten the heart.

And I thanked her for all she had taught me. I had been collecting her lessons in silence. And I told her I regretted my silence. And I asked her forgiveness. I believe that I saw a faint smile on her lips, and I took it—I needed to take it—as forgiveness.

As the light in the bed chamber dimmed from dusk to that sad, first murk of night, I sensed the midwives leave, taking the body of Isabel's stillborn son with them. The priest had come and gone. Silently sitting vigil, I had hardly noticed. Alone, staring into the dark, I thought back to Bodiam when I first sensed Isabel's gift, when she supported me without words and made it possible for me to look forward to an uncertain future. So I again asked her forgiveness for doubting the depth of her gift, for waiting instead for further proof.

It was then that Richard came into the room. Putting a hand on my shoulder, he said sorrowfully, "My lady is gone."

I looked up into his face in the gloom and said, "I had so much to tell her."

Richard shook his head and sat next to me. Still holding Isabel's hand, I took up one of his hands. I felt his pulse thud as slowly as a death drum. Bowing my head, I strengthened my grips on Isabel's cold, limp hand and on Richard's strong, warm hand. And I did what Isabel would have done. I released myself to feel Richard's anguish as he felt it, and it was then my own grief came flooding back, grief for my father's death, grief for the death of Sir Roger, and grief for the deaths of so many others, and in that desolation, I added Isabel's name to the list. And I became buried in what I dreaded most, the anguish felt by my father and stepfather in their last minutes. And in the chasm that opened up below me, I felt my mother's anguish on learning of their deaths. I saw death all about me, and I swam in its depths, and I heard its discordant note tolling finality.

Bringing Richard's hand up, I gently rested my cheek on it. Grief became our bond. Shortly, I felt my grip on his hand grow slippery.

Past exhaustion, I was weeping, for at the moment Isabel died, so much of me died with her. My hope for the renewal of our family died. My contentment with Bernersbury and its routines died. And yes, in the hour of Isabel's death, my youth died. And it was at that moment that the urgency of the future pressed in on me.

In time, Richard's sobs quieted and his gaspings became less frequent. The clean scent of frozen woodland and meadow swept through the open window and drove away the smell of drying blood. And the wan light of a rising half moon fell onto Isabel's face and onto the white sheets covering her. Her amber hair, splayed about her pillow, grew luminous as the moon grew brighter. And her tranquil face glowed afresh as if she were asleep.

Spent, Richard stared at Isabel now transformed. After a time, he said, "Thank you." Hugging his hand, I felt his words pierce me. Would that I had said these same words to Isabel even a day earlier.

And so it is when I enter a dwelling today, I feel Isabel beside me. When I duck my head to enter a lowly toft or hear my sandals scuffing the tiled floors of the wealthy, I sense her footsteps keeping pace with mine. And my eyes with hers search for signs of lavished care. The children, the kitchen, the linens, and so much more that comes to a wife's hand. I search for signs of Proverb's "good wife." She with the "strong arms" whose "lamp does not go out at night." She who makes "linen garments" for others, clothing her own self in "strength and dignity." It is she I find "teaching of kindness." For "she opens her hand to the poor, and reaches her hand out to the needy." And when I find that selfless woman, I find she bears the face of Isabel.

SISTER CLARE BRINGS Psalm 18 to life with the words that have often returned to me over the years during the odd moments of my day.

Therefore the Lord has rec-om-pensed me according to my righ-teous-ness;

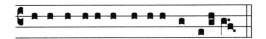

Ac-cord-ing to the clean-ness of my hands in his sight.

With the loy-al you show your-self loy-al;

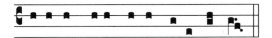

With the blame-less man, you show your-self blame-less.

Isabel's funeral was unbearable. Many came for the Mass, and we strained to entertain them. Edward and Philippa arrived with a great train of servants, and during the service, they sat apart, distracted and whispering. I guessed the village choir did not meet Philippa's approval.

The sky, the fields, and the very air mourned. Hard, stinging snow fell as her body and her son's body were lowered into the ground, and in our great hall, a damp and cold so profound took charge that blazing fires in every hearth and brazier could not dispel it. After greetings, Richard, my mother, and I stood among our agitated guests to answer questions, incapable of offering warm cheer. Cold meats went untouched on side boards, and trays of untasted cheese tarts steamed quickly to ice. No one sat.

Philippa was the first to seek me out. "Juliana, the queen offers her condolences," she said. The message delivered, she stood waiting for my response.

"Please thank the queen for me," I said. "It is very kind of her to remember us this day."

"I will take your gratitude back to her," she said.

"Please do," I replied with feeling. I reached out to touch her hand but teared and drew my hand back to wipe my eyes. Philippa offered a handkerchief. I took it, dabbed my eyes, and with a great sigh handed it back to her. "This is so hard. I worry about Richard," and then choked out, " . . . and my mother. I do not know how many more such deaths she can withstand."

There was a long silence. "I worry about you, Juliana," Philippa said. "I never imagined seeing tears in your eyes."

Smiling, I said, "Since Isabel's death, I am even less polite."

Philippa smiled back and said playfully, "You were barely polite to begin with."

"I have been working on kindness instead," I replied.

Philippa's smile disappeared.

"It is Isabel's death," I said. "Every moment of my day passes, shouting its eclipse into my conscience. Each of those passing moments is now real for me. I keep asking myself if what I am doing is worth the loss of those moments. Every night since Isabel's death, I total up my day, weighing its empty moments against the absolute value of each beat of passing time. And I am ashamed when the empty wins out."

"I do not understand you," Philippa said gruffly, searching my words for an insult.

"I never fully accepted Isabel," I said. "I hung back, distant from her, even when I knew she deserved my appreciation." I fumbled with my necklace. "But I waited. And I blame myself for waiting. Now I am afraid."

Philippa's eyes widened.

"Yes. I am afraid there will come a day when I will be asked to account for all the moments I spent marking time," I said hurriedly. "I hope you understand. I want to have something to show for each moment of my life."

Now fully on guard, Philippa hesitated, trying to assemble a conventional response, one she could repeat later at court to her credit. I said to relieve her of the effort, "I take your words and your queen's words for what they are, acts of kindness. And kindness is always worth the time."

Philippa relaxed but was interrupted by Richard, who bowed and thanked her for attending. I drifted away to one of the side tables, where Edward found me. As I took a sip of wine, Edward said, "Should I apologize for my wife?"

"No," I said. "She is a comfort."

"Philippa has taken an interest in your family. It was she who informed the queen of Isabel's death," Edward said.

"Philippa is the queen's finest advocate," I said.

Edward grew thoughtful. "The queen found two ladies that suited her, and they are now at court. But I have since made inquiries and found several other positions the queen may be opening. One is for an expert falconer to attend her when the queen's court hawks. She could do no better than you."

"I am not interested, Edward," I replied tersely. "On this of all days, I do not wish to discuss my future."

"As Henry's Master of Game, my recommendation carries great weight with the queen," Edward said, ignoring my protest.

"Edward, stop," I said firmly.

"Just a simple 'yes,' and I will take care of the rest," he pled.

"No," I repeated heatedly, my voice rising. Philippa and other guests nearby glanced over. We fell silent, and in the break I cooled enough to repeat tonelessly, "And you have no one to blame but yourself."

"It is your ingratitude I blame," he whispered.

"Edward, you taught me to ignore caution when we hunted together. You never pulled back, and you expected me to follow head-long into danger," I said. "And I learned that lesson well. The quick thrust carries less risk than standing back."

"You could learn so much more at my side," he pressed me.

"You are not taking my meaning."

"Speak plainly then," he shot back.

"With Isabel's death, I have decided to take my future into my own hands," I said. "I will wait on no one. I would rather be thatching a tenant's roof than waiting for the queen's party to select the proper wardrobe for a day of hawking. I am now committed to the doing, no matter how humble. That is my quick thrust at life."

"You are talking nonsense," he said.

"Waiting leads to a meaningless life," I said. "Since Isabel's death, I now see this clearly. If I spend hours every day waiting for others to decide my day, I will occupy myself in the meaningless—idle chatter, flirting, and all the other ways the court marks time. I added vehemently, "To speak plainly, Edward, I will not be wasting any more time."

"Are you saying I am wasting my time at court?" Edward asked.

"Each must make that judgment for himself," I said.

"Thank you for your absolution," he said sarcastically. "I have no more business with you." He looked about and saw my brother Richard with Philippa. "You will be joining me at the royal court. I will see to that." With that threat, he approached the two of them. I could hear him complaining to my brother about my rudeness and stupidity. I did not hear my brother's responses, but I did hear Philippa's.

"Edward, the only rude person here today is you. Have you forgotten the purpose of our visit? Richard's wife, Juliana's sister-in-law and good friend, just died," she said. "They are thinking of her and do not wish to discuss your plans."

Edward went silent. The rest of the afternoon he gave me wide berth.

In the weeks following the funeral and the departure of friends and kin, we fell back into ourselves. As happened so often in the past, my mother handled her grief by retreating to her room. Richard spent long days out inspecting the manor's properties, returning home exhausted. I read.

One spring day, that changed when Constance, Eleanore, and Catherine arrived. They took it upon themselves to plan our days, and in the evenings appointed themselves our minstrels, carrying me, my brother, and my mother along in their merriment. We began to thaw.

One close afternoon, when hints of moist meadows and low-growing chartreuse shoots of field grass drifted through the manor, we gathered in a small chamber off the main hall. It was our music room, holding psalteries, recorders, and lutes, and it was a refuge from the business of the manor. Dark storm clouds were low on the western horizon, and we watched them build with the promise of rain. Having exhausted talk of relatives, neighbors, and rumors from the court, I proposed the subject of my future, a subject my cousins enjoyed spending hours discussing. They had no end of advice.

To shock them away from their usual reassurances about dowries and eager young men, I said, "I am moving to Sopwell Priory, where I will profess my vows as a Benedictine."

Constance was not taken in by my ploy. She laughed but then caught herself and played along with me, saying in all seriousness,

"You would make a good nun. You love your schedules and your books, and you have a fair singing voice."

Eleanore and Catherine just stared at the two of us. "You cannot mean it, Cousin Juliana," Eleanore blurted out.

Not wishing to dispel their shock just yet, I added, "My mother will be against it, but no matter, I can learn to read Latin there. Sopwell is a part of the prestigious St. Albans Abbey, where, as you probably know, England's first martyr is buried."

Eleanore and Catherine were speechless, so I went on with more irrelevant historical notes to feed their gullibility. "During his reign, Pope Adrian, our English pope, gave St. Albans precedence over all other British monasteries and removed the abbey from local episcopal rule. Sopwell, its women's convent, has many patrons."

Narrowing her eyes, Eleanore said, "You're joking."

"Yes, finally," I said, grinning. "You are too involved in planning my future."

Both cousins relaxed, and Eleanore went on, "Juliana, I cannot imagine you locked up forever in some dreary convent."

"Nor I," I replied. "I have already visited Sopwell. And I can say without reservation it is not dreary. Rather it is a delightful community of well educated, talented, and spiritual women. Sopwell and St. Albans have extensive libraries to which I have access when there. While a student there, I will be free to read and write and under no obligation to celebrate the hours."

"No matter what you say, Juliana, there is no future in reading and writing," Catherine said. And Eleanore added, "You must remain patient. Your brother and my father will find you a dowry."

"I have been waiting," I said with exasperation. "I do not fault your father or my brother, but how much longer can I wait? A year? Two years? Every day I wake with a mounting urgency to get on with my life. I make up long lists of chores, and then spend frantic days dispatching them one by one. And I read and reread our books and all the books loaned me by our neighbors out of pity. There is not a book in Essex I have not read more than once."

"I know you are reluctant to accept the Duke of York's patronage," Eleanore said, plainly unsure of how I would receive the remark. "I do not wish to upset you, but it would solve your problem."

"You do not upset me," I said. "No doubt Edward's plans for me would solve my money problems. He has inherited his father's estates, and he is daily at Bolingbroke's side. I just do not wish to pay the price for his patronage."

"I should think your family has had enough of Edward," Constance said crossly, looking over to Eleanore.

"They have. But I have read his book, *Master of Game*, and it has inspired me to write about hunting," I said. "Oddly enough, Edward has pointed my way forward, although not in the way he hoped. *Master of Game* is a book for experienced hunters. I see the need for a beginner's book for England's young nobles, an introduction to the language of the hunt. My introduction will also praise chivalry, reminding our young nobles of Lord Tristan's virtues. I plan to write a poem as if Tristan had authored it."

"So you will fill up your days writing an introduction to hunting," Catherine said.

"No, I will fill up my life writing," I said. "Right now I am making notes in my daybook about hunting and hawking. I think I can write a better book on hawking than Edward."

"What then?" Philippa asked.

"I don't know," I said. "Perhaps fishing?"

"What could you say about fishing?" Constance asked incredulously. "A good net is all you need." We all laughed.

Before I could answer Constance's question, Eleanore asked, "Why not write here at Bernersbury?"

"Bernersbury has no library to speak of," I said. "There is so much more available at Sopwell. To write about hawking, I will need to study *De Arte Venanci cum Avibus* by Emperor Frederick. St. Albans has a copy, but it is in Latin, which I have not yet mastered. It will take some months before I can read it intelligently. Books that are not found in St. Albans's and Sopwell's libraries can be borrowed from other Benedictine monasteries as far away as Germany."

"So you really do not plan to become a nun," Eleanore said.

"Not now," I said.

"We want you to say 'no' absolutely," Eleanore said plaintively.

Gesturing at the musical instruments about the room, I said, "I believe life at Sopwell will put me in tune to sound a harmony in my writing."

WE PRESS AHEAD with Psalm 18. Sister Clare smiles to encourage us.

Yes you will light my lamp;

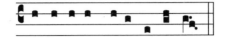

The Lord my God lights up my dark-ness.

MY CONVERSATION WITH my cousins found my mother's ears. And when Uncle William arrived at Bernersbury to escort his daughters home, she prevailed on him to argue me out of Sopwell. Late one morning, he found me in the stables repairing a saddle and drew me apart for a walk and privacy.

"Your mother finds it difficult to speak with you about certain subjects," he said. His massive figure, the frame of a tested warrior, towered over me. His bare head showed new signs of gray since his last visit, and his eyes had grown more kindly.

"You mean the subject of marriage, Uncle," I said.

"Yes, Juliana, your mother is firm in her desire to see you married," he said.

"Her firmness would mean more if it came with an estate," I said sharply.

"That is all your brother and I think about. But I am surrounded by marriageable young women and must first provide for Eleanore and Catherine. I can barely manage their dowries," he said apologetically.

"Uncle, I do not blame you or my brother," I said. "It is what my father's death took from us."

"Please do not blame your father," he said. "It was his love for King Richard that led to his impeachment. His death was hardly foreseeable. Even I, one who has kept an eye on the politics of the royal court for years, was shocked to discover your father's life was in jeopardy, because of Richard's partiality to him. How can that be treason?" Then in a low voice, he said, "What was most reprehensible was that Richard soon forgot your mother's needs, making only, after much prodding, a slim allowance for her. He should have done more."

"Uncle William, this is the history that circumscribes my day to day," I said. "It is inescapable, and it is obdurate."

"Your curse, Juliana, is being clear sighted. You should have children so that they may share in your realism," he said. "It is in short supply, and Britain needs a new infusion."

"I know that is my mother's hope, but I am finished wrestling with the immutable. I foresee nothing that will change my circumstances. I must move on to embrace what choices I do have," I said with finality.

"You are being rash," he said quickly. "Wait another year before going to Sopwell, even as a student. Right now your studies could become one more impediment to marriage. Your mother is very concerned." Then he added, "I have paid you the compliment of recognizing your clear-sightedness, but, in the extreme, that virtue becomes cynicism and despair."

"Will you not talk with her on my behalf, Uncle William?" I asked. "I cannot wait any longer. I need strike ahead. Right now I believe my path is to study and to write."

"Your mother will never agree to it at this time," he said.

"Does Mother not realize that the longer I wait, the greater the estate will be needed to interest a spouse?" I said pleadingly. "I am getting too old for marriage."

"Never say that," he said. "Wait a little longer."

"But I have waited, Uncle William," I said.

"I know," he said sadly. "And your patience has been admirable. I suggest you try to live in the present. And for my part, I will try to convince your mother to begin considering realistic alternatives for you. Remember, you will need her agreement for us to pay Sopwell's fees."

"She can be so stubborn," I said. "But I can match her."

"I am sure you will," he said, a smile playing across his lips. "Why do you think I listen to you? It is not just because you are my niece. No, it is because you are a virtuous woman like your mother."

We stopped a distance from the hall. He swept his arm across the landscape and said, "For the time being, I suggest you continue your work here, writing your observations of the countryside. Make notes on your hawks and falcons. Make notes on your fishing. I understand you have taken it up again."

A lark was calling regularly and, as we walked, ground-nesting birds, skylarks and corn buntings, scattered before us, gliding to new cover as grasshoppers do when set off by grazing horses.

"Thank you, Uncle William," I said, but as I opened my mouth to say more, he cut me off with a wave of his hand.

"I know well your mother's fascination with pilgrimages and relics. I know you have your doubts about her consuming fervency. At times, even I hold what I consider her superstitions against her. But Juliana, whatever has supported her good character, I do not challenge. After mentally stripping away whatever illusions or myths feed her virtue, I am still left with her good habits. They endure no matter what she believes. It is her good habits alone I judge," he said. "So it is with you. I judge not your bluntness, but I approve your reliable good sense."

With that, I took Uncle William's hand, and we made our way back together to the hall. Frayed, scudding clouds dappled the fields with fleeting sunshine, and my singing heart challenged Uncle William to a foot race. Indulging me, he accepted and lost.

psalm 119, the third and last Psalm for Sext, reaches its end. Sister Clare relaxes, shuffling notes to the back of her psalter. She will spend her work hours this afternoon reviewing next week's feasts. Later she will consult me on her choices. Psalm 119 concludes:

Sev-en times a day I praise you,

For your righ-teous judg-ments.

Today's feast recalls for us St. Thomas's martyrdom. As a novice, I admired him. Thomas's persecutor, King Henry II, was publicly flogged in retribution for instigating his murder. Once I was chosen prioress of Sopwell, I began to look on Thomas differently. I no longer thought about King Henry's infamous question, "Who will rid me of this troublesome priest?" I no longer thought of the grotesque assassination scene.

Instead, I began to pity St. Thomas. As prioress I took notice of other details. Well educated and from a middle-class family, Thomas won his place at the royal court through talent. And by that talent, he won Henry's friendship. But Henry miscalculated when he appointed Thomas Archbishop of Canterbury, our most influential see. Henry's miscalculation was judging Thomas's conscience forever malleable in the king's service. Henry had pulled him from the lower ranks and raised him up to a place at his side. Thomas was indebted to him. When he appointed Thomas chancellor and then archbishop, Henry believed he had bought and paid for Thomas's conscience once and for all. He had not.

What Henry had not counted on was that without notice Thomas had pulled his integrity from the auction block. Angrily, Henry concluded Thomas was a traitor. The obligations of archbishop dominated Thomas's conscience. The logic of the demands of his office drove him. He could no longer act as he felt. The sacred office dictated new, all-encompassing demands on him personally. The obligations of the office conflicted with the debauched life he had pursued with Henry, and so Thomas withdrew from Henry. Henry became a temptation, and there were others in Henry's life that could fill this void. But worse than the estrangement between the two was that Thomas's counsel to the king changed. The Crown was no longer Thomas's first thought. His loyalty to the office of the archbishop took precedence over his loyalty to his king.

But Thomas had his own traitor. What Thomas had not counted on were his wayward feelings. Memories of his indulgent life as Henry's closest companion in debauchery hung on the edges of his consciousness and without notice invaded a careless reverie in the half world he traversed between waking and sleeping. His very affections threatened him. He believed that his affections for women, for the pleasures of the table, for the pleasures of his friendship with Henry were demonic powers requiring total annihilation. And he also believed that with demonic powers there could be no half measures. All his affections must go.

Once archbishop, Thomas spent his last years methodically eradicating his memories not only of indulgent nights spent carousing with Henry, but every other pleasurable feeling as well. His prescription for achieving a pure life, a life of pure thought and feeling, free of obsession, was the extirpation of all past memory of pleasurable feeling. He worked to bury the residue of his early indulgences.

For Thomas, the solution for his obsessions was pain. The Martyrology states that when Canterbury's canons disrobed him to prepare his body for burial, they found a hair shirt worn next to his skin. Thomas had replaced his pleasurable affections with the constant pain of rough wool cutting into his skin. For sure, strong pain overcomes strong desire. The deeper his desires burned within him, the greater the pain he inflicted on himself. Eventually fasting and flagellation, thirst and flayed nerve ends distracted his mind, but at a terrible price.

Often in the first days of my life at Sopwell, I too thought back about my early life and its pleasures. The wild thrill of the day's hunt, the new foods and wines from Brittany and Burgundy, the bouts of flirting, the glittering array of gowns and jewels dazzled me. These memories have never left me.

To this day I miss the minstrels. The best of them knew all the Arthur stories and could sing them for hours, improvising new scenes and melodies for us. On winter nights, with cooking smoke hanging redolently above our heads, our families sat transfixed by the magic of the old romances. These were our forebears. We dreamt of their deeds and the days of Arthur and Tristan. And we saw ourselves in their halls by their sides, silent and worshipful of their selfless heroism. As the voices of the minstrels filled every corner of our halls, we young people sipped good Burgundy wine and promised ourselves to live like Tristan, Gawain, Arthur, and Isolde.

This was all good. During my first years at Sopwell, I visited St. Albans's library to relive those nights by rereading de Troyes. His tales bring back for me the intense bright eyes of my mother and aunts as they sat erect and silent, wrapped in furs. And they bring back the faces of my brother, cousins, and uncles as they fondled the hilts of their swords while listening intently to scenes of battle. I see even now their broad smiles at the triumphs of true chivalry. I see it all as if it were just yesterday. And I feel it as if it were yesterday. Yes, those were good evenings, but they have passed. I am one of the few left who remember them as they were, when we proclaimed unashamedly to all in minstrel song our deepest aspirations.

I grew to pity Thomas because I know a more wholesome cure for his debauchery. Holy Benedict does not ask his followers to uproot their memories and feelings. We are at liberty to retain all our affections for this life. I am at liberty to love deeply my mother, father, and brother. And I am at liberty to feel the haunting absence that came with their deaths. I am at liberty to take pleasure in the songs extolling Tristan's deeds and virtues, the memories of Edward's wild eyes as he urged his horse to a reckless gallop, and the polite picture of Bernersbury's head table, where Isabel smiled quietly as she listened to the story of Richard's day. Just as surely, I am at liberty to feel the perfection of a psalm well sung. And I am at liberty to feel deep pleasure in catching a vibrantly colored trout. Just as I am at liberty to mourn its death as its colors fade in my hand after I kill it.

My day courses with feeling. I would never banish a one, and as a follower of Holy Benedict, I am not asked to banish any. I pity Thomas because with each feeling, with each aroused affection uprooted, his world lost color and vibrancy and his life became by degrees bleaker. What a desolate prospect his life offered once pain pushed aside all his feelings.

The hours with their psalms order my affections. Countless small joys—the breath of the morning breeze carrying the fragrance of roses, the moist smell of a riverbank, soft drops of rain on my face, our voices chanting as one the hour's psalms, the smiles on my sisters' lips, a well-turned stitch, a countryside shrouded in fog, a heartfelt prayer—all become a river of feeling, transforming by the hour my deepest affections.

These small pleasures—this profound river of affections—course through me. This river of gladness weds my affections to the demands of my deepest commitments. Thus I do not flinch at the prospect of past memories of burning pleasures. Nor do I worry if such feelings invade my reveries. I worry even less if they invade my dreams. My day and its joys flood my mind, carrying all feelings before them toward that shore where the ebb and flow of each day balances and stills.

SEXT IS ALMOST over. I catch Sister Clare's eye. She understands I wish to recite the Collect for this feast day of St. Thomas. Leaving her place in choir, she stands in front of me holding up the prescribed page. I begin my recitation,

Al-mighty God, who sees our man-y weak-ness-es and de-fi-cien-cies

And who under-stands how our man-y mis-deeds op-press and bur-den us,

Hear Bless-ed Thom-as of Can-ter-bur-y your cou-ra-geous mar-tyr and learn-ed

Arch-bi-shop when he in-ter-cedes with you on our be-half.

Sext is finished. We file out of chapel to take up our work. This is the point in the day when I review my most pressing chores.

It is time for me to write Lady Elizabeth Howard, the mother of the Second Baron Berners. Cousin Elizabeth is pregnant. Her first marriage to Humphrey Bourchier, the eldest son of John, the First Earl of Berners, ended at the Battle of Barnet in 1471 when Humphrey died, securing the throne for our present monarch, King Edward. She is in great favor with the royal court. After Humphrey's death, she married Sir Thomas Howard, the Second Earl of Surrey and the Third Duke of Norfolk. With Howard, she has given birth nearly every year of their marriage so far.

At first glance, she seemed another beautiful, shallow girl who, like Isabel, married well. Yet she has proven herself astute in business matters. She is privy to the latest intelligence on trade and is familiar with the operations of the king's cabinet. I am at a loss with what to do with Lady Alice's bequest. I want to put the farm to its best use for both Sopwell and the Marshes. Prices for agricultural products are stagnant. Labor is in short supply. Coin is scarce. There are no signs these conditions will change, although Abbot Wallingford holds out for a turn in the markets. Overseas trade seems Sopwell's best opportunity for profit, but what to make and what to sell? These are questions I hope Lady Elizabeth will answer.

Also, I must review the larder's inventory with Sister Anicia.

And the last item on my list is a visit to Sister Margery.

Conversation has become too taxing, so I read to her. Until yesterday I put a brave face on my visits, but she has grown disgusted with me. Once she asked, "Have you never talked to death before?" I ignored the question, hoping to overwhelm her pain with cheerfulness. She no longer enjoys the Gospels, the Acts, the Fathers, or the Lives of the Saints. She requests poetry and literature. The psalms are constantly on her lips, and fleeting smiles punctuate her enjoyment of Chaucer and Christine de Pizan.

Yesterday, pressing her as I do every visit for a description of her pains, her eyes flashed angrily, and she turned away from me. After a moment she whispered, "Psalm 41."

I began to recite Psalm 41 from heart. When I reached the words, "The Lord protects him and keeps him alive; he is called blessed in the land; you do not give him up to his enemies. The Lord sustains him on his sick bed . . . ," leaning forward with great effort, Margery signaled me to stop by waiving a single index finger from side to side.

Then falling back she whispered, "Psalm 55."

With the words, "O that I had wings like a dove! I would fly away and be at rest; yes, I would wander afar . . . ," my enforced cheerfulness broke as I finished the verse: "I would take up residence in the wilderness." I finally understood her and saw her fate. My breathing stopped and my heart screamed for comfort.

She smiled vaguely at me and began the verse, "But it is you, my equal . . . " when her voice fell away.

As tears trailed down my cheeks, I took the verse up quickly as if we were chanting together in chapel: " . . . my companion, my familiar friend. We used to hold sweet converse together; within God's house we walked in fellowship."

We were sitting on the veranda of the infirmary, looking across Sopwell's orchards hanging with half-ripened apples and pears. Rocking forward and backward, my arms crossed and my fists clenched, I wept. For how long, I do not know. Always the stoic, Margery sat silently. An eternity passed as two old nuns, shrouded in black, wordlessly faced their destiny.

In the end, I turned to Margery again and for a moment saw the sweet, intelligent novice I had first come to love. Breathing shallowly, she was composed and at peace. Rising, I kissed her. It was the last real conversation between us. Her constant pain struck her mute. There is no one to replace her.

With the words of Psalm 55 still on my lips, I carried my sorrows to the Ver. Trudging down Sopwell hill, I began to chant under my breath:

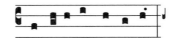

My heart is an-guished with-in

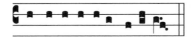

The ter-rors of death fall up-on me.

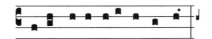

Fear and trem-bling come up-on me

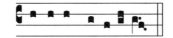

And hor-ror o-ver-whelms me.

Nearing the river, I saw flights of shell fly rising from a long riffle upriver from the Sopwell Bridge. The shell fly is a green bodied caddis fly that for most of the year encrusts the Ver's rocks with its tiny, cylindrical sand cases. During July, they break their cases and swarm up from the river bottom. Springing into the air, their wings became shimmering silver blurs. Their first order of business is to flee to bordering bushes and trees, where they rest. They are found clinging to bridge abutments and the underside of leaves, their light beige wings folded over their backs. By late morning, they hear the call to dance and to mate, sowing their yellow eggs hours afterward. Within a day or two, they disappear. The return of this annual show gladdened my heart.

Trout fed rhythmically. But my first casts brought no takers. Hundreds of natural flies glutted the Ver's riffles, and trout fed deliberately and steadily. Perhaps preoccupied with thoughts of Sister Margery, I did not notice that the fish refused the floating naturals and not surprisingly also my artificial fly, a reliable pattern fashioned out of green wool wound about with peacock herl for the body and snippets of hawk flight feather for the wings. I cast and cast without luck.

I had disobeyed the most fundamental rule of angling. Every angler must stay alert to the river's surface. The rules of water, rock, and plant inexorably etch their meaning on the surface of the water, moving over them just as the rules of word, sentence, and metaphor form the story told on the pages of a book. The angler must study the movement of the water and the resistance of what lies beneath, whether it be rock or fish, to read the river's story, just as the story-teller observes the rule of composition to tell her story. Water speaks a plain text. When it encounters a feeding trout, it explains its feeding strategy.

This day, the day of the shell fly, I had no excuse for not reading the water correctly. It is true that by July the page of the river becomes harder to read. The water is clearer and lower. Too much is written on it. And especially then the angler need study the disturbances left by the feeding trout. My flaw was an old one with me, trusting in the power of my artificial fly. An experienced angler must not only select the right bait but must also stay alert to how trout and grayling feed. And that was the rule I had forgotten. I cast my fly before closely observing the fish. At first gauging the rise rhythms of individual fish, I was able to fool only two small ones by throwing my fly on their noses. But this early success just confirmed me in my sloppiness. I should have recognized that even these fish were reluctant risers. They took my fly, I concluded later, out of surprise. I made more and more accurate casts, but the trick ceased to work.

Fish are always forthright. In the pattern of their disturbances, the fish speaks truly to the angler. Rises for surface flies, especially mayflies, usually leave a ring and bubble on the surface. There were none on the open page of the Ver. When fish lift to feed on insects inches below the river's surface, they raise a momentary humpbacked bulge of water. Instead of a bubble and a ring, the observant angler notes, as I should have noted, the rolling crease at the head of the bulge. The crease repeats every time the fish feeds.

After a while, frustrated, I focused on the bulges. The shell flies were not being taken off the surface but from just under the surface. Then I did what I should have done earlier. I resorted to surgery. Hurriedly taking the two small trout from my satchel, I opened their stomachs with a small knife and squeezed the contents into the palm of my left hand. Rolling the debris about with the knife point, I separated out the crushed bodies of several shell flies. Examining them closely, I found stiff casings clinging to their lower bodies. The caddis flies were able to pull their wings from the casing but apparently could not wriggle all the way out. The stomach debris did not reveal any flies fully freed from their cases.

I returned to the Ver excited. Roughing up my dubbed shell fly, I teased out wool strands, leaving them disheveled to stream behind the hook. Then I wrinkled its wings and splayed them out to the side. Finally I wet my bedraggled fly so it would ride just under the surface. Only then did I cast several feet above the bulge of the nearest rhythmic riser.

Swinging my rod tip with the fly as it swept down the run, I felt the pleasant throb of a large fish. It was heavy and used its weight to run below me. I followed until it stopped and held against a deep undercut bank. Patience and constant pressure drowned the trout, and I slid it in my satchel. I repeated this performance once more. The four trout were enough for Sopwell's supper.

Scrambling up the bank, I stood erect to catch my breath. Looking north, I saw the crenellated walls of the abbey and the roof of the great abbey church within. As I entered Sopwell's gate, I thought of all the young women who would need Sopwell's serenity in the future,

as I once needed it. Without that serenity I could not have reflected
. . . nor have written. If Prior Thomas has his way, none will come
to know it. Instead he plans for them to kneel at his brother's tomb
contemplating just one more abbot's death before they return to the
confines of village life.

none

Feast of St. Mary Magdalene
3:00 p.m.
July 22, 1477

None recalls us from work. When the bells announce this midafternoon hour, we drop what we are doing. If within the convent, we return to chapel. If outside, we sing this short hour where we stand. I have recited its psalms and antiphons humming them under my breath on roadways in St. Albans, alongside rivers and ponds, and in fields and pastures. It has been a week since Sister Margery's funeral Mass, and my spirits are at low ebb.

SISTER CLARE LEADS us into the invitatory, after which she intones the hymn *Pater superni luminis*, Father of Heavenly Light. Sopwell is dedicated to Mary, the mother of Jesus. Today is the feast of Mary Magdalene, Blessed Mary's faithful companion and close friend. The third stanza for today's feast reminds us of Mary Magdalene's fidelity and passion.

Fear-less she would not leave the Cross,

Griev-ing she would not leave the Tomb.

She did not fear the cruel watching soldiers

For from her love all fear had fled.

I have known young women like Mary Magdalene. Living in small towns, like Bethany and St. Albans, they become "sinners" once they cross the stifling boundaries set for women's conduct. It matters not whether the boundaries mark out the true limits of spiritual living or simply the unexamined legislation of a town's intolerance. According to local scolds, stricter than most Pharisees, young women misbehave when risking their reputation by committing indiscretions. Scolds never examine the motivations for "sin," for such inquiries lead them into moral confusion.

So it was with Mary Magdalene. The Gospel authors never described her "sin."

Misogynists, clerical and otherwise, assume her sin was sexual, possibly prostitution. Their conclusions point up their own misunderstanding of human nature because prostitution is more a sin of greed than sexual intemperance. At least this is what I have learned from nuns who left a life of prostitution to dedicate themselves to the Rule of St. Benedict. They struggle not with their passions for men but with their passions for comfort. They struggle harder to keep their vow of poverty than their vow of chastity.

Even the most superficial reading of the Gospels leaves no doubt that her "sin" was not greed. Mary was no hoarder. She gave freely, unashamedly and, worst of all, indiscreetly, and so became a public sign of extravagant generosity and . . . scorn.

So, I keep my own counsel on Mary Magdalene's sin. As prioress, I often think of Jesus's reproof to the Pharisee who invited Mary to meet Jesus and, so, test him. Jesus said, "He who is forgiven little, loves little." I am always more lenient with my sisters who fail while striving

aggressively in their love. It is more important that they wholeheartedly love their work, the beggars at our gate, and their sisters.

Extravagant generosity strikes the divine spark. Our ancestors
counted on the annual runs of thousands upon thousands of salmon,
wilderness forests forever rustling with coursing deer and boar, soaring
flocks of geese and ducks blotting out the sun, gushing pure springs
of water, forests of towering trees, and so many other signs of God's
interest in us. I remember hunting in trackless woods as a teenager. I
remember, also, the annual return of salmon on which every manor
and their tenants feasted. Such signs bolstered our ancestors' faith in
the divine, thousands of years before Mary Magdalene thoughtlessly
emptied her alabaster jar of ointment without remorse.

This is all changing. Our dense wilderness forests have been grid-
ded and graveled. Fewer salmon swim our oceans and seas. It is still
true that every year thousands of salmon enter hundreds of our rivers
to spawn. Along our coasts, they swarm, stage at the mouths of our
rivers and streams, and then run up them to where they find aerated
gravel riffles and runs to dig their redds and drop their eggs. They leap
dams, weirs, and set nets to return to where they were born. They have
done so even before man inhabited this island. The greatest salmon
river is the Thames, with its tributaries. It fed London more surely
than Roman agriculture.

Salmon runs are diminishing by degrees. And as they diminish
by degrees, we lose by degrees our sense of nature's generosity. There
will come a time when the runs can no longer be described as extravagant, instead of thousands we will be counting hundreds. When that
day comes, a sign of the divine shall vanish forever from this land. We
will be thrown back on ourselves, on our fleeting emotions, to prop
up that secure sense of our place on this earth, the very floor of our
faith. When the day comes that salmon no longer climb our coastal
rivers, then the most obvious sign of the universe's interest in us will
disappear forever. And unutterable loneliness will challenge our faith
at every turn.

Faith will never substitute for that feeling of elemental belonging.
Our sense that we belong in this world is more ancient than our faith.
Our feelings of faith build on it. Now the signs that we belong here
are everywhere: the oceans, the forests, the very air we breathe and

water we drink. These signs are constant reminders that we are the earth's rightful tenants. When these signs dim and disappear, when air and water threaten us, when wilderness forests are leveled to a bleak horizon, then our sense of security will disappear altogether. And we shall overtax our faith to salve our profound loneliness.

As nature's generous brilliance falls into oblivion, as we lose the divine spark, we build up our liturgies. We look to the liturgical show for that sense of place that is the natural ground of any faith. But such emotions are fleeting. We will pick at them to enflame certitude as we pick at scabs that itch, achieving, in the end, only renewed bleeding, infection, and anxiety. Bedrock certainty inevitably followed by blind fear will become the minute by minute cycle of our lives, once the annual cycle of the salmon is gone.

On this feast of Mary Magdalene, therefore, I pray for her intercession and the return of extravagant salmon runs. Through her, may my sisters and I overcome the obstacles frustrating our headlong rush toward achieving divine extravagance. Let our passions loose, so that we might pour out all that we are and so become a sign of divine interest in this earth.

SISTER CLARE LEADS us, announcing the antiphon for the None.

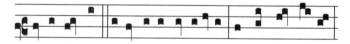

Ma-ry there-fore a-noin-ted the feet of Je-sus, and wiped them with her

hair and the house was filled with the o-dor of the oint-ment.

Today Sister Anicia and I fish our ponds as we have every July. She fishes for bream, and I fish for tench. Each pond is over two acres, fed by spring water, and ringed with a screen of rushes. During the year, we feed the fish kitchen scraps. Lately, in preparation for harvest, Sister Anicia has been scattering groundbait, the same bits of food that we will use for our baits.

Our bream have fattened over the summer. We take the older

bream, thin as a plate with a distinct small head and a forked tail. They are generally bronze. The bronze on their upper back tends to a brownish black but lightens to a grayish white on the stomach. All summer I have watched their shoals patrol the silt-bottomed weedy edges of Sopwell's upper pond. Spawning is now complete, and their sticky yellow eggs cover the shallows.

Our tench are omnivorous and prolific. Their numbers must be reduced before the late fall, when the water cools, and they begin to hibernate in the pond's mud bottom. Cylindrical in shape, our tench wear a deep olive, almost bronzy cast throughout, darkest on the back turning a yellowish olive on their belly. By late July, they give away their location by emitting thin streams of bubbles. Where bubbles appear, the angler lets down his lure. An occasional twitch helps.

Sister Anicia and I sit with our backs to each other, she fishing the lower pond and I fishing the upper pond. The verge dividing the two ponds is hardly four yards wide, so we talk over our shoulders to each other. I cast above, in the slight current where the upper pond drains into the lower, and she fishes in the slight current where the trickle from the upper pond enters.

In years past, Sister Anicia giggled with each fish. Should a bream escape her after taking the bait, she laughs and waves it good-bye. Sister Anicia, more than anyone else, adds to my merriment. We sit near each other chatting back and forth. Sometimes we sing songs remembered from childhood. Sometimes we plan meals. Sister Anicia is tired of mustard sauces for our fish. She believes in cooking with herbs.

But this afternoon, she is subdued. "Two more months and we will know our fate."

"Yes," I said. "Come what may, I will savor the memory of each day spent fishing with you. What are your plans if Sopwell is disbanded?"

"I have written to my son in London, and he has offered me a room in his house. There is a nearby inn that needs a good cook," she said. "I can do no better than that. My family put up all its silver to place me here at Sopwell, and the family has no money to interest a new convent." She hesitated.

"It would not be the same," I replied, and I saw her eyes had grown moist.

"Yes. Once I leave here, the best part of my life will be over," she said, wiping her eyes with the hem of her habit. "What about you, Mother?" she asked. "What are you planning?"

"I have no plans," I said flatly.

Startled, she turned and asked, "Why not, Juliana?"

"I fear my resolve to see this matter through will evaporate if I take comfort in my plans for a new life," I said. "So I have put such considerations off. I need all my apprehensions."

"What will happen to you?" she asked.

"I have no idea," I said. "Now let us plan Lady Elizabeth's meals."

Sister Anicia giggled. Another bream went free. "I should have been paying attention," she said.

"We should be paying attention to the menu for Lady Elizabeth Howard's visit," I said. "She will be here in a few weeks with her children."

"What dishes does she prefer?" Sister Anicia asked triumphantly, sliding a large bream up the verge.

"Cousin Elizabeth is especially fond of chicken and partridge," I said.

It was then Sister Anicia got down to business. For roast fowl, she suggested a galantine sauce made from grated bread, pulverized cinnamon, ginger, claret wine, and vinegar, to which she adds a pinch of shredded galingale root. In small quantities, the root increases the aromatic flavor of the sauce while adding a pleasant bitter aftertaste. There would be a few fish meals. Sister Anicia suggested flounder in a sugar sauce, which she will make more complex by adding rose hips simmered in a very dry white wine with a little minced rosemary.

As the menu grew, Sister Anicia pointed toward the gate. "I believe Sister Joan needs you."

"Could you take the fish to the kitchen while I confer with her?" I asked.

"Of course," she said. And by the time Sister Joan joined us, Sister Anicia had gathered up our baskets and equipment.

"If you could give me some time with Mother . . ." Sister Joan said to Sister Anicia.

"We have just finished," Sister Anicia said cheerfully.

After Sister Anicia was out of earshot, Sister Joan said, "Another note from Prior Thomas."

I took it, broke the seal, and read aloud:

> Your delays with regard to Lady Alice's gift to Sopwell concern
> the abbey greatly. You took title to the property personally as Lady
> Alice intended. But you have not transferred your title to Sopwell as
> she also intended. This is a breach of the trust Lady Alice placed in
> you. You have held her property beyond the time needed to make
> the transfer to Sopwell or to the abbey. We have made allowances
> for your age. We now put you on notice that the necessary docu-
> ments must be drafted and the necessary signatures must be added
> to effect the transfer of Lady Alice's bequest. We direct you to make
> the transfer immediately.
>
> Should you not comply, the abbey has one of two courses open
> to it. It may petition Rome to have the abbot declared the guardian
> of your estate, which would permit the abbey to execute the neces-
> sary documents to preserve Lady Alice's gift for the use of St. Albans.
> Or the abbey may petition Parliament to have an attainder issued
> against you for breach of trust, fraud, and theft. If this alternative,
> the abbey will charge you with stealing abbey property. Our good
> king has in the past lavished the Abbey with gifts and would only be
> too happy to assist us with Parliament.
>
> The abbey respects your past services but is very concerned with
> your delays in this matter. We choose to believe it is due to your age
> and what we deem to be the early signs of mental incompetence.
> Abbot Wallingford urges you to put an end to this matter before he
> is forced to take the necessary steps to preserve abbey resources. In
> your declining years, you are risking your good name and the future
> of Sopwell.

Pondering the threat for a moment, I looked up at Sister Joan and
said, "Remember this day when as Sopwell's Prioress you deal with
the abbey."

"They are heartless," Sister Joan said. "They show no compassion
even to their own."

Sister Joan then stood silent.

"Was there more?" I asked.

"Prior Thomas said that St. Albans is enjoying the rumor that
you kept a man overnight inside the convent. An old Lombard, his
marshals reported."

"That is true. The town drove him out, and following St. Benedict's
words, I allowed him to stay in one of Sopwell's guest rooms," I said.

"You probably remember him taking supper with us."

"Yes," she said, plainly distressed. "I cannot bear the slander."

"If Prior Thomas took the charge seriously, he would have put it in writing," I said, waiving the note.

"Perhaps he is storing it up for another day," Sister Joan said.

"Perhaps," I replied. "There will be more slanders until the abbey gets its way."

"There is one more thing," she said thoughtfully. "Prior Thomas wanted me to repeat his warning about selling off any of Sopwell's properties. He specifically warned me to say his directive included wool."

"Anything else?" I asked.

"I must report back to him your answer."

"You may report that I fully understand his message. And also compliment him for warning me about overgrazing our fields. Taking his advice, I find that I need shift parts of our flocks elsewhere," I said.

"That will be an easy message to carry back," she said, relieved.

"On your way out, instruct the herdsman to find me." I said with a smile.

SISTER CLARE QUICKLY leads us into Psalm 15. Its words call to mind Constance and the days before her marriage to my brother Richard.

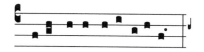

O Lord who shall so-journ in thy tent?

Who shall dwell on thy ho-ly hill

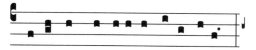

He who walks blame-less-ly and does what is right,

And speaks the truth from the heart;

The storms that brought memories of Bernersbury beached a story that I did savor. It was a quiet moment. I recalled it one afternoon while rearranging benches and cupboards in Sopwell's workroom. Constance's image came to the fore as I had so often seen her, her ashen blonde hair draped over the chair back, looking up smiling as I entered Bernersbury's music room.

I could hear her say as she said so often in those days, "Oh there you are. I was wondering when you would join me." Constance returned to Bernersbury late in the fall after Isabel's death. For once, I had the manor to myself. Richard was at Bodiam, the guest of Constance's father, Sir John.

That summer, after observing the mourning period following Isabel's death, Sir John invited Richard to hunt at Bodiam and, once, even arranged for Richard, Edward, and Prince Hal to hunt his forests together. Sir John's invitations to Richard grew more frequent. Hunting no longer the purpose, Richard accompanied Sir John on business to London and on visitations to his tenants.

Relaxed after a breakfast of wheat cakes, dried currants, and honey, Constance and I sat in Bernersbury's hall, facing its great hearth. Piled high with dried oak and elm, the fire kept us company as we sat wrapped in fur-lined capes. Mine, wolf, and hers, fox. A cold snap had followed Constance to Bernersbury, and the drafty hall stung our shoulders and exposed hands. Occasionally the kitchen brought us warm wine as we sat huddled near the flames like worshipping supplicants. We did not venture out except to exercise our hawks. For days we talked.

As Constance related, Richard's frequent invitations to Bodiam were a test. Richard and her father enjoyed each other's company. Did Constance enjoy Richard's company as well? Always the doting father, Sir John would not force a husband on her. Yet he was protective and would screen her likely choices before arranging a marriage.

Richard never spoke to me about Constance. And when he was

with the two of us, he was always correctly cordial and attentive to us both. He never contrived to catch Constance alone.

So Constance sought me out. "Would your brother make a good husband for me?" she asked. "He is always congenial, but I feel something is missing. My father has genuinely warm feelings toward Richard in spite of their age difference. But I do not feel I really know Richard, and the routine at Bodiam leaves me no opportunity to test his feelings and thoughts. We are always with other people. Do you understand? He does not avoid me, but every second of my life at Bodiam is so organized that I can never venture a personal question without embarrassing him."

"Such as?" I said.

"Oh, how he feels about Isabel's death. Is there room in his heart so soon afterwards for someone else?" She replied, clearly agitated. "This is the question foremost on my mind."

"Do not be offended, Constance, but I cannot answer that question. I only know Richard as a brother," I said vaguely, not wanting to upset her.

"But you know him so well," she said, stroking the red fur of her cape.

"I know him well as a brother, and he has been a good brother. Whether that would make him a good husband for you is a question I cannot answer," I said.

Growing more agitated, she pressed me, "Please try!"

"No," I said. "It is very simple. With my family members, I do not judge. They did not ask to have me as a sister . . . niece . . . or daughter. We have been thrown together without a choice in the selection. I discipline myself to have no expectations for my family. It would not be fair."

"I really do not understand you," she said, deflated.

"You are asking me to assess my brother as a husband for you. The long and short of it is that I would be a traitor to judge him. All I can say is that he has been a good brother."

Constance relented and thought for a moment. "Let me try another question."

"Make it an easier one," I said.

"Do you think Richard will be my Tristan?" she asked and then waited for my response.

"No," I said without hesitation.

Constance's smile disappeared, and she said dejectedly, "You feel certain of this."

"Yes," I said. "Richard is no longer the enthusiastic young man we knew before Isabel's death. He now shows greater restraint in all matters. I do not doubt he will be restrained in his attention to you," I continued. "But that is only my opinion."

Constance frowned with disappointment before rousing herself and asking, "Did you ever entertain the hope of finding your own Tristan?"

"Yes. When I was younger," I replied, "When I hunted with Edward . . . before Conisbrough. But since spending months at a time reading and writing at Sopwell, I have concentrated my spirit on what I can accomplish there. Sopwell is the eye of my needle, through which I must pass before finding a new life. A life in which I study and write."

She grew silent again. I picked up one of her hands and said, "Shall I tell you of the happiest day of my childhood? It is a kind of romance."

"Of course," Constance said, staring into the fire. "Will it help?"

"It might," I said. "My family and I were returning from visiting relatives in Hertford. It was August, and I had just turned five. My mother and father were riding horses while I and most of the servants rode in wagons loaded with our baggage."

"This does not sound like a romance," Constance interjected.

"I said it is a kind of romance," I replied, smiling. "I grant you that it will not be put to verse and sung by minstrels, but it is my romance. The day had started bright and sweltering. We rode down dusty roads past fields of desiccated crops, silently sympathizing with the peasants resting here and there in bits of shade. My parents pushed us on because storm clouds suddenly appeared, black and menacing, on the western horizon. For a time, we flew ahead of the storm. But it overtook us—hurling winds, then darkness, and then scattered raindrops. Finally the torrent drove in on us with its full force. My parents, taking the lead, disappeared now and again between sheets of rain.

"At first, we fought the relentless, sodden sea of rain. The roads became a mire, and whips whistled and snapped over our horses, urging them to keep pace. Sail cloth covers unfurled over the wagons, and my parents pulled their green linen cloaks over their heads. But it was no use. The rain was warm and intimate, soaking us through and through. Soon our baggage sloshed about in the wagon box, and my parents gave up trying to hold their cloaks away from the prying hands of the wind. As we came up to Bernersbury, my father signaled the servants to take the wagons into the stables, and my mother and he sat on their dripping horses as we passed.

"It was then I looked back and saw my father pull his horse up next to my mother's, pick her up with one arm, and place her gently on the ground. Rivulets of water dashed through our graveled yard, and great puddles covered the roadway. My mother looked up in surprise. No dry island rose up from the sea of water. But, laughing, my father jumped down beside her, splashing; embraced her; kissed her; and hugged her. All the while the warm rain inundated everyone and everything. I will never forget when afterward my father and mother, with arms about each other's shoulders, led their horses toward the barns. My mother's gown, soaking with rain and mud, clung closely to her, and my father, joyful, opened his mouth skyward to catch a drink, pure and soaking down his black beard.

"I see even now the two of them, smiling at each other, walking unhurriedly through the torrent. My father then took me by the waist and lifted me up. When I opened my arms like a bird, shouting ecstatically into the cloud burst, he ran about, splashing in circles and holding me aloft so that I flew. I have never felt so light since.

"That is the romance of my childhood. And it is how I best remember the marriage of my father and mother."

We both fell silent.

"You are not leaving the rest of us behind," Constance said anxiously.

"Never. You fuel my happiness and buoy my hopes."

psalm 135, one of None's three psalms, reminds me of de Worde and London's book market. Sister Clare compels us with her quick hands to move through it crisply. I sing,

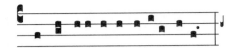

The idols of the na-tions are sil-ver and gold,

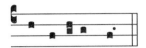

The work of men's hands.

They have mouths and speak not,

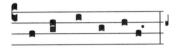

They have eyes and see not,

Last week de Worde returned to argue for permission to print my *Treatyse*. He tells me that Caxton plans to offset the losing sales of his scholarly works by the more lucrative sales of general interest books like my *Treatyse*. Otherwise, de Worde admits Caxton may need to close his printing business. Printing and selling my *Treatyse* would bring income to Sopwell and solve Caxton's financial problems.

But I must tell him no. His arguments have made an impression on me. But they have not convinced me. If I knew who would buy my *Treatyse*, I could resolve my doubts. But de Worde is of little help on this question. And to be fair to him, he cannot be, for he cannot say with any certainty who will purchase the *Treatyse*. As he told me, "With each new book, a new group of customers comes to Caxton's shop. The books determine the customers." Caxton has not yet published a book on field sports, so he does not know which customers the *Treatyse* will attract. He is certain there will be many, because the king permits Londoners to fish the Thames and many of its tributaries.

I believe de Worde when he tells me that the *Treatyse* will sell well in London. Many anglers reside there. And many of them are gentle and reflective—true anglers—but some are not. I must keep in mind those readers who will abuse its instruction when I speak with de Worde. I will not be able to control the lessons of the *Treatyse* once Caxton publishes it. This is what I foresee, and no amount of money for Sopwell, in the short run, can justify empowering the unethical sportsman.

Thus my answer to de Worde will be no. This is not a hard answer for me to give. I have given that same answer often enough to the Second Duke of York. It was the answer I gave him, vehemently, when we met at Bodiam attending Richard and Constance's wedding.

One morning in the week after the wedding, I went out early to fish. Bodiam's riverkeeper suggested that during late summer the best bait for trout and grayling is a combination of maggots and worms. A single maggot is first strung on the hook, and then a worm is snugged up behind it. He directed me to a nearby section of river that held trout, and I made my way to it in the silent dark, waiting for the first faint cast of blue sky to appear overhead, waking the birds. The river gurgled while I sat in tall grass wet with dew. Finally, when the dawn crawled overhead and cascaded rosy golden to the Rother's curling surface, and when the willows along the river's margins took on a brilliant green, I swung my bait into the current.

A slight weight carried the maggot and worm down to the bottom of the nearest deep hole. Not long after, I saw my line twitch and move forward in the current. I pulled back, and before long, a heavy trout was in my basket. Replacing the maggot and worm over and over, I took trout after trout. Sir John would have trout for his breakfast.

Maggots and worms are also effective earlier and later in the year. Thinking about the success of this combination, I began to see them rather as combinations of colors, white and red. That morning I wondered if the contrast between the two colors was what enticed the fish. I experimented using redder and redder worms and whiter and whiter maggots. The whiter and the redder were more effective.

My basket was nearly full when I heard galloping horses, drawing my attention toward Bodiam's gates. The hollow sound of hooves clambering over the drawbridge warned me someone else was out in the dawn, threatening my solitude. It was Edward looking for me.

Sitting among the reeds in my sage-colored gown, I saw him before he saw me. Dressed in a white tunic, he was leading an empty saddled horse, which slowed his progress. Both were spirited blacks. Always the hunter, Edward was on my scent. In the past, finding myself his prey exhilarated me, but now the idea brought only resentment. A guest at the wedding and still childless, he had tried to corner me all week, but I eluded him with polite excuses.

His persistence only increased my resentment. I disliked him most for pursuing me after it was clear to everyone at Bodiam that I did not want to speak with him. Through all his pestering, however, I never felt disadvantaged. Edward thought like a hunter, and I knew how hunters thought. The problem for me was to determine what sort of prey he believed me to be. Was I the hare, the hart, the boar, or the stoat?

My guess was he saw me as the hart. His plan was transparent. He wished to corral and pin me to his side. My resentment toward him turned into disgust when I realized that he believed me frightened of him. In his arrogance, he guessed I was fleeing his company like the hart before hounds, and so he wished to stymie me from using the hart's ploys to escape. The hart will run up streams and rivers until dogs lose the scent. Or it will double back on its track and jump onto another hart's trail, hoping the dogs pass him by. Finally, the hart will push another hart out of hiding and take his place in his cover, forcing the fresh hart to lead the pack away. I did not need any of these ruses to lose Edward.

It was not in me to flee. And I had no intention of further bloating Edward's already inflated sense of himself by fleeing. As he rode me down at a gallop, he pulled up just short, working his reins in an effort to intimidate me but only succeeding in spilling my basket of trout. Angered, I resolved to play the boar, the most dangerous game in the forest. The boar will flee only to find a thicket in which to entangle pursuing hounds. Then the boar stands his ground, waiting for its moment to kill the hounds one by one, and when only the hunter is left, it charges with speed and purpose to upend him. Then it gores him as the hunter tries to stand. The boar believes in confrontation. And so do I when dealing with the arrogant. Today the river bank was my thicket.

"Finally I caught you," Edward shouted as he dismounted. My suspicions were confirmed.

"How do you know that my beaters did not drive you to me for the kill?" I asked.

This was not the response Edward expected. Suspiciously, he circled me. I squared my shoulders and faced him, waiting for a response. None came. Continuing to play the boar, I pressed him again, "Have you come for Sir John's trout?" I said, pointing to the scattered basket.

He did not wish to duel with me over his purpose. "No."

"Then tell me why you are here." I said coyly.

Lying, he said, "I was out surveying Sir John's forests for today's hunt."

Not wishing to lose the advantage, I said, "Come now, Edward, you can do better than that. When do morning rides require a spare horse?"

"I came to see you waste your time fishing," he said, now clearly caught off guard.

He was now at bay and sought to free himself by one quick block. I thrust, pressing him. "That is better, Edward. So you have come to mock me?" I said. This remark hit home.

"No, no, no. I came just to speak with you," he said, chastened and retreating from my parry.

"I know you have no use for fishing," I said. "For me it makes more sense now than hunting." Referring to his *Master of Game*, I reminded him, "It keeps me busy when I am not hawking."

"I cannot sit and wait for fish to bite," he said apologetically.

His eyes shifted about, looking to escape this conversation. He was putting on a show of humility, buying time for the moment to catch me off guard. Now was the time to lay the groundwork for the boar to upend him. "Do you know why I study fishing?"

"No," he said, confused.

"Too easy an answer, Edward. Try again. Why do I study fishing?" I repeated without pity. "Tell me."

"I have no idea why you study fishing," he said belligerently. "You tell me, Juliana."

"Not right away," I said imperiously. "Once you admitted a high regard for my knowledge of hawking. Is that not true?" I asked.

"Yes," he said. "I have told you so already. Get on with it."

"In my own time," I said. "What will happen when I finish my

163

books on hawking or hunting?" I waited, "Edward, please answer my question."

"You are playing games with me," he shot back.

"Yes, I am playing games with you. If you do not like my games, then get on your horse and leave," I shot back immediately.

"All right, I will humor you. Your treatise will be praised. I am sure you have many useful things to say," he said.

"You are wrong there, Edward," I said. "First it will be compared to your book, *Master of Game*, then to de Foix's *Livre de la Chasse*, and finally to Emperor Frederick's *De Arte Venandi*. If my book is at odds with the opinions found in any of these honored texts, it will be disregarded. No matter the strength of my evidence and logic, my words will be disregarded because I am a woman.

"Let us start again. Why am I writing a book about fishing?" I asked.

"I have no idea." Edward said flatly and waited for my thrust.

"It is all there before you, Edward," I said, taunting him into a final rush. He did not take the bait. "I want to write a different kind of book. My books will be based on what I observe . . . what I see, feel, and touch," I said. "I do not wish to fill up the interstices between what the authorities have pronounced."

"Do what you like, but few will read your books if they do not square with our traditional authorities," Edward said.

"Now do you see why I will write about fishing?" I said.

Edward's eyes told me he did. But he stood silent.

"Yes, now you understand. I study fishing because there are no authorities."

Punching his chest with a finger for emphasis, I said, "I can write what I see, and no authority, no man, can contradict me. Each sentence I put down will be tested by what I have experienced and nothing else."

Angrily he batted my finger away. "I wish you luck, but I doubt if anyone will read your fishing book," Edward said with thick sarcasm in his voice.

"It does not matter. I will write it anyway," I said. "At Sopwell."

"You are determined to hide yourself away there," he said scornfully.

"Think what you like. I am not asking for your advice," I said. When Edward grew silent, I added, "I will not need your horse. I can make my own way back."

Edward finally said, "I have no doubt." With that, he mounted and rode off, his horses kicking up clods of meadow as he increased their pace.

PSALM 24, A short psalm, was coming to an end as we chanted.

Who shall as-cend the hill of the Lord?

And who shall stand in his ho-ly place?

He who has clean hands and a pure heart

EMBOLDENED BY MY confrontation with Edward, I rode my self-righteousness to my mother's chamber. She looked up as I entered and then drew back, sensing the heat of my rage.

"Should I be happy to see you?" she asked.

"It does not matter," I began. "I have come to give you the courtesy of hearing from my own lips what I just announced to Edward."

"And what would that be?" She asked, steeling herself for my words.

"I intend to live and work permanently at Sopwell," I said. "You will have Richard and Constance with you now. You do not need my help managing Bernersbury."

"I want to see you married," she replied firmly.

"There will be no marriage, Mother," I shot back. "There is no dowry and there will never be a dowry."

"We can only hope . . . and pray," she said quietly, almost to herself. "We could make a pilgrimage—"

"I pray, Mother, but I have lost hope," I said, cutting her short. "More importantly, there is no reason to hope."

"It is my dream to see you married," she pleaded.

"It is your dream but no longer mine. My own dreams do not include marriage," I said. "Do you hear me, Mother? I can live your dreams no longer. I have tried." Choking with anger, close to tears, I paused and chose my words carefully, "I have tried, but your dreams stifle me."

My mother sat silent, immobile.

"One more thing. This I did not tell Edward. Once Richard and Constance have a child, I will take my vows and profess myself a Benedictine."

"I beg you . . . ," she began.

"There is nothing more to discuss," I said, shouting. Afraid, I moved to leave, not to evade her arguments, for I had heard all of them before. No, I was livid with defiance. Looking back after I turned to go, I saw that my words, as a fleshing knife, separated her from her dreams for me as I had so often severed the hide off a deer preparing to butcher it. The room grew cold, and I saw her sitting at a great distance as a lonely star bravely marking its place in the vast firmament. I quickly left before pity softened my heart and made me take back my words.

With the afternoon before me, I did not trust myself in the hall where polite conversation was expected. Walking the battlements alone, I made a circuit of Bodiam's walls. From that vantage, the golden meadows of the Rother beckoned. Descending to the workshops, I retrieved my fishing equipment, searched a sodden pile of fodder for worms, and left again for the Rother's meadows unnoticed.

That afternoon I cast off forever my mother's hold on me, feeling more deeply than ever my own purpose. The wandering walk along the meadow cow path calmed me, and by the time I reached the Rother, I had forgiven Edward and my mother their plans. For I realized my anger began not in their plans but in my distrust of my own strength of purpose. And I further realized that my anger, my defiance, brought me new strength, and in that strength, I allowed myself to be drawn to Sopwell and my new life there. To celebrate this new clarity, I decided to angle for a difficult fish, a storied fish that earned its reputation by thwarting the Rother's anglers for years.

The legendary trout resided under a downstream bridge. The bridge, a massive stone arch, pinched the river. Consequently, the current slowed above the bridge before it rushed through the arch. In the slow section above, matted water plants choked the flow, but as the river raced under the bridge, the current picked up speed and gouged deep holes along its abutments. My ancient fish lived in one of these holes protected on one side by masonry and on the other by the depth of the water. It was well over my head.

Difficult fish are the angler's best master, and she must apprentice herself to them. Difficult fish have survived because they do not follow the rules. They have earned their individuality by staying alive. It is the angler who must change, keeping her mind open in the face of their refusals. The angler's mind seeks the predictable, and it is what she finds predictable that blinds her to the habits of difficult fish. So often what she thinks she sees as regular patterns are in fact temporary events. Finding true patterns in the habits of fish makes the angler more efficient, but each river, each pool in that river, and each and every fish breasting that river's currents will dispute her conclusions and resist conforming to her formulae. Instead they stamp their individuality on the flow. And on the angler's day. The difficult fish above all has learned this lesson practicing its individuality by refusing the angler's predictable offerings.

Hawthorn bushes protected the bank above the bridge. I sat behind one, first to observe and then to form a plan. No insects were evident, and the great fish did not show itself. Others had tried fishing from the bridge but were unsuccessful. The reason was clear. At this point in the summer, the drop from the bridge to the river was severe, and at this time of day, the sun backlit any angler, thus casting a moving shadow over the fish's hold. There was the possibility of cautiously following the bridge walls down to the edge of the river and then flicking a cast into the hole from above. This tactic presented two problems. The first was the appearance of the rod tip above the hole; the second was the splash caused by the bait and lead weight needed to carry the bait down into the deep hole before the driving current took it below. I was stymied.

By happenstance, wood chips littered the ground around my hawthorn bush. Wood cutters had taken out a nearby tree. The chips suggested a new tactic. I added several lengths of braided, three-hair leaders to my line, affixed a large hook, and crept closer down, to a bush that grew next to the river. Using the bush as a screen, I impaled a large, lively worm and twisted on several inches of lead strip above it. Then placing the worm and the lead weight on the top of a wood chip, I floated it like a small boat in the current. It slipped down the river gradually and then started to pick up speed. Paying out line so as not to disturb the chip, I let it travel down to the bridge, where I carefully tightened the line so that the worm and the lead dove to the river bottom without a ripple.

Blinded by the novelty of my ruse, I had not considered landing the fish. After a short interval, my line began moving to the side of the deep hole. Waiting a moment, I struck. The ponderous weight at the end of my line told me I had hooked the legendary trout. It came to the surface immediately and jumped once and then again. Framed by the stone arch, even in the shadows its arching body promised a great fish for my basket. In my joy, I ran to the edge of the bridge abutment to land the fish. What I had not foreseen was the rush of the trout into the rapids below the bridge. Ordinarily, by keeping a fish under her rod tip, the angler can draw a fighting fish to the surface and so drown it. But my extra leader lengths made this impossible. No matter how hard I tried to force my rod tip up, there was still slack in the line, which allowed the fish to run. With the great trout below me in the current, I was at a disadvantage, fighting both the fish and the river. I could not wade down under the bridge and fight the fish below because the water was too deep. Once the fish ran beyond the slack, my line parted where I had knotted the lowest leader.

That night at supper I told Constance and Richard the story. Even my mother was amused but remained silent.

SISTER CLARE PUSHES us to complete Psalm 24, and we follow so that we can return to work—the sewing we have put aside, the tilling of our kitchen garden, or the bread left to rise.

He will re-ceive bless-ings from the Lord,

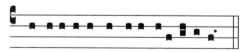

And vin-di-ca-tion from the God of his sal-va-tion.

I saw Edward one last time several years later at Sopwell. The prelude to his visit was a visit from Philippa, who appeared the week before I professed my vows. She brought the court's compliment on my hawking book. We met in Sopwell's visitor's room.

"The queen and her court think very highly of your work," she said.

"Thank the queen for her approval," I said. "Tell her I will keep her in my prayers this most blessed week."

"Blessed week?" Philippa asked. "You do have a glow about you."

"Within a week I will profess my vows as a Benedictine nun," I said.

Philippa rose and embraced me. Tears glittered in her eyes. "I am so happy for you," she said.

I hugged her and began to tear also. Finally, I stood back, my hands gripping her upper arms, and said, "Look at us. Two very silly girls."

Philippa laughed, "Juliana, you make me so happy." She grew thoughtful, "When I first met you, I disliked you. It was that awful Christmas at Conisbrough."

"I remember," I said. "A tragic Epiphany followed."

"Yes, Edward and his whims. I was jealous of you and talked myself into believing that you were just one more of them," she said.

"But I was," I replied brightly.

"No," she said. "His romantic feelings for you have remained constant. Perhaps the only constant in his life."

"It is not important now," I said.

Philippa's eyebrows went up. "Did you ever love him?" she asked.

"As a young girl, I was . . ." I searched for the right word for the court gossips, "infatuated with him," I said. "And I shall always be grateful to him for all he taught me."

Philippa sensed I was trying to lead her away from talking about Edward, but she would not let the subject go, "You must have hoped for more," she said hesitantly.

"I did," I said with a smile. "I did," I repeated, not wanting to pursue this conversation any farther, "And I found it. Friendship with his wife." Philippa was not fooled but sat back, studying me, waiting for more. I remained silent. Through reflection, I had herded my feelings for Edward into the cupboard where I stored my youthful memories. To rummage through that storehouse now would risk distracted prayer and more unruly daydreams. This was not the week for that.

"Enough of this," Philippa said, sensing that although there was more, I would not be talking about it.

"Yes. Let me show you the cloister garden," I said. We spent a very pleasant day together discussing books and promising poets. At one point she said, "Now that the court knows you will be here permanently, we will recommend Sopwell's school to our young women."

Philippa returned to Windsor with the news I was taking my vows as a Benedictine nun. I was not surprised when a few days later Edward appeared. I met with him also in the visitor's room. He was pacing furiously as I entered.

"You cannot go through with this," he pled. His desperation showed true enough, and it pained me. "Your vows are forever. You cannot undo them without the approval of the Pope."

"I am aware of that, Edward," I said quietly. "Please take a seat," I said, offering him a chair.

"No," he shouted. "You have no idea how frustrating you can be."

"My mother has told me that many times," I said, trying to make light of it and so soften his mood. He kept pacing, so I sat down.

"You are doing this to spite me," he said. "You will come to regret it."

"No, Edward, whatever my feelings for you may be, I need to set a course for my future," I said, moved by his anguish. "This is my next logical step."

"You keep talking about your future. Stop being so narrow-minded!" he shouted. "There is no future for you here. You are hiding away from the world . . . and from me."

Stung, I said, "I am not hiding from you."

Edward growled, "You have forced me to pursue you. I am the Duke of York. The king values my counsel." Then, shaking with emotion, he spat out, "You are humiliating me."

Ignoring the accusation, I said, "You are an important man, Edward. You will always be an important man regardless of my actions. The fact is there is no future for us."

"Stop thinking about the future!" He shouted, "There is the now." And then he begged, "Come to court. We can make a life of many nows."

"What exactly are you proposing?" I asked.

"Come to court, and we shall find out . . . together," he implored.

"You and I are so different," I said, defeated, and before I realized it, I was weeping. Gathering myself, I said stoically, "Edward, you flatter me by coming here today, but there is too great a chasm between us. There always will be. No matter my feelings for you, no matter the romantic feelings we may have for each other, I will never trust being swept up in the now."

"Do you not trust me?" he cried.

Hesitating, I felt my tears drying, "I do not trust you." I then added with conviction, "I will never join you at court."

"You cannot hide away here for long. You will tire of it. You can read through the abbey library just so many times, and once your ideas are exhausted, you will grow bored with writing," he said, adding triumphantly, "And when you come out of hiding, I will be waiting for you."

"I may become bored with writing, but that is why I am taking my vows," I replied.

"You are taking your vows because you are a coward. You cannot face the world," he said angrily.

"Edward, you have had your say," I replied. "Now I will have mine. Let me tell you what it is really like living here."

"I did not ride for a day to hear about the beauty of the countryside and the sweet pleasures of chant. I have those every day at Windsor," he said sarcastically.

"Edward, we once measured ourselves by our prey," I said. "We praised each other for thrusting more forcefully than the scrambling boar or for being more agile than the lunging hart." I paused.

"Is that all you have to say?" he shot back.

"I am just making sure you are with me when I get to the point," I said.

"Please," Edward said with disgust.

"You see here a much regulated community. Tomorrow, if all is well, will be like today," I started. "But our need for order does not come from cowardice. It is not some substitute for a worthy cause. It is born of discipline."

Then I glared at him and said, "Our orderly routine is the regulation of a military encampment." And then I added unkindly, "You feel tranquility once through our gates, but you have been fooled. We confront the real world here—the ugly, obdurate world. It is the world that Windsor shrinks from facing."

Then I stood up and said, "And this is my point, Edward. Every day we confront want and ignorance and too often, death."

"So what?" he said, rearing back. "Those are everywhere, and they will be everywhere as long as we live."

"I do not accept that," I said with feeling. "Edward, you once said you measured yourself by your enemies. The greater the enemy, the greater your own stature. When we hunted together, these were the wild animals of the forest. In truth, not much in the end to measure ourselves by. I have passed beyond wild animals and am now struggling with greater adversaries.

"My enemies are want and ignorance," I said sternly. "Yes, they are pervasive, but I measure myself by my victories over them." I fixed Edward and whispered angrily, "I contend daily with death. Lengthening a life, bringing comfort to the dying, these are' my triumphs now. When allaying the pain of the dying, for a brief moment, I have surpassed death. When I teach a child to read, I have surpassed ignorance. And when I hand out food and clothing at our gate to the needy, I have overcome, however briefly, want."

"You will tire of it," Edward said soberly. By now he had stopped pacing and faced me.

"You are right," I said triumphantly. "That is why I am taking my vows next week," I replied. "I have no doubt I will falter. Every day I see so many faces bearing the scars of our greed and superstition. Famished children, the leper, the confused illiterate, the vacant eyes of starving mothers, the hardworking debtor incarcerated for his bad luck, the drunk. Doubtless, I will lose heart from time to time. But it is then I will remind myself that I have sworn a vow to continue the struggle against my enemies here at Sopwell."

I felt my tears starting again. "And after reminding myself of my vow, I will take up the fight once again. In the end I will measure myself by my conduct in the face of death." My voice was rising.

"Do you hear me, Edward?" I shouted. "Do you hear me?"

"Yes," Edward said reluctantly. He swayed and went silent.

My last words to him were, "I will contend to the end. That is my vow."

He stared at me and, before turning to go, said, "I will be waiting for you. I will always be waiting for you."

There was nothing more to be said. Recalling the pleasant day with Philippa, I walked the cloister. With every step, I thought of Edward's horse stepping back to London, putting with each step greater and greater distance between us. It brought, as it brought before, a great longing, but luckily today, my passion for Edward had turned to anger, an easier emotion to shelve. I never saw him again. He bravely died holding Henry's center at Agincourt.

SISTER CLARE PUSHES us to complete Psalm 24.

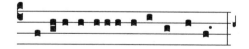

Such is the gen-er-a-tion of those who seek him,

Who seek the face of God.

How the abbey's attitude toward nuns has changed. Lately I have been thinking of St. Albans's anchorite women. They were the first "generation" of women to "seek the face of God." Just after the turn of the millennium, a time of great upheaval, anchorite women took up a precarious, solitary, and prayerful residence near St. Alban's shrine. They won favor and protection from St. Albans's Norman abbots. This was before Sopwell. Shambling wood huts at crossroads nearby the abbey marked their dwellings. Trust in their neighbors won them bread and gruel. And they stayed apart from everyone to pray and meditate, true contemplatives. Truly alone. Truly silent.

They lived to worship all day and every day. They made no exceptions. Their work was their prayer, and their prayer was their work. Embracing a single purpose, they achieved a total purity of life. If no one gave them food as alms, they did not eat. They prayed through their hunger. And when hunger pangs woke them from their sleep, they prayed all the harder until exhaustion and weakness brought sleep.

Their journey to St. Albans was not mine. I was a hunter, a falconer, and an angler, and I became a writer in Sopwell's sheltered quiet. Certainly I pray, certainly I worship as the anchorites did. But I have embraced complexity, and my triumph is to balance the complexity of my day. Working, studying, praying, eating, sleeping . . . and writing in balance.

My life is coming to a climax. The review of my youth is finished. I saw myself once again pursuing hart through thick forests; I saw myself lifting my gauntlet to throw a hawk into flight; I saw myself fighting a lumbering barbel. I have seen my past. Yes, and I saw myself as the dutiful, sometimes rebellious daughter helping to manage my mother's manor. My memories of Isabel, Constance, and my Uncle William and his daughters will not return to invade my idle moments with such force again.

No more reveries, no more dreams. I vaguely sense a future where I need scramble for community and the basics of life. These losses the anchorite women did not fear, and their courage sustains me. I do not yet see the full shape of my future, but I will stride the path ahead, not as leading to doom but as another turn in the river. I anticipate the surprise of the next bend.

I am looking forward to Lady Elizabeth's visit. She is bringing her three children, Margaret, John, and Anne, my family's next generation. It is the children I wish to see, for I will be looking into their faces for incarnate memories of my family and even myself, as we were so long ago. And I shall look even deeper into their eyes. For there I seek to find that vision of the future that only children have in full measure. An ecstatic expectation of the next day.

chapter seven

VESPERS

Feast of the Transfiguration
6:00 p.m.
August 6, 1477

t was lady Elizabeth's last evening at Sopwell, and she with her children took their places in chapel to celebrate Vespers. Lady Elizabeth, her elder daughter, Margaret, and younger daughter, Anne, were dressed in hooded traveling cloaks and short gowns, all the cheerful blue of the Borage flower. John wore hose under a long tunic covered by a sturdy surcote, a study in forest green and gold.

Each held Psalters in their hands, poised to begin. As is the habit with so many of my family and kinsmen, they stood intently perched, with flicking, penetrating eyes scanning all, especially the corners and doorways of the chapel. They took on the aspect of falcons on their blocks at the moment their hoods are removed and jesses loosed. They live in anticipation of movement, the slightest flutter, the vaguest blur.

SISTER CLARE ANNOUNCES the antiphon for the feast of the Transfiguration. Tonight Elizabeth, her children, and Sopwell repeat it.

Je-sus did take Pe-ter, James, and John his broth-er, and brought

them up on-to an high moun-tain a-part and was trans-figured be-fore them.

Today we visited the Westby farm. Lady Elizabeth's party appeared at Sopwell's gate at dawn, all mounted. She was accompanied by her children, maidservants, and a groom who led a horse for me—a young energetic mare.

The inspection held a surprise. Drawing into the close, we joined a great bustle. Will rushed to take the reins of our horses, and behind him was Laurentio, who bowed gracefully to Lady Elizabeth and then helped me dismount, kissing my hand.

The close was crowded with oxcarts and workmen furiously bagging piles of wool.

"It is as you say. Fine Chiltern Rylands," Laurentio chattered, waving toward the Westby field where dozens upon dozens of shorn sheep now grazed.

Lady Elizabeth looked over to me. I smiled hesitantly and said, "This is Laurentio, a Florentine wool buyer."

Laurentio bowed again, saying, "My Lady." Then turning to the children, he bowed again and again, saying, "My young Lord. My young Ladies."

Turning to me, Laurentio said, "The shearing, sorting, and weighing is done. Now we bag and load the wool. Many clove." Offering me a clinking leather bag, he said, "You are as good as your word. And I also. One hundred pounds in gold coin for you."

"Thank you. I never doubted your word," I said.

Elizabeth said, "Dame Juliana, I understood that part of your money problem was that you were forbidden to sell off your animals or their wool to raise cash."

"Not quite. The abbey directed me not to sell anything off Sopwell land," I replied, emphasizing the "off." "This is not Sopwell land as we stand here today. It is mine."

"So you did not disobey the abbey," she said in admiration.

"No. Prior Thomas's directions have been observed to the letter," I said firmly.

Will interrupted, asking whether Lady Elizabeth and the children wanted a tour of the croft. Pushing through the milling sheep, Will led Lady Elizabeth's horse so that she might inspect the fields. At one point, she dismounted, searching the ground with her eyes and scuffing the earth as she went. Once, she dug the toe of her linen shoe into the ground where water from a recent rain had settled and dried. When she withdrew it, wet clay clung to the sole, which she dislodged with a stamp of her foot. It fell off in a ball. Stooping, she retrieved the lump, kneaded it in her gloved fingers, and then sniffed it before discarding it.

Remounting, Lady Elizabeth led us back to the busy croft close. After briefly inspecting the woodshop, she fixed her attention on the Marshes' small foundry. At length, she questioned Will and his son, Edward, about its workings. Will demonstrated the stages for fashioning and hardening the iron hinges, corners, and locks needed for his wood chests. When Will finished, Edward offered completed items for our inspection. Carefully, Lady Elizabeth turned these over in her hand. She was clearly impressed with Will's skill and praised his work.

The children followed their mother about with upturned faces full of curiosity. They hung on her every question and Will's every reply, looking first to her and then to him. They were permitted to tentatively finger the finished steel products as Elizabeth pointed out to them their light weight, graceful lines, and strength. Then she directed they return them to Will with a thank you.

Turning to me, Elizabeth said, "I am done, Cousin."

Hurrying to leave, I reminded Laurentio to return next year and received his "Certamente" in reply. And after placing two pounds into Will's hand, I said, "This should get you through the winter and help with any construction costs."

"You are too generous, Mother," Will said, showing the coins to his wife, Mary.

Lady Elizabeth was thoughtful on our way back to Sopwell. But at the gate, she said lightheartedly, "Let us have a picnic in Sopwell's meadow." I agreed, and she directed her maidservants to the kitchen. Then I went to the workroom, where I had stored my three gifts for Elizabeth's children.

SISTER CLARE DRAWS my mind back to chapel with the opening verses of Psalm 111, and we all chant:

Great are the works of the Lord,

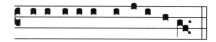

Stud-ied by all who take plea-sure in them.

In Sopwell's meadow, the maidservants rolled out a bright blue carpet for us. Lady Elizabeth and I sat next to each other, facing down the slope toward the Ver, watching the children as they explored the edges of our ponds. Jokingly, Elizabeth confided, "It would ruin a perfect day if one of them drowned."

I laughed but added, "It would take a very talented child to drown in our ponds. They are so shallow."

"I am afraid John could find a way. Unlike my girls, he is not bothered by mud and wet clothes."

"I see so much of my brother, Richard, in him," I said.

"Yes, unlike my daughters, who are fair, taking after me and my family, John has the dark hair and green eyes of your family."

"And his curiosity. His grandmother, Lady Margaret, would be so proud of him," I said, calling up the picture of Richard's daughter, now dead. She was so like me, short in stature, lithe, and dark with mischievous green eyes and black hair.

Motioning to her maidservants to stand at a distance, Elizabeth said, "Aunt Juliana, I want my daughters to attend school here. Let me propose an arrangement."

"Of course," I replied.

"We have paid heavy taxes on John's taking of Bernersbury as well as other taxes the Crown levied to fund its campaigns in the north. We have little coin. I hope you understand," she said apologetically.

"I do understand. That is why I have been wrestling with the terms for accepting the Westby property," I said. "I am fully aware of your problem."

"Do not misread me. I am not proposing you take my daughters for free or even at a reduced tuition. As part of our arrangement, there are things which my husband can do for Sopwell," she said.

"You would do these things in exchange for your daughters' education?" I asked hopefully.

"Yes," she said. Motioning to her closest maidservant to attend her, Elizabeth said, "The children are returning from the ponds. Please occupy them for a few more minutes. Take them for a walk to the deer park," she said, gesturing toward nearby Eywood.

"You probably noticed the virgate set aside for crops includes substantial clay loam deposits," she said.

"Yes. Very poor cropland," I replied.

"This property is not one of Westby's best. The clay loam reduces its income substantially. If it were not for the intelligence of the tenants, it might even be regarded as wasteland."

"I understand. The Marsh family exhibits intelligence in all their undertakings," I said. "They are probably the bequest's greatest resource."

"That was my conclusion, and so I propose we build an enterprise based on them and the good quality clay loam found there," Elizabeth said.

"Is not the clay a hindrance?" I asked, puzzled.

"Aunt Juliana, these days our most profitable enterprises pursue trade with the continent. English pewter is very highly valued there. I believe the Westby farm could turn out pewter products, which will do very well overseas. Clay loam is essential for producing pewter products."

I was taken aback. "How can that be?"

Elizabeth said, "Pewter's attractiveness is that it can be easily worked into many different products—plates, tankards, and so on. The first step in that process is to pour molten pewter into clay loam forms shaped to the product desired. The clay on the Westby farm is perfect for such molds."

"You will help Sopwell start a pewter business in exchange for the education of your daughters?"

"Yes. And I will do better. The clay loam not only is necessary for manufacturing pewter, but it also reduces the value of the Westby property as cropland," she said excitedly. "My husband will have our notaries petition the Crown to reassess the value of the Westby property. As you know, Lord Henry, the older brother of Humphrey's father, the First Baron Berners, is Royal Treasurer. He never forgot your courage after his younger brother was captured during the Second Battle of St. Albans. You alone interceded immediately with Queen Margaret to save Baron Berners's life." She paused. "Margaret made you pay for your audacity by sacking Sopwell."

"I have never asked for any consideration," I said.

"Yes, but you are due it."

"I do not wish to seem ungrateful with this question. But pewter is a mix of lead and tin, expensive to obtain," I said.

Excitedly, Elizabeth turned to face me. "But worth the price. There is a new type of English pewter. It is a secret mixture of lead, tin, and brass. Our new English pewter is stronger and has a lustrous color. It sells well on the continent, and they have not yet discovered our secret."

The children's voices carried on the breeze. They were returning from Eywood. Elizabeth and I smiled at each other. "We will be happy to have your daughters here," I said with a great aunt's pride.

AS WE APPROACH the last verses of Psalm 111, I hear the high voices of Lady Elizabeth's children following each word in their Psalters. With them we sing,

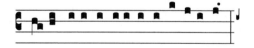

The fear of the Lord is the be-gin-ning of wis-dom;

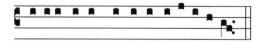

A good un-der-stand-ing have all those who prac-tice it.

The cold partridge and honey cakes filled us up as the ale loosened our tongues. The children filled all our pauses with questions. They expected thoughtful answers. It was tiring.

As we were finishing our meal, I brought out my three gifts. To Margaret and Anne, I gave my treatises on hunting and hawking.

Without a word, they ran their fingers along the binding and carefully turned the pages.

"Your mother has decided to send you both here for school. These books will be your first textbooks. We shall study them all next year."

Margaret asked, "Do you think I can become a great huntress like you?"

"Of course. When you come to Sopwell, I can help you learn the old way of hunting. Sister Carol and Sister Joan also were raised as hunters before professing their vows, and they are thoroughly familiar with my treatises."

"How did you learn to hunt?" she asked.

"I had a great teacher, Edward, Duke of York, who taught me and my brother, Richard, to hunt. He pushed us to risk ourselves, running dangerous game to ground and then dispatching them with pike and sword."

Anne interrupted, asking, "We will hunt from horseback?"

"Yes," I said.

"Where will we find our hawks?" she asked excitedly.

"In the early spring we will hunt for peregrine eyas," I said.

Turning then to John, I said, "I have not forgotten you. I have for you my book on heraldry."

"Dame Juliana—" John began.

"Now, John, if you call me Dame Juliana, I will need to address you as Baron John. I suggest you call me Auntie or Mother," I said gently. He ripped off the ribbons. He was much struck with the colored illustrations and identified without prompting many of the coats of arms found there.

"Thank you, Auntie," he said. Lady Elizabeth gave me a quick glance, surprised by his show of manners. I expected no less from her children.

After leafing through the book, he came to the last page and looked up to me, very puzzled. "Auntie, you have not signed your book."

"That is true, John. A long time ago I made a decision not to sign my writings."

Margaret and Anne then leafed to the back of their books and, finding no signature there, looked up at me quizzically.

"Why would you make such a decision?" Margaret asked.

"Margaret, as you know, I am a follower of St. Benedict," I replied. "I strive every day to achieve humility, as he has urged us. I stopped signing my manuscripts in order not to draw attention to myself."

"Is humility that important?" John asked.

"It is the heart of living together amicably," I said.

"If we ask you to sign your gifts, will you?" Margaret asked.

"Of course. It will be another gift for you," I said, flattered by the children's request.

"But Auntie Juliana, why would you write your books if you do not want anyone to know you wrote them?" John asked.

"John, when our people first came to this country with William, our families spoke French. These days English has now taken hold among us. King Henry V even made it fashionable at court."

"We still speak French among ourselves, Auntie Juliana," John said.

"I know, John. I even speak it here with my sisters. But future generations will not remember it. I see it as my work to preserve our French literature in English. My humble efforts have been few, dealing mainly with sport, as you see," I said, pointing to their manuscripts.

"Is it that important, Aunt Juliana?" Margaret asked.

"Yes. It is part of the heritage of this land that will be lost except for the few who speak French and Latin, a few nobles and their clerks. When we lose our heritage, we will become confused as to who we are."

"So you believe people like us should make it their work to translate our French stories into English," John said.

"Yes, John," I replied.

"What French works would you translate if you had time?" Margaret asked.

"I have not thought deeply about this question, but I believe Froissart's *Chroniques* and any book lauding the noble ideal of courtesy would make a valuable contribution. *The Boke Huon de Bordeuxe* would be another good book to translate. You will have no problem finding a printer to publish it," I said.

in memory of Sister Margery and as a comfort to us all, Sister Clare substituted Psalm 23 for the last Psalm of Vespers. We chant resolutely,

The Lord is my shep-herd,

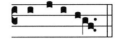

I shall not want.

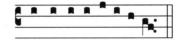

He makes me lie down in green pas-tures.

He leads me be-side still wa-ter.

He re-stores my soul.

I, as so many other anglers, have been led beside still waters. One day the angler will walk along a nearby river once too often. Forever after, when bound indoors by January's snows, her river will remind her of warmer, greener days. During a mild spring, thoughts of dancing olive caddis will distract her. During late summer, she will be suddenly arrested by visions of grasshoppers falling into its slow, placid pools. In all seasons, she will fall asleep imagining the slashing rises of its trout, the subtle nibbles of its bream, and the charges of its pike.

Love has swallowed her up. During her spare moments, she will plan trysts with her river. She will live for the moment when she is physically and absolutely reunited with it . . . when she sits on its banks and views its sinuous form stretched out beside her. On chill, overcast days, her desire will become unbearable. She will yearn for the moment when she can step into its riffles and be swept up passionately in her river's swirling caresses.

The angler's river reveals many secrets to her. But the angler soon discovers that her river discloses them piecemeal. So it has been with me and the Ver. Day by day, season by season, I docilely take in the short lessons that the Ver chooses to teach. The angler learns to live with the fact that she will never fully understand her love. And that she will never be a better angler than the one her river allows her to be. My *Treatyse* is simply a compendium of the many brief lessons the Ver taught me.

But make no mistake, these lessons are not just about hooks and baits and dubbed flies. Each time I am on her banks, the Ver teaches me hope. Tomorrow's time sits at my cell's threshold, whispering to me as I go forth that today's deeds shape our future. With its endlessly sounding play of water, the Ver forever calls on me to stir the stagnant pools of hope. Few casts bring fish. But I cling to the memories of those few casts that do. As I cling to a few memories of trust rewarded. As I cling to a few memories of transfiguring love.

While Sopwell sharpened my taste for reflection, the Ver taught me the engine of reflection, its ebb and flow. The contemplative drinks and drinks at life's rivulets for days, even years, without enlightenment until that unexpected moment when the vagaries of the spirit move and show us our meaning, when they show us the face, the countenance of God. As a sudden blow, enlightenment transforms our experiences, revealing the pulsing golden thread of meaning that enlivens us and all we perceive.

Angling is built on a life of such realizations. Day upon day, the angler experiences events opaque to her mind. These experiences sit within the angler's memory and nag her. They cry for significance. But neither the angler nor the contemplative can force the rhythmic ebb and flow of perception and meaning. Reflection is a will-o'-the-wisp. The angler must wait. The contemplative must wait. She must be patient, for she cannot call up the cresting torrent. She cannot name the day or the hour when all is laid bare, transfigured into her new truth, her new meaning. So she waits for the moment of enlightenment.

And while waiting, all—all anglers and all contemplatives—

cultivate the sense of anticipation that is hope. And so, each day, they remain fully attentive to what they see and what they hear, whether it be on the river or at their studies or in chapel. They live day to day, hour to hour, feeding their reflection and patiently awaiting the hour of abandon, the moment of transfiguration.

WE ALL CONTINUE chanting Psalm 23.

Thou pre-par-ed a ta-ble be-fore me in the pres-ence of my en-e-mies;

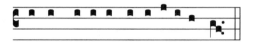

You anoint-ed my head with oil, my cup over-flows.

Sopwell is dedicated to Mary, the mother of Jesus. We invoke her protection daily at Mass and recall her name hourly when we recite the Hail Mary. Her name comes to my lips scores of times daily. But my feelings for Mary were, from the beginning, tepid. For me she was no more than a distant, passive thought, a name easy to ignore. I earnestly sought to fan the slightest spark of warmth, but no matter how hard I fanned, my feelings were as damp wood, and the spark died.

There were days I became frantic with my lack of feeling for Sopwell's patroness. But this all changed one day. After Edward, after my waiting years at Bernersbury, and after my firm decision to live out the rest of my life at Sopwell, by degrees my life became conformed to the eternal cycles. Day by day, my hours were numbered by St. Benedict's hours of prayer. Month by month, my days were marked by the feast days of the Church. Year by year, my seasons were marked by nature's changes. One flowed into the next. When the dreams of Edward ended, I had new dreams, but these were of fish, bees, and tighter stitches. Visits from Eleanore, Catherine, and, of course, Philippa became less and less frequent as their families grew. And I, I clung to the hours. I had gained equilibrium.

One day, cleaning out hives, I was informed that a visitor was waiting for me in the parlor. Taking off my work clothes and boots,

I hurried to the front gate of the convent running through a list of likely guests. Eleanore, Catherine, Philippa, Richard . . . My list was not long enough. It was my mother, one name I left off. She rose to meet me. Flustered, I bowed slightly, lowering my eyes. My humble posture, now reflex to me, shocked her, but she did not remark on it. Instead she gathered my hands in hers and kissed me.

Motioning me to sit, my mother began to relate, without prompting, the family news. She went on familiarly as if following up on a conversation interrupted yesterday. Old suspicions put me on my guard. But I listened to her rambling monologue, laughing with her when she laughed and posing questions when she lost the thread.

Finally, I could stand it no longer and asked, as gently as my impatience allowed, "Can I help you, Mother?"

She looked at me with a smile playing on her lips. "No," she said without elaboration.

I let her cryptic answer pass. Instead, I weighed her smile. "Will you be staying long?" I asked.

"I would like to," she said.

"Our guest rooms are not up to the manor's," I replied, mystified. Then on a lighter note, I asked, "You're not here to join the convent, are you?"

She laughed and said, "No. I am here to visit my beautiful daughter." Then she choked out, "I have missed her face and her troublesome energy."

I did not know what to say. The silence lengthened. Finally I mustered, "I am very happy to see you, Mother."

She dabbed her eyes. "Prioress Letitia promised me a tour. Would you care to join us?"

"I would like that, if Dame Letitia approves."

She stayed for a week. We took walks together during my free time and supped together in the guest dining room with Prioress Letitia. The rest of the day she spent by herself. One day she rode to the Town of St. Albans and explored its shops. Another day she visited the abbey church to view St. Alban's reliquary. Fashioned in the twelfth century by the goldsmith Dom Anketil from gold, silver, and jewels, it was surmounted with a silver eagle and a gold canopy. She was impressed.

Long after she left, I realized the meaning of her visit. There was no talk of my father, nor Sir Roger, nor Edward, nor kings and court intrigue. There were no apologies for her absence from my childhood. There was no talk of marriage. There was no talk of my books. Instead, our conversations sounded a single theme. We talked of the years before my father's death. She was starting over with me. She was picking up the loose yarn of our lives, which had unraveled with my father's execution. She was trying to knit us back together again by recalling those first years at Bernersbury. She had a deeper purpose, I was sure, but I could not then divine it. That came much later.

When she rode out from Sopwell, a gray lady on a gray horse, I felt her presence as I never felt it before. The impasse was crumbling. What events prompted her to visit Sopwell I will never know. But from that day on, I began to feel a new current in my life. Its gentle flow even warmed my prayers naming Mary and promised glowing days ahead.

My mother's visits continued. Without notice, she would appear and stay for a week. Regularly unexpected. One year she visited me six times. Her routine varied little. One trip to St. Albans's shops; one trip to the abbey church. The remainder of the time she stayed at Sopwell in the guest house. She never complained of her room and her meals even though I knew they were not to her liking.

Once I apologized for the brief time we were able to spend together.

She replied, "You are following the rules of the convent. It is not your choice. I do understand convents and the way they are run."

"But I am afraid your days will be empty," I said.

Her response puzzled me. "It is just good to be near you."

"I do not understand," I said.

"Being . . . near is all I ask," she said. "Being near." Her eyes spoke of an inner frustration. She set her lips as though to speak, but no words came. She struggled with herself and then signaled defeat with a vague wave of a hand. She never returned to the subject.

I turned her words over and over again. I made no headway until I realized that it was not her words that I should be exploring. It was the pause in her words. Her pause was a silence. Of silence I believed I knew much. Holy Benedict favored it. After Compline, Sopwell observed the Great Silence. It was then the silence of night invaded our cloister, and on our beds we retreated within ourselves, where we picked over the day, repeated prayers, or just drifted in our own great darkness. For certain, there were times during the day where we spoke, but always for a purpose. We never conversed to pass time. Silence was our way of life. We had words, but we chose not to use them.

But my mother's silence meant something else. She could not find the words. It was then I came to realize that her silence was born of awe. Something overwhelmed her and silenced her. Benedict writes of humbling silence born in the fear of God. Quoting Psalm 37, he reminds us that being in God's presence "is all my desire." This is the silence where expression fails. Unlike Benedict's awe, however, my mother's awe was not reserved just for her Creator.

All my mother wanted was to be with me. Being near me filled her days. She was never bored at Sopwell knowing I was nearby. She did not need to talk to me, nor did she need to touch me. Her mind was filled with me being nearby. It was enough for her. And so, she continued to visit, regularly unexpected. She continued to talk about our days at Bernersbury and about her grandchild, Margaret. She talked to me of plants and honey. And she talked to me of my favorite books. It was all so forgettable.

The slight warming current she brought on her first visit began to swell in me. It filled me up imperceptibly as the slow lowering of water gates fill up a lock. Before I knew it, I was drowning in it.

She had converted me. The awe of being . . . with her, of being . . . with my sisters at Sopwell, of being . . . close to the waters of the Ver . . . struck me dumb. I no longer have the words to explain my existence even to myself. Silence has welled up in me, and the prospect of my life extends out infinitely to a silent horizon. I am no longer a professional at silence. I have become a groping amateur, incapable of the simplest speech.

WE ARE NEARING the end of Vespers. I glance at the children and see that they are beginning to flag. I turn and point at them just as we begin the Magnificat, Mary's hymn. They come to attention while Lady Elizabeth questions me with her eyes. "Am I unhappy with them?" I smile a "no" to her. Then, having their attention, I wave my arms to lead them in song. They chuckle, as my sisters chuckle, and with mirth we sing joyfully and wholeheartedly the song of Mary, the song of my mother, and now my song.

My soul mag-ni-fies the Lord,

and my spir-it re-joices in God my Sav-iour,

For he has re-gard-ed the low es-tate of his hand-maid-en.

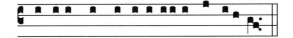

For be-hold, hence-forth all gen-er-a-tions will call me blessed;

For he has done great things for me,

and ho-ly is his name.

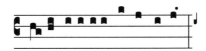

And his mer-cy is on those that fear him

from gen-er-a-tion to gen-er-a-tion.

We tumbled out of chapel and crossed the cloister, its four walls echoing with our laughter. We are looking forward to Sister Anicia's gallantyne chicken and honied tench. The reading tonight is from St. Bede. In it he describes the early days of Britain, its wild tribes and wilderness forests. Adventure enough for any child's dreams.

chapter eight

compline

The Feast of St. Michael the Archangel
7:30 p.m.
September 29, 1477

Yesterday evening, abbot Wallingford and his brother returned early from their annual vacation at Redburn. No need to speculate on the cause of their early return, for next morning Prior Thomas was at Sopwell's gate demanding I attend him.

"This is the day the abbey takes over management of Sopwell," he said.

Waving the reminder he scratched months earlier, I said, "We have until five o'clock to pay your fee."

"If that is what it says, I stand behind it, but why drag this unpleasantness out?" he said condescendingly. "The marshals will be here any minute to take possession of the convent and inventory its contents. I assume you directed the community to find a new home."

"No," I said.

"No?" he shouted, "Your obstinacy will be punished."

"No," I said agreeably, "We have your money. You must acknowledge its payment before I hand you the coin."

"Let me see your coin before I set my seal," he said, jumping down from his horse, his black robe whipping about him.

From my right hand I dropped gold coin after gold coin clinking into my left palm. "By my count, a hundred pounds as requested," I said evenly. "Do you want me to go through them again? You seemed fascinated with the way they flashed in the morning sun."

He advanced on me. I put the coins behind my back.

"Set your seal here," I said, offering his written reminder. "Then I can balance my books."

Sullenly he pulled ink, pen, and seal from his saddlebag. As he handed the reminder back to me fully acknowledged, I handed him the coins.

"Thank you," I said. "I believe that is all the business we have together today."

"There is the matter of the Westby farm," he said angrily, hurling the words at me.

"That will be our business tomorrow," I said.

"You will attend our parliament tomorrow with the documents of title," he threatened, "or there will be repercussions."

"I will be there with our documents. Now I have a pressing errand that cannot be put off without inconveniencing others."

I did not tell him the purpose of my errand, which was to deliver three documents to the Marsh family: a copy of the deed naming Sopwell and Will Marsh joint tenants of the Westby bequest, a copy of the papers forming our company to manufacture pewter products, and a copy of the formula for English pewter. The papers were Will's defense should the abbey challenge his partnership rights.

At that moment, I stood at Sopwell's gate as on the fault line between my past and my future. I saw myself as a child hanging on a river's ledge, judging when to slip over, to dive into the plunge pool waiting below. My life at Sopwell stood balanced against Wallingford's order to take the property as Westby left it. I chose not to follow his order, and with the child, I slipped over the ledge trusting myself to the churning currents beneath me.

For days now, I have asked myself, "What will be the sum of myself should I die today?" Or to put it another way, after totaling the additions and subtractions, I have asked myself, "What will be my final tally?" I have always taken pride in being clear sighted, in facing the hard facts. Once my hard facts led me to Sopwell. Now they were leading me away. Monasticism as we knew it at St. Albans was dying. The tide was going out on our world. With its ebb not far off, the tidal flats of our world will reveal the detritus of empty castles and ruined monasteries. Of this I have no doubt.

So all came down to this moment. I would trust myself to the churning currents of the world beyond Sopwell. For I am . . . I am . . . the woman who hears the gears of reflection turning within at every moment. That is who I am. That is my final sum. I am the woman who reflects on all. Not just overpowering fact, but also the humble. Nothing is so small that I will not reflect on it. I contemplate the bent beggar, the wren, and the caddis fly too small for my hooks.

Once Wallingford read the title documents, I would deliver tomorrow, the abbot would remove me. One more dotty old nun too confused to do what she was told.

And so I need let Sopwell go. And as with the diving child, I know that once I am immersed in the churning water of the plunge pool, there will be the struggle to right myself and swim upward toward the light. That struggle will bring one last question. Will I breathe again? Whether I do or not, I trust that I shall surface in the light.

Pilgrims crowded the road to London. I fell in with a family returning home after two days at St. Alban's shrine. Our conversation was of weather, vestments, and shops. Before long we came abreast of the road to the Marsh croft, and I turned off, leaving them with my blessing.

The yard of the croft was a shambles. Will had torn the foundry apart and was moving a wall of his workshop. "They were too small," he explained. "I need to enlarge the furnace and build storage space for the molds."

As always, the Marshes were good hosts. Their son, Edward, was in London consulting his uncle, but Will and Mary received me warmly. Their plans were well thought out, and I was as enthusiastic as they about our eventual success. When I withdrew from my satchel the copyhold document as well as the papers inaugurating our business together, they could barely contain their joy. Will ran his fingers respectfully over the sheaves of parchment and handed them reverently to Mary for her inspection. Overjoyed, Mary asked, "Where shall we keep them? The mice would love to line their nests with these."

Will quickly replied, "I will make an iron box. For the time being we can store them in one of our tight wood chests."

Throughout the afternoon, unease crept over me. At first I could not identify its genesis. Finally, over a cup of the Marshes' delicious ale, I realized that I had been avoiding my immediate problem, settling on the amount of wood for Sopwell's winter. I needed to make the trip to the woodlot. Sensing my unease, Mary inquired if I "had other errands."

"Yes, Mary," I said. "I cannot delay any longer dealing with Sopwell's wood shortage. Our need for wood, however, will be a distraction from readying the foundry."

Will immediately interjected, "No need to worry. The extra work this year is to be expected. The foundry will be in operation the day after the Feast of the Epiphany. I have scheduled extra help then."

"But how will you pay for it all, Will?" I asked, concerned.

"The two pounds will cover all our expenses."

Appreciatively, I replied, "Will, I have no doubt you will make a success of this enterprise."

Mary looked at Will and then back to me, "You promised to visit the woodlot last time you were here. It will do you good. Sometimes there are fish in the spring pond."

I turned to stare in the direction of the woodlot. Clouds had been building throughout the afternoon, the wind had slackened, and the air grown thick. It was a dark, lowering sky and promised an early evening. "Well I had better take a look. A fish or two is all we need." I rose to leave.

"Good luck, Dame Juliana, and thank you," Mary said as she busied herself clearing the table.

Will offered to guide me, but I told him, "No, just point out the path." He led me past the woodshop and gestured to an opening that disappeared quickly into fenland.

Striding confidently, I set off. His last words were, "We will keep watch for your return." His concern was evident.

The wooded virgate rested on a spur of land more than a quarter mile from the Marsh croft. The fens surrounding it extended for miles south and east. The woodlot was directly accessible by Will's well-worn path, more a narrow road scraped smooth by Will's oxen dragging tree trunks and branch bundles. It was easy walking, but the featureless horizon, scored here and there with shallow, wandering waterways, was forbidding.

As evening approached, the low, gray clouds darkened further. I increased my pace while distant bells from a nearby parish church announced Compline. Alone, I began singing the hour quietly,

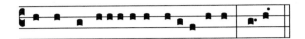

Please Lord grants us a qui-et night and a per-fect end. Amen.

September's frosts had wilted all the greens of fern, grass, and reed to browns and rusts. All was dying. I recited the Confiteor.

> I confess to God Almighty, to blessed Mary ever Virgin, to blessed Michael the Archangel . . . to all the Saints and to you, my sisters, that I have sinned exceedingly, in thought, word, and deed; through my fault, my own fault, through my most grievous fault. Wherefore I pray blessed Mary ever Virgin, blessed Michael the Archangel . . . and all the Saints, and you, my sisters, pray for me to the Lord our God.

Composing myself for a moment, I then recited my own absolution.

> Almighty God, have mercy upon me, forgive me my sins and bring me to everlasting life. Amen.

The first psalm of Compline, Psalm 4, calmed, as it always did, my anxieties,

You have put in-to my heart a great-er joy,

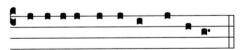

Than the god-less have from much wheat and wine.

I will lie down in peace and sleep comes at once,

For you a-lone, Lord, make me dwell in safe-ty.

Underfoot, fallen leaves of scarlet, gold, and yellow cushioned the fall of my sandals. My step became rhythmic once the stiffness that came from sitting too long loosened. About halfway to the woodlot, I began the second psalm of Compline, Psalm 91, singing more loudly now to fluttering evening moths and calling blackbirds.

He will de-liv-er you from the snare of the fowl-er;

And from the dead-ly pes-ti-lence.

He will cov-er you with his pin-ions and under his wings you will find refuge;

His faith-ful-ness and truth will be your buck-ler and shield.

You will not fear the ter-ror of the night,

Nor the ar-row which flies by day,

Nor the pes-ti-lence which stalks in dark-ness,

Nor the de-struc-tion which wastes at noon-day.

On this, his feast day, the wings of Michael the Archangel, God's falcon, reassured me. As evening deepened, my time for fishing grew shorter, and my hopes for a few meals dimmed. But I was determined to see this excursion through to its end.

Coming to a break in the trees, I saw a spectral mist blanketing the fen. Thickest along the watercourses, the mist mushroomed yard by yard into bordering reed beds and grass plots. The leaden skies colored all a deepening gloom. Before long the mist would surely sweep into the woodlot. I doubled my pace. I needed every minute of what little light remained.

Sister Margery is always in my thoughts. Hers was a seasonable death. She would be the first to say that she lived a full life, a complete life, although she rarely stepped out of Sopwell. Until her illness struck, every day was a joy to her. We all accepted her loss as we accepted the turn of the seasons. If I should die on this path, whether by accident or an overly taxed heart, my sisters would accept my loss also as seasonable. They do not know what plans my imagination conjures for the morrow. With so little time left me, I scramble to realize them.

As it entered the woodlot, the path turned left, following a wide, gravel-bottomed stream, much wider than I expected—easily as wide as my rod fully extended. The gravel was clean, and the water ran fast and absolutely clear. It flowed west, toward the Ver. I, however, clung to the path turning east deeper into the woodlot. The many huge oaks surrounding the path were stately reminders of our ancient forests. Here and there the trunks of the downed trees Will left to dry stood as high as my waist. Three would be more than enough for Sopwell.

Venturing deeper, the oaks thinned and pine and yew dominated. I saw a glimmer of water ahead.

Overjoyed, I began Psalm 42, my personal addition to Compline. It is my prayer every night when I retire to my cell at Sopwell, breathing in with each step the overpowering silence of the night. With the stream on my right, I shifted my attention between the path and the water, glancing first for exposed roots and then for sign of fish.

And I chanted,

As a hart longs for flow-ing streams

So my soul longs for you, O God.

My soul thirsts for God, for the liv-ing God,

When shall I be-hold the face of God?

The path ended in a great spring pool, easily several acres in size. Balancing on a slight promontory supported by tree roots, I stood where the pool welled and bubbled into my companion stream. Hemmed close in by dark green yew and pine, the great pool glowed, its bottom fine white sand and gravel. Even the leaden skies could not dim its luster.

Scattered over the pool were shoals of dark-backed salmon. Great fish in size. It was a late run up from the Thames, the last of the season. They were spawning over the pool's gushing springs. Everywhere the bottom's fine sand pulsed as a boiling kettle, sending continuous streams of spring water bubbling upward, covering each fish in silvery, joyous beauty.

The pool churned. The gravid hens hung above their redds, releasing clumps of orange eggs while excited cock salmon, thrusting and charging about, sprayed trails of white milt. Trout waited below each nest to snare stray tumbling eggs carried along by the pool's relentless currents.

But the fish were not alone. Drake mayflies appeared sporadically on the pool's edges. As I watched, dark amber flies popped to the surface and then hopped about, finding quiet places where their wings could dry. Cock salmon and trout fed on the less nimble. But many drakes escaped upward, flying directly into the lowering mists only to be eaten by silent swallows and chattering warblers that flashed and skimmed, taking drakes at will.

The rising fish awakened me to ready my gear. I unfurled my rod and affixed a fifteen-hair, green leader. Time was short. Digging worms was out of the question, so I tied on an artificial drake fly. It was tied with a dubbed black wool body and black mallard wings, its body segmented by black, silk thread wrappings. I only needed one salmon to make the day a success.

Swinging along the edge of the pool, I crouched beside a redd with a large hen and several cocks. I cast my fly ahead of them into the current. The fly swung past them, not just once, but several times, with no response. The lowering clouds grew darker as a thick mist rolled from the fens and invaded the woodlot.

Hurriedly, I searched my satchel for a strip of lead. Finding one, I bit off half an inch and twisted it on my line just above the fly. Casting into the bubbling springs, I watched it sink and bump along the white gravel, coming to rest on the nest's edge, where a cock salmon daintily picked it up. Before the fish could turn and drop the fly, I struck hard and then led it downstream to a shallow bay. After I forced its head above water, its gills working hard, the salmon soon gave up its thrashing. Sliding the fish up onto the bank, I struck it with a piece of limestone, and it fell still, enough meat for the whole convent for a day. Twice more I cast my weighted fly into the pool. And twice more I led thrashing salmon into the shallows. As I slid the last great fish up the bank, I knelt to tie all three together.

So intent on fishing, I had not noticed that the mist had engulfed me and the woodlot. I could hardly see my hands working to string the fish. Turning, I stood and peered into the stark white landscape. Just then the wind quickened and played through it. Shapes billowed and disappeared. The wind blew again. I stood at attention, my senses on alert. More shapes appeared and disappeared.

I whispered my chant to its end,

By day the Lord com-mands his stead-fast love;

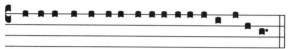

And at night his song is with me, a pray-er to the God of my life.

The billowing shapes steadied, and an absolute calm fell over all. Familiar shapes appeared, and my eyes searched their features.

Before me, I beheld the person of my father.

And I beheld the person of my mother.

And I beheld the persons of Isabel and Constance and my brother, Richard.

Yes, and I saw Philippa and Edward, and my Uncle William with Eleanore and Catherine, and so many more.

And I reached out with my hands to draw the lines of my father's face and to caress my mother's cheek.

And I heard my father ask, "Do you remember the day you flew in the rain?"

And I whispered, "Yes."

"Daughter, you are the one who soars with hawks."

The wind quickened once more, and the mist billowed and lifted. My family was gone. And I looked at my hands. Drake mayflies covered them. Gently, I shook the flies loose, and all but one flew off. And I drew this lone drake close. It quivered, its smoky brown, upright wings and its amber body suffused with light. I stroked its wings and then looked up to the see a brilliant moon and my drake and a host of drake mayflies winging upward, transformed into sparks of light, each its own colored crystal, points in the night of amber, gold, and brown. Thousands of drakes danced above me. Braving nightjars and dragonflies, they held to their destiny, their fleeting moment of life, proving again and again nature's elegance and courage. For how long I stood transfixed, I do not know. The croak of a night heron ended my reverie.

A mayfly's graceful wing, the salmon's determination, a falcon's reckless dive.

explicit

dame juliana berners

the great silence

Sopwell
Feast of St. Cecilia, 1487

How I miss my friend Juliana. She took great care deciding with me the psalms and hymns for Sopwell's hours. It has been ten years since Abbot Wallingford deposed her. The official reason given was incompetence due to her declining mental powers. She was very old and set in her ways, it is true, but she was rarely mistaken.

Wallingford summoned her to the abbey the day following Michaelmas, 1477. What transpired at the meeting I learned later at Dame Juliana's last chapter meeting. Apparently Abbot Wallingford and his brother disapproved of the arrangements Dame Juliana made concerning the Westby bequest to Sopwell. They were unhappy that she transformed the bequest to join Sopwell with the tenants as partners to manufacture pewter items for sale abroad. They wanted a fixed return rather than the fluctuations of foreign markets.

The abbey found these arrangements too risky. Nonetheless, it later took a quarter interest, half of Sopwell's interest, in the enterprise, over Prioress Chapelle's protest. The abbey then deposed Prioress Chapelle, again due to her age. Apparently she also was old and set in her ways. The abbey took an interest in Sopwell's metal works on the rationale that it had expended great amounts of money and time reviewing the legality of the underlying transaction. The abbey's impress of notaries advised against challenging Dame Juliana's arrangements, for Lord Howard's notaries had done their work well. While the Marsh pewter venture prospered, Wallingford's own attempt to found a printing business did not. After publishing but six books, it failed. Only its last book, the *Boke of St. Albans*, Dame Juliana's collected works, turned a profit, but by then it was too late.

Dame Juliana was saddened by her deposition but not surprised.

She often evinced pessimism when predicting human behavior. Within a week and with the abbot's approval and relief, she left Sopwell on an "indefinite sabbatical." I spoke with her frequently during her last days here and learned that she planned to return to Bernersbury "to teach Lady Elizabeth's children to fish for barbel."

Her next destination was Cornwall. She repeated several times the words of Psalm 55: "I will take up residence in the wilderness." I took this to mean that she planned to join a convent there, but this is simply my surmise. Concerning Cornwall, Dame Juliana was quite clear about her itinerary. She looked forward to visiting the Tristan sites. She mentioned Tintagel, the Island of St. Samson, the stone called Tristan's Leap, the Malpas, and the Forest of Morrois. She even suggested she would build a "leafy bower" in the Morrois "and wake in the morning to birdsong and the fragrance of pine." Her greatest desire was to explore Tintagel. "Just once," she said, "I want to stand on the ramparts of Tintagel and watch a scarlet sun sink into the western ocean. Then when the evening star appears above the darkening horizon, I will sing the Ave Stella Maris."

All the while she planned to fish. She looked forward to catching salmon and sea trout, "silver fish from a silver sea," she said. In the Morrois she planned "to eat salmon steaks grilled over a pine fire." Unlike the Thames and many of its tributaries, Cornwall's salmon rivers were shorter and narrower, allowing her to fish her dubbed flies. She grew excited with the prospect of fishing the Tamar River and, when she "tired" of it, she intended to walk the coastline, fishing its rivers as they rushed down Cornwall's craggy heights to the sea. "It could take the rest of my life," she said.

My last view of her was walking through Sopwell's gate. She looked back and shouted, "Keep a merry spirit. Always." With her fishing satchel swung over her shoulder and her staff firmly in her right hand, she turned into the lane and, with a wave, set out, a determined, diminutive black figure, trooping toward London. I heard the thud of her staff and waved until its sound died in the noise of the road.

It has been a great sorrow for me that Dame Juliana has not contacted Sopwell since. Most likely, she ended her days in one of Cornwall's Celtic convents. They are famous for taking in the itinerant religious, especially ones with her learning. From her reputation among the older nuns here and the people of St. Albans, I can say without hesitation that Dame Juliana continued the daily observance of the hours. The only book she took with her when she left Sopwell was her Psalter.

explicit

dame clare

Glossary

agincourt   A battle fought between the English forces under King Henry V and a numerically superior French army on October 25, 1415. Edward, Duke of York, one of Henry's field commanders, died during the battle.

ale   An alcoholic drink commonly served in medieval England. It is made from water, barley, hops, and yeast. Monasteries often served half ale, a very low alcoholic version of ale similar to near beer. Very likely half ale was served at Sopwell. Dame Juliana also used it to dye her leaders.

almoner   The monk or nun designated to distribute alms or gifts to the poor.

barbel   A freshwater fish from the cyprinid family that is most closely associated in the United States with carp and minnows. The barbel is similar in shape to the carp, with four barbules hanging from its mouth. Very popular among British anglers, they run from two to five pounds, although they may grow to over ten pounds. There is no close

American cousin. Its back is green to gray in color, with golden flanks and a white belly. Its roe is poisonous to humans.

BENEDICTINE HOURS   See the essay directly following this glossary.

BOAR   A wild member of the pig family, whose fur runs mostly to brown and black with an average weight of 110 to 200 pounds, although larger specimens are regularly taken.

BREAM   Another freshwater cyprinid, prized by British anglers, usually running one to three pounds, although they can grow to over ten pounds. It has no close American cousin. Its back tends to black or brown, which lightens by degrees to a grayish-white belly.

BROADCLOTH   Strong, smooth, glossy woolen cloth, 1.75 yards wide and from 24 to 30 yards long. The best of it is made from short hair wool, felted together. It was a staple of English foreign trade during the Middle Ages. Benedictine habits were made from black broadcloth.

caddis fly

An aquatic insect that builds a case for protection. Some species attach the case to underwater debris. Its larva develops in the case, which, depending on the species, is made of one type of debris or another, from sand grains to bits of leaves. Usually the cycle from egg to adult takes a year, but there are many species of caddis, eight hundred in North America alone, and the cycle varies from species to species. The adults generally have two pairs of hairy wings and many combinations of body and wing color.

cadges

A wooden frame, sometimes padded, on which hawks or other birds of prey perch. The cadge was carried by male servants called cadgers. The size and shape of the frames varies from a few thin, pliable tree branches to sturdy blocks of wood, depending on the size of the bird of prey.

chamber knight

A noble title awarded by a sovereign during peace time, often to members of his household. The award was done privately.

chapter house

A large, often much ornamented room on the east side of a monastery or priory cloister, where the monks or nuns met every morning after mass to discuss business. The agenda for the chapter meeting included public confessions of error and a reading of the Rule of St. Benedict.

chubb

The chubb family has many subspecies in both the United States and Europe. The chubb Dame Juliana mentions in the *Treatyse* is a prolific freshwater cyprinid, averaging one to three pounds, although it can reach over ten pounds. It often feeds in water temperatures not congenial to other fishes. The chubb has a black or brown back, silver sides, and a white belly with fins of pink or gray. It has a few cousins among American cyprinids.

cloister   A rectangular open space often established on the south side of the monastery church, surrounded by a covered, enclosed walkway, in northern climes especially. It is a favorite site for ornate gardens. The cloister was the crossroads of the monastery; the buildings fronting on the cloister were the ones most essential for monastery operations.

convent   During the medieval period, the word *convent* referred to the entire assemblage of monastery buildings and residents of either sex, thus it was used interchangeably with the word "monastery." Later "convent" was used to refer to female communities, replacing the word "nunnery."

coursing   Sight hound hunting, usually with greyhounds. In some instances where the coursing was set in parks, stands were set up for spectators to watch the dogs pursuing the game, usually deer. Coursing was distinguished from venery, where scent hounds were used for pursuit of the game.

croft   A small, enclosed farm plot including a residence for the farmer.

dormitory   A large room in a monastery or convent where residents slept in common. Where separate rooms were built for individual residents, the rooms were referred to as cells.

dubbed fly Dame Juliana's word for her twelve artificial fishing flies, probably derived from the wool yarn for the body of the artificial fly, formed by repeatedly rolling the loose wool between the tier's fingers until it thins to a very small diameter.

eel In the Ver, Dame Juliana would have encountered the freshwater or river eel. It tends to be black in color with a silvery belly. Dame Juliana disliked the taste of eel.

fulling Repetitive pounding of woven wool cloth to compact it and smooth it out. Water mills were geared to drive the hammers. St. Albans had a mill dedicated to fulling.

gauntlet The falconer's thick leather glove, her protection against a bird's talons.

grayling A freshwater fish that thrives in cold, well-oxygenated water. It is a delicately colored, silver fish with patches of gray blue and gray green dappled with black spots. One identifying characteristic is its beautiful, large dorsal fin. The grayling will attain a size on average of one pound by its fourth year. America had a number of grayling species, but most are extinct or close to extinction.

hare A species similar in shape to the common rabbit, but they are larger, with longer ears and black markings. The European hare has fur that is generally brown in color. It has never been domesticated and will attain speeds of 45 mph when fleeing predators.

hart A mature European male Red Deer, the largest deer in Britain.

hawking Hunting with birds of prey. The different species of accipiter were by law assigned to nobles by their rank. The higher in rank, the better, usually bigger, the bird. A low-ranked noblewoman like Dame Juliana would have been allowed a merlin. Kings could keep gyrfalcons; emperors alone were permitted eagles.

herbalist Persons who collected and tested the properties of plants, the medieval pharmacists and healers. If the monastery was large enough, a monk might be assigned full time as its herbalist, raising herbs, testing them, preparing them, and making salves and tinctures from them.

horsehair leaders Medieval anglers used lines made from horse tail hair. The *Treatyse* illustrates Dame Juliana's preferred device for weaving horsehair lines. Most likely, Dame Juliana would have collected light-colored horse hair for the last section of line, namely, the section of line to which the hook was attached and today called the leader. The lighter-colored hair could then be colored as she directed depending on the color of the water fished.

hover Collective noun used to describe a group of trout.

infirmary The room of a monastery or priory where the sick were treated, usually attached to the monastery itself. Sometimes, where there was danger of infection, like leprosy and the Black Death, the infirmary building was sited apart from but nearby the monastery. St. Albans's leprosarium was run by Benedictine nuns at St. Mary de Pre Priory located about two miles from Sopwell.

mayfly   An aquatic insect that lives most of its life underwater, clinging to rocks or burrowing into silt. It does not construct a protective casing like the caddis fly but develops freely from egg to emerger, when it swims up from the bottom of the river or pond to turn into the adult mayfly. Within a day or so, it molts, mates, and spins its eggs back into the river for the cycle to start all over. The cycle usually takes a year, but some species have several cycles within a year and other species will extend the cycle out over two and three years. Depending on the species, the mayfly takes on various colors, browns, grays, yellows, and olives being the most prevalent.

merlin   The bird of prey trained and hunted by lower-level noblewomen. They are a robust bird about a foot in height, with a wingspan of two feet. Their color varies from blue black to silver gray.

monastery   The complete assemblage of monks or nuns, buildings, and gardens essential for running a worshipping, disciplined religious community.

moot hall   A large building, centrally located in manorial towns, whether religious or secular, often housing shops on its lower level while the upper story was dedicated to the operations of the lord's or abbot's court.

nocturn   In the depths of the night, it was customary for two bible readings, one from the Old Testament and the other from the New Testament, and a third reading from the commentary of a recognized saint to be read. These with the prayers and chants surrounding them were the nocturns.

notary   During medieval times, notaries were church-appointed clerks who worked with judges to authenticate deeds and other documents. Their principal work was to record court proceedings and other official meetings, but depending on their training, they also prepared legal documents.

par force   The noblest type of medieval hunting, usually done in royal forests, where a hart was pursued by scent hounds with the hunters following on horseback until the hart tired, was brought to bay, and turned on the hunters to defend itself. Usually one hunter, the most prominent personage present, was then selected to dispatch it on foot with a sword or spear.

peacock herl   A long strand of feather taken from the tail of the peacock. Iridescent, a dark green in color but with a bronze cast. Dame Juliana wrapped it about the bodies of her dubbed flies.

perch   A European freshwater fish, very similar in size, shape, and coloration to the Yellow Perch found in the United States. Its back is generally colored a greenish yellow with a white belly, its flanks exhibiting four to five vertical, dark bars. It inhabits all types of water and grows to a size of one to two pounds on average, with some specimens running to four and five pounds.

pilgrim A person journeying on a religious quest. The goal of the quest was usually a holy site, where the pilgrim received enlightenment or a cure for some ailment or deprivation.

pike Dame Juliana's pike is a freshwater fish distributed throughout Europe with close cousins in America, in structure long and thin with a head shaped like a duckbill, and bearing many sharp, long, bony teeth. The quintessential aquatic predator, in medieval literature sometimes called the luce or waterwolf, widely distributed in rivers, lakes, and streams, both in America and Europe, running on average from five to ten pounds, but many larger ones of twenty pounds or more are taken by anglers.

prioress A woman elected by her community to perform the same functions as an abbot within the priory yet all the while subordinate to the abbot. Where the female community was autonomous, the woman in charge of the community was called an abbess.

priory A satellite community of a monastery, usually set apart due to the specialized function it performed. Sopwell Priory was set apart to house the female religious. Priories answered to their sponsoring monastery.

refectory The monastery dining hall, usually associated with a nearby kitchen and buttery.

Reliquary   A receptacle, usually of silver or gold, holding relics: bits of saints' bones and holy objects such as the true cross. It is most often used to display relics during services at a holy shrine. Sometimes pilgrims were allowed to touch it in the hope they would partake of its power.

Roach   A European freshwater cyprinid found in rivers and lakes. Very popular among British anglers. Its back runs from gray to blue green with sides and belly a bright silver white, and its average size is half a pound to one pound. Specimens over two pounds are rare.

Salmon   The Atlantic Salmon is Dame Juliana's favorite fish, probably due to its size and food value. It is an anadromous fish, spending a good part of its life in the ocean and then entering freshwater rivers and streams to spawn. After the eggs hatch, the young salmon lives for a time in freshwater until it gets the urge to travel. Then it descends its nursery river to the ocean, where it quickly puts on weight. From time to time it may return to its river of origin before it returns finally to spawn. In the ocean, it has a dark back and silvery sides, but on the spawning run, its sides darken by degrees as time passes to red in males and black in females. The average size of the Atlantic Salmon is twelve pounds, although much larger fish have been recorded.

Snare   A trap for catching small animals, where a loop of wire is hung at the animal's head level over a run it frequents in the hope it will poke its head through the loop and strangle itself while pulling on the wire trying to break free.

sounder   Collective noun referring most often to a group of boar.

stonefly   An aquatic insect, usually brown or black, growing to between one and three inches, sometimes over a multiyear cycle underwater, usually in rivers and streams. Smaller species are also yellow and green. It hatches out most often by crawling out on rocks and shoreline shrubs and trees, where it splits its hard shuck and flies off to mate and lay its eggs. The adult has six legs and four wings, which lie flat over its back at rest. The adult survives over many days.

subprioress   The nun who, in matters of business and liturgy, stands in for the prioress in the event of her absence. The prioress mentors the subprioress in managing the priory.

tench   A popular European cyprinid, usually inhabiting still waters and slow rivers. Its average size is one and a half to four pounds. It is colored olive or forest green on its back, becoming more yellow on its belly. Its scales will flash gold in the sunlight.

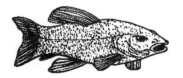

timber construction   A method of building construction common in the medieval era. It is similar to what is popularly called today pole barn construction. Heavy timbers are joined together to form the frame of the building. Walls and roofs are then hung on the timber frame. Often in Britain during the Middle Ages, the timber frame remained exposed, with the walls, usually wattle and daub, filling the spaces between the frames. The spectator saw such buildings as large spaces of white framed by the darker timbers.

toft A peasant's residence on which his or her dwelling and outbuildings stand.

tower hill An elevated place close by the Tower of London where executions of important persons took place during the Middle Ages.

tristan Prominent figure in Arthurian romance literature, renowned as the greatest hunter and singer among Arthur's knights. The story of his romance with Isolde is just one of many lays, stories set to poetry and music, in which he figures. Dame Juliana has a poem celebrating him. The Isolde romance is set in Cornwall.

trout Dame Juliana's second favorite fish. Her trout is the brown trout native to Britain. Its general coloration is a brownish yellow, with the yellow predominating along its side. It is spotted with red and black spots, and its size varies from water to water depending on alkalinity. Most caught in the United States are one pound or less, although the record is over thirty pounds. It is a fish known for feeding selectively and therefore being difficult to catch.

villein

A feudal and later manorial social ranking. The villein is a higher level of peasant, above a serf, who was tied to and obligated to work his lord's land. He had the right of possession of the land on which he lived and worked as his own, usually about thirty acres. Once the lord sold his manorial property, the villein's services went with the land to the new landlord. Villeins usually paid for their use of land with days of labor or produce. The closest institution in the United States is the sharecropper, but unlike the sharecropper, the villein could never leave the manor to which he was obligated, whereas the sharecropper can move once his annual contract expires. Most of St. Albans's peasants were villeins.

wattle and daub

Wattle is a type of medieval wall construction. Often hung on timber frames, wattle is constructed from branches interlaced in a woven pattern and affixed to the timber frame. The daub is usually a mixture of clay, dung, and straw smeared on the wattle, and when dry, coated with a lime wash, leaving it a bright white.

the Benedictine hours

AS PRACTICED IN FIFTEENTH-CENTURY BRITAIN

By the time of Dame Juliana, Benedictines had been chanting their hours throughout Europe for nine hundred years. The name "the hours" refers to eight shifting temporal points in the progress of the day. These points in time the Benedictines celebrated with the chanting of psalms and the recitation of Biblical passages and other similar approved writings. They were not clock hours, for until Dame Juliana's time, mechanical clocks were rare. St. Albans erected one of the first in Britain during Dame Juliana's life. Thus it is misleading to think of the Benedictine hours as the hours marked by a clock. The mechanical clock has twenty-four, while the Benedictine Rule recognizes only eight. In fact, most of the Benedictine hours do not correspond neatly to any clock hour.

The Benedictine hours were a flexible measurement dependent on the rising and setting of the sun. Monasteries were first and foremost agricultural enterprises where sunlight was critical for most field work. Artificial light was expensive. St. Benedict advised his monks to make adjustments in the hours for the shorter days of winter and the longer days of summer. Some of the adjustments for the summer allow for more uninterrupted sleep following a long day of heavy labor needed for planting, cultivating, and harvesting.

Psalm 119 provided St. Benedict with scriptural support for celebrating the hours. The relevant passage reads, "Seven times a day I give you praise." The scriptural seven hours Benedict took as the numbers of his daytime hours. As he calculates, these are Lauds, Prime, Terce, Sext, None, Vespers, and Compline. To the seven daytime hours he added an eighth, Matins, which is usually observed at midnight.

Inclusion of the eighth hour Benedict based on a second passage from Psalm 119, which reads, "At midnight I arose to confess to you."

Lauds, the first of the daytime hours, was originally celebrated as day broke. But by Dame Juliana's time, it was shifted back to follow Matins. Thus, by the late medieval period, Prime took the place of Lauds, becoming the first hour of the day, celebrated at dawn. Following Prime, the community ate a light breakfast or Mixtum and attended a daily Chapter meeting. Terce was celebrated between the Chapter meeting and morning high Mass. Following Mass, the community ate dinner silently, for a reading always accompanied dinner. Following dinner, a period of talk and relaxation was allowed, and afterward the community observed Sext. Then serious work began, interrupted once in midafternoon by the celebration of None, a short hour. Toward dusk, earlier in the Winter and later in the Summer, Vespers was celebrated, although this varied from monastery to monastery. The last meal of the day followed Vespers. At the very end of the day, Compline was celebrated, after which the community quietly went to bed. They remained quiet until Prime the next morning. This was the Great Silence.

Originally Matins was the lone nighttime hour. It was, throughout the history of the Benedictine order, always observed at midnight and is the longest of the hours, dividing the monks' sleep time into two parts. During Matins, Benedict's Rule and long-standing tradition ordered the chanting of many psalms and the oral recitation of many readings, or nocturns, ornamented with short chant pieces. By Dame Juliana's time, Lauds had floated backward in the day to assume what became its regular position just following Matins. A short pause between the two hours was observed to keep the distinction between the two hours.

In all, the celebration of the Benedictine hours took about two and a half to three hours of clock time. Matins and Lauds usually took more than an hour together. The daytime hours were short, some taking only five to ten minutes, with Vespers and Compline being the longest, but by the time the community celebrated them, the work day was over and only supper and bed remained. Compline fostered calm and trust in sleep and, probably for this reason, remains a very popular hour to perform.

who was dame
Juliana Berners?

This essay by John Gubbins won a national award from the British Studies affiliate of the American Historical Association. The essay provides substantial historical and academic support for the substance of this historical novel about Dame Juliana.

Dame Juliana Berners was the first woman author published in print in English. In 1486, a press associated with St. Albans Abbey published her treatises on hunting, hawking, and heraldry in a work entitled *Boke of St. Albans*. In 1496, Britain's most successful commercial printer, Wynken de Worde, republished the *Boke of St. Albans* with the addition of Dame Juliana's fishing book, the *Treatyse of Fysshynge wyth an Angle*. Her fishing book was the first of its kind ever published in any language. For a century and a half, Dame Juliana was Britain's bestselling author. In whole or in part, her *Boke of St. Albans* went through twenty editions, more than any other book of the period.

For two hundred years thereafter, antiquaries, those who collect and study old books, made entries into Dame Juliana's résumé. Beginning with John Bale in the early sixteenth century and ending with John Hawkins in the eighteenth, she was described as "an illustrious female, eminently endowed with superior qualities." She was compared by Bale to "a Minerva in her studies and a Diana in hunting." More helpfully, her biographers provided her full name, Dame Juliana Berners, and her lineage, the daughter of Sir James Berners and the sister of Sir Richard Berners. All were agreed that she wrote field sports books. And finally, the respected antiquary William Burton disclosed that she was, for a time, the Benedictine prioress of St. Mary Sopwell Priory, a community of St. Albans Abbey.

Yet Dame Juliana, England's first woman author and its first bestselling author, has been largely forgotten. Except for a few academics, it is angling historians who have kept her literary legacy alive. They agree that Dame Juliana's fishing book, the *Treatyse of Fysshynge wyth an Angle*, is a highly original work and a fitting start to the proud tradition of English angling literature. Her fishing book went into eclipse during the seventeenth century with the publication of another bestseller, *The Compleat Angler* by Izaak Walton.

Each new generation of anglers claims to discover Dame Juliana. They must do so because every generation also forgets her. They forget her because scholarship has turned her into a wraith. In the name of certitude, her critics have excised her personality from her works. Recent scholars have ignored the biographical details of her life, leaving readers no stimulants for their imagination. Her early biographers, while praising her, described her as a fifteenth-century Benedictine prioress, a little understood and so a forbidding career for today's reader. With no idea of how she lived, it is near impossible to identify with her person, a necessary prerequisite for any piece of literature to have lasting impact.

Before looking into the dynamics of rediscovery, it is time to lay to rest one concern. No scholar, no critic, has disproved the existence of Dame Juliana. All the most rigorous scholars, all the most cynical critics conclude that Dame Juliana did exist and did write about field sports during the fifteenth century. What they have attacked is the story of her life. Thus, the question is not, "Did she exist?" That question has been answered emphatically in the affirmative. Rather the question is, "What sort of person was she?"

The critics are no help, because they prefer to say who she was not. The linguist Rachel Hands has pursued the question of Dame Juliana's identity. But Hands's inquiry begins and ends in the text of the *Boke of St. Albans* and the genealogy of its source documents. She gives no credence to Dame Juliana's early biographers, and she makes no reference to the cultural history of her time. Even so, Hands concludes from the text alone that, at a minimum, much of the hunting book and, perhaps, some parts of the hawking book were "more likely to have been assembled by a woman" during the fifteenth century. She further concludes that the association of the hawking section "with Dame Juliana therefore seems more probable." In sum, for Hands,

Dame Juliana was a fifteenth-century woman who knew something of hunting and hawking and wrote it down. For most readers, these slim facts will not breathe life into her memory.

One fatal shortcoming of those who seek Dame Juliana's identity solely through textual analysis must be flagged. The textual analysts do not survey the whole of the 1496 edition of the *Boke of St. Albans* for clues. They do not consider the illustration, the frontispiece to the *Treatyse* published by Wynken de Worde in 1496. This illustration, the first in the history of English printing, depicts a streamside angler catching a fish with rod, line, and hook. The fish is slim and its upper back speckled and, therefore, it is most likely a trout and thus, the stream depicted a trout stream. On his left, the angler is flanked by an edge of masonry work, and on his right, by the profile of a great hall.

In a highly original piece of detective work, Frederick Buller and Hugh Falkus compared the terrain pictured in the introductory illustration with the terrain near the site of Sopwell Priory. In 1974, after clearing the vegetation obscuring the ruin of Sopwell Hall, they photographed the scene from the perspective of the de Worde illustration. The resemblance between de Worde's woodcut and their photograph is uncanny and persuasive that Sopwell and the River Ver are linked to the *Treatyse*. The perspective is correct, and the geometry of the graphic elements is a match.

The link between the woodcut and Sopwell could only be through Dame Juliana. In 1496, de Worde's print shop was located in Westminster. The easiest course for him would have been to picture an angler on the banks of the nearby Thames. The Ver and Sopwell were twenty miles away. The reader need ask why de Worde would commission a woodcut of a scene so far from his printing shop and London, the locale of his customers. As a highly successful printer, de Worde may have included the illustration of the Ver and Sopwell because his customers expected it. The customers already knew of Dame Juliana and her sports writings.

Beginning with William Oldys in 1748, a new school of antiquaries challenged the legend of Dame Juliana. This new school initiated their argument by working off the generally accepted description of Dame Juliana as the Benedictine prioress of St. Mary Sopwell. Oldys was the first to raise the argument that the roles of knowledgeable sports woman and pious Benedictine prioress were not just incompatible, but fully irreconcilable. Without reference to any historical underpinnings supporting this pronouncement, Oldys argued that fifteenth-century Benedictine nuns rarely left their cloister and, therefore, had no opportunity to hawk, hunt, and fish. Thus he concludes Dame Juliana's authorship of the *Treatyse* was dubious.

Oldys's argument was taken up by William Blades in 1881. The harshest of Dame Juliana's critics, Blades concluded that the only facts that could be safely recounted about Dame Juliana's life were that she "probably lived at the beginning of the fifteenth century, and she possibly compiled from existing MSS [manuscripts], some rhymes on hunting." Agreeing with Oldys that a nun could not reconcile sport and prayer, Blades discredited all biographical facts recounted by the proponents of her legend.

Oldys's and Blades's error was to conceive the life of medieval nuns too narrowly. Medieval Benedictine nuns were not walled up in convents. Contrary to the monochromatic vision initiated by Oldys and carried forward by Blades, the practices of medieval nuns cannot be encapsulated in a few absolutes. As the scholar Penelope Johnson, an expert on female monasticism, has written, "The criticism that medieval religious women ignored claustration is valid; they continually bent and broke the rules of enclosure." The medieval period was a time when idiosyncrasy and exception were the rule. The bald assertion that medieval nuns were under a kind of house arrest in their convents does not begin to take into account the rich diversity of female religious orders then operating in Britain. By the fifteenth century, Britain was home to numerous religious orders with female convents: Benedictines, Cistercians, Augustinians, Franciscans, Dominicans, Gilbertines, and others.

Nor does it take into account the rich diversity within female Benedictine convents. The Rule of St. Benedict encouraged the autonomy of each community. With autonomy came differences, which were reflected in the occupations of the nuns, in the prayers selected for the hours, in the times for marking the hours, in their dedication to scholarship, in their architecture, and so on. The reforms of Cluny and their popes encouraged the Benedictines to reform and regularize their practices. Still, the culture of each monastery never approached the standardization that the modern corporations require of their franchisees. Benedictine monasteries were small communities, many with no more than a dozen residents, shaped not only by St. Benedict's Rule but also by the personalities of their superiors and residents.

The picture of the isolated, silent, cloistered nun is more reminiscent of the modern-day Carmelite than the medieval Benedictine. Although living together as a community, Carmelites are eremitical, meeting together infrequently. Many did not even eat in common, observing strict rules of abstinence, silence, and retirement. On the other hand, Benedictine monks and nuns were cenobitical, strongly communal, observing their Rule each day by praying and working together. Including shared work as part of the monastic's day was St. Benedict's greatest innovation.

Very often their work brought monks and nuns outside their cloisters. Benedictine nuns had businesses to manage, sheep to shear, wool to full, gardens to tend, herbs to collect, and crops to harvest. They had beggars to feed, plague victims and lepers to succor, and students to teach. They visited and were visited by their own families, traveled to conferences, looked in on widows, and performed countless other tasks that took them outside their cloisters. Sopwell, Dame Juliana's convent, would have been no different. Benedictine nuns were individuals before they professed their vows, and while embracing the goals set by the Benedictine order, they did not give up their individual attitudes and talents.

Chaucer, writing in the time of Dame Juliana's childhood, provides instructive examples. Of the thirty pilgrims traveling to Canterbury, he includes a prioress and a nun. He portrays them telling stories and presumably listening to stories. Apropos Juliana's biography, Chaucer's prioress, Madame Eglantine, is a highly cultured, French-speaking lady. She dresses fashionably, eats in public, and mingles freely with her fellow pilgrims, including the earthy wife of Bath. The prioress's table manners are impeccable, and she is attended by three "tame" priests, a nun as her secretary, and lap dogs. Oldys and Blades would not have recognized her as one of their cloistered nuns. Chaucer is a much more credible witness to the Benedictine practices of Dame Juliana's time.

Most medieval Benedictine communities would have encouraged Dame Juliana's love of field sports. They would never have ordered Dame Juliana to chapel to quell her love of hunting, hawking, and fishing. Dame Juliana's skills were an asset to the community. Fish were essential to the Benedictine monastic diet. The Benedictine Rule forbade the eating of flesh meat. By interpretation, fish and fowl were not considered flesh meat. Thus in an average year, Benedictine convents served fish on 215 days. At a minimum, convents served 570 fish dishes each year. Even in a small community, the numbers of fish needed for the Benedictine diet were staggering. To ensure a steady supply of fish, Benedictines fished rivers, lakes, and oceans with nets and with hook and line. They dug fish ponds, breeding fish for their table. In their ponds, they bred carp, tench, roach, perch, breams, eels, and pike. In the late tenth century, hundreds of years before the appearance of the *Treatyse*, a Benedictine abbot named Aelfric wrote the *Colloquy on the Occupations*, which included the occupation of fishing. In a medieval Benedictine community, there was no irreconcilable conflict between praying and fishing. A competent angler saved them money. It is ironic that Oldys and Blades deny Dame Juliana authorship of the *Treatyse*, the most valuable of her books from the medieval Benedictine point of view. With respect to hunting and hawking, a nun with Juliana's skills only enhanced the reputation of a convent school. Given the choice, noble families would rather have entrusted their daughters to schools that competently taught the language of the chase. Young noblewomen could then converse with their fathers, brothers, and future husbands. Many noblewomen hawked, and the school that taught their daughters superior hawking skills was especially attractive. It is possible that some of the commonplace books Hands studied as sources for the *Boke of St. Albans* were written by Dame Juliana's students as memory aids.

The British antiquaries writing closer to her time describe Dame Juliana as a Benedictine prioress, a high-ranking member of the religious order founded by St. Benedict in the sixth century. This fact is a difficult imaginative leap for today's reader. The difficulty is compounded by the additional fact that few records about English Benedictine nunneries are available. Beginning in the early 1530s, Henry VIII began to dissolve Britain's monasteries. Britain's religious communities either migrated to the continent or were disbanded and their residents pensioned off. By the mid-sixteenth century, therefore, the memory of English monasticism dimmed slowly to ignorance with each succeeding generation. With the end of the living tradition also came the destruction of monastery records in the upheaval that followed dissolution. To fully reconstruct the daily life of any one English convent is now impossible. As an example, the fifteenth-century records for Sopwell are nonexistent.

While Sopwell's own records are nonexistent, fragmentary records from the town of St. Albans and St. Albans Abbey hint at life within Sopwell. Some conclusions may be safely drawn. First, Sopwell's nuns were, for the most part, high-born Norman women. The abbey's partial list of Sopwell's prioresses records many Norman names. As with high-born Norman women of the time, many probably read and spoke several languages, principally French with some Latin. Thus, Dame Juliana would have been surrounded with women like herself. Second, Sopwell's operations extended well beyond the walls of its cloister. Sopwell owned two inns in St. Albans, probably to discharge their obligation to provide safe haven for travelers, and it is safe to assume that these businesses did not run themselves. Also, Sopwell owned many farm properties some distance from the convent. Sopwell's prioress, or her representative, would have inspected them and inquired of the tenants concerning their health and the health of their herds and crops. In all these matters, the convent would have kept accounts and verified their tallies. Third, according to St. Albans Abbey and town records, many of Sopwell's nuns were superb seamstresses. English nuns were known throughout Europe for their fine work, supplying vestments to popes and other high church officials. Fourth, Sopwell's relationship with St. Albans Abbey was contentious from time to time. Fifth, Sopwell was a few hundred yards from the River Ver and owned two fish ponds connected with it.

From the very first, Dame Juliana had many supporters within the publishing world. Her first biographer was John Bale. His book, *Scriptorum Illustra Majoris Britanniae*, was published in 1559. The Dame Juliana that emerges from his biography is a virtuous woman, a writer of books on hunting, hawking, heraldry, and fishing, and living in 1460. Successive biographers adopted these facts and expanded on them. The first was Raphael Holinshed in 1577, followed by John Pits in his *De Illustribus Angliae Scriptoribus*, published in 1619. Both reiterate the same facts about Dame Juliana.

The angling historian John McDonald researched the underlying documentary sources for Bale and the proponents of Dame Juliana's genius. He settled on two. According to McDonald, the trail of reliable documentation for Dame Juliana's legend begins with John Leland and ends with William Burton. Henry VIII commissioned Leland to catalog and collect books and manuscripts owned by Britain's monasteries, then recently dissolved. This commission became his life's work. From time to time, John Bale assisted him in his researches. In 1612, Burton came into possession of Leland's copy of the first edition *Boke of St. Albans*, possibly retrieved from the library of St. Albans Abbey itself. This copy bears Burton's notes confirming that Dame Juliana was a Berners and the prioress of "Sopwell, a Nunnery near St. Albans." Burton's copy of the *Boke of St. Albans* traveled to Bishop Moore's library, then to the University Library of Cambridge, where its catalog designates Dame Juliana as its author, without reservation. Thus, McDonald found early documentary support for Dame Juliana's authorship of the *Boke of St. Albans* and her life as a Benedictine prioress. His arguments are persuasive and should be read in his own words.

No critic of Dame Juliana's legend has offered a competent argument against Bale and the other proponents of Dame Juliana's legend. Today's reader need not follow Blades and company into the void. The question is what credibility is owed the words of Bale, Holinshed, Pits, and Burton. Broadly speaking, today's reader expects proof of events by contemporaneous documentation, video tape, or audio tape. The sixteenth-century scholar had no such expectations. Few people read or wrote, and most evidence submitted in court, where it really counted, was oral. Issues disputing the boundaries of property, the meaning of contracts, and criminal liability were determined by words that dropped from the mouths of unlettered peasants and tradesmen. More often than not, the oral evidence jurors heard was secondhand. Today no court would accept such evidence, but it was the usual order of business in British courts during the sixteenth century.

Between the fourteenth century and the eighteenth century,

Britain shifted from a culture that proved facts by secondhand oral reports to a country that relied more and more on documentary proof and firsthand experience. This change in attitude went hand in hand with the rise of printing and literacy, affecting law courts, government, education, and commercial life. It is seen played out in two legal developments. The first development was to accord documentary proof greater credibility than oral testimony. British merchants and judges spearheaded this change. In Dame Juliana's time, written contracts, even deeds, were considered at best ancillary forms of proof to eyewitness accounts of the underlying transaction. If a written contract conflicted with any oral testimony elicited at trial, the oral testimony trumped the documentary proof. This changed when in 1678, Parliament legislated the Statute of Frauds and Perjuries, requiring documentary proof—and only documentary proof—of certain types of agreements and real estate transactions. Oral testimony could not even be considered by the fact finder. As issues arose, triers of fact and academics looked more and more for documents to support their positions.

The second development was to accord firsthand eyewitness testimony greater credibility than hearsay testimony. During Dame Juliana's time, the bulk of testimony accepted in Britain's courts was hearsay or secondhand testimony. A summary witness, a witness with secondhand testimony, or an attorney, would recite the facts to the jury as told them by witnesses not present before the court. In the 1603 trial of Sir Walter Raleigh for treason, hearsay testimony from one of the two witnesses against him was accepted by the court and became a basis for his conviction and eventual execution. By the eighteenth century, law courts, as a matter of common law evolution, excluded hearsay witnesses because these witnesses could not be cross-examined and thus have their credibility assessed by the fact finder.

Bale's account of Dame Juliana's life bears the earmarks of the traditional sixteenth-century jury trial verdict. Britain then trusted what was called the *ex scientia* verdict to deliver accurate outcomes. The ex scientia verdict was a jury verdict based on witness testimony that was either firsthand knowledge or secondhand knowledge derived from a survey of the community for their understanding of local custom, reputation, and fact. It did not distinguish between first- and secondhand evidence. The survey witness summarized information collected "through the words of their fathers and through such words of persons whom they are bound to trust as worthy." With respect to the *Treatyse*, Bale's account of Dame Juliana signals such a survey on his part when he prefaces one of his factual statements with the word "dicitur." This word does not, as some suggest, qualify his confidence in the facts recited. Rather, it signals that he surveyed a community familiar with her. Such an intergenerational survey is confirmed when he also states that she was alive in 1460. Although Bale's book on British writers was published in 1559, he may have done his community survey earlier, since his works were banned off and on between 1546 and 1558. The community survey on which Bale relies could have been done by Leland in St. Albans. If it was, Leland related the results to Bale when they were working on Leland's account of his journeys to the dissolved monasteries. It is also likely that Bale surveyed the community of London's printers, authors, and antiquaries. He was a prolific writer and translator always looking for a publisher. He very likely knew de Worde and Dame Juliana's other publishers and could have spoken with them about the genealogy of the *Boke of St. Albans*. London publishing was a small world. Between 1486 and 1557, there were no more than a hundred master printers at work in London, and not all of them were operating at any one time. Someone with Bale's interests and energy would know the inhabitants of London's publishing world well.

To judge Bale, Holinshed, Pits, and Burton by today's standards of proof is dishonest. If Bale and company played by the rules of the sixteenth century, a transitional period in the shift to more rigorous proof, then care should be taken to treat them fairly. The issue is whether his facts are wrong and not whether the method he used was unreliable. Just because Bale used a different method than scholars use today does not mean that what he wrote down was false. What will scholars four hundred years from now say about the methods today's scholars use? It is elementary decency not to judge a scholar by a newer standard of proof without providing that scholar a chance to meet that standard.

Where the issue is a simple one, namely the identification of Dame Juliana as an author, sixteenth-century methods are acceptable. The researcher need only poll the relevant community. The critics need to explain how, in Dame Juliana's case, Bale was wrong on his facts. They have not done so. The critics' demand for proof by today's standards comes from the arrogance of the living counting on the silence of the dead. If Bale knew how he would be judged four centuries later, he could have satisfied today's critics by recording the identity of his sources and their testimony, and could have even gone to a notary to have their statements sealed. Beginning with Bale and ending with Hawkins, a long string of scholars, antiquaries, and librarians supported Dame Juliana's authorship of the *Boke of St. Albans* and the *Treatyse*. This period spans two hundred years. Over that period of time, no one challenged her biography.

Is today's reader to assume, as Dame Juliana's critics appear to assume, that the early proponents of the legend were gullible, biased, or lazy? What proof that meets today's scholarly standards allows Dame Juliana's critics to dismiss the early antiquaries out of hand? There is none. To jump to such a conclusion without providing an evidentiary basis worthy of today's scholarship is truly shoddy. The critics should look into their own mirrors, judging their own arguments, thin as they are, by their own standards. Two hundred years of uncontradicted written proof is enough to claim title to land or to subvert a treaty.

Consideration of the cultural winds of the sixteenth and seventeenth centuries further enlivens our picture of Dame Juliana. For Bale and his successors to attribute the *Boke of St. Albans* to Dame Juliana was to buck prevailing literary currents. If any of the antiquaries had doubts about her authorship, they would have resolved them against her.

In the two centuries following Dame Juliana's life, publishing was a man's world. Women writers were an oddity. As a bestselling woman author, Dame Juliana was an oddity among oddities. The principle commercial printer during this period was Dame Juliana's publisher, Wynken de Worde, who died in 1535. During his career, he published approximately seven hundred books. His output was 15 percent of the total of five thousand books published between 1486 and 1557 in England. Nonetheless, among the authors of those thousands of books, only eight women writers were published. For a printer or an antiquary to come out with a book attributed to a woman was an extraordinary event. It happened once a decade in London. Attribution to a woman was not a casual act or a slip of the pen. It was not done on a "perhaps" or a "maybe."

Further, during Britain's late medieval and early renaissance period, women were being progressively marginalized. They were more and more confined to work done from the home. New laws prohibited women from practicing the professions of law and medicine, and the guilds restricted women from earning guild masterships. To restrict competition, women were excluded from the job market except for work done under the supervision of a husband. In spite of these trends, antiquaries attributed the *Boke of St. Albans* to a woman.

To sum up, Dame Juliana Berners was a "luminous woman, overflowing with mental and physical gifts and with an arresting, graceful figure." So wrote John Bale, one of Britain's first generation antiquarians and a companion of John Leland, who was charged by Henry VIII with saving Britain's monastery libraries. Bale's purpose in life was to win over the English to Luther and the Reformation, a hostile witness to all things Catholic, yet he was generous when assessing Dame Juliana's accomplishment, namely, her four books, including the *Treatyse*. His description was accepted by antiquarians for hundreds of years. C.S. Lewis praised Bale's objectivity in the matter of Dame Juliana. The cumulative corpus of Bale's work and those who followed him is the British antiquarians' tradition. Some recent scholars, hundreds of years removed from Dame Juliana's world, ignore this tradition, arrogantly refusing to address it and choosing instead in their own writings to begin with assuming she barely existed. Their verdict is that she was a real person but author of only a few fragments of the books attributed to her. Their animosity to her has no basis in fact or tradition. They have produced nothing—no fact, no statement—running counter to the record supporting Bale's conclusions.

The heart of this book is the mind of the person who wrote the *Treatyse*. That mind was a font of genius. The relentlessly tough, practical approach of the *Treatyse* adopts a format copied by angling authors ever since, namely, equipment, places to fish, a checklist in the event of failure, and baits by species and months of the year, including artificial flies. There was nothing like it before in the history of books and angling. It is the seminal work from which all our fishing literature follows. Additionally, the novelty of the writing points to a deeply reflective mind, one that was emotionally independent of the political and economic currents of the time. This is the mind of Dame Juliana Berners, the contemplative, the Benedictine prioress. I have tried, as best I could, to portray the history of that mind—the mind of a genius—but not being a genius myself, I can only hope this book will give the reader a brief glimpse, at best, of her person and her writings. I would caution the reader as Plato cautions all us cave dwellers. This book has at best thrown on the cave wall a shadow, a poor reflection of the idea of her mind. So take my thoughts rather as an invitation, especially to the geniuses among you, to make your own explorations into Dame Juliana's life and her *Treatyse*. And do so in the firm conviction that both are worth your best efforts.

suggested readings

Buller, Frederick, and Hugh Falkus. *Dame Juliana: The Angling Treatise and Its Mysteries*. Devon: Fly Fisher's Classic Library, 2001.

Byrne, Lavinia. *Women at the Altar*. London: Continuum International Publishing Group, 1999.

Chaucer, Geoffrey. *The Canterbury Tales*. Edited by Nevill Coghill. London: Penguin Books, 1951.

Eckstein, Lina. *Woman under Monasticism*. New York: Russell and Russell, 1963.

Foggia, Lyla. *Reel Women*. New York: Random House, 1995.

Hands, Rachel. *English Hawking and Hunting in the Boke of St. Albans*. Oxford: Oxford University Press, 1975.

Johnson, Penelope. *Equal in the Monastic Profession*. Chicago: University of Chicago Press, 1991.

Knowles, Dom David. *The Religious Orders in England*. Cambridge: Cambridge University Press, 1961.

McDonald, John. *The Origins of Angling*. New York: Lyons and Burford, 1957.

Steele, Michelle. *The Abbot and the Rule: Religious Life at St. Albans*. Burlington: Ashgate, 2002.

about the author

John GUBBINS lives with his wife, Carol, alongside the Escanaba River in the Upper Peninsula of Michigan. His historical essay, "Dame Juliana Berners: The Case of the Missing Sportswoman," was recently recognized for its scholarship and originality by the North American Conference on British Studies. Spending his teenage years studying traditional theology and philosophy, Mr. Gubbins later attended the University of Chicago, where he received a graduate degree in humanities, and Columbia University Law School, where he received a Juris Doctor degree. After pursuing a big-city law career, he came to his senses and settled his family near some of the Midwest's greatest trout streams. He and Carol spend their free time fishing, camping, and reading poetry with their family.